Daughters of Ruin

K. D. Castner

MARGARET K. McELDERRY BOOKS
New York London Toronto Sydney New Delhi

MARGARET K. McELDERRY BOOKS
An imprint of Simon & Schuster Children's Publishing Division
1230 Avenue of the Americas, New York, New York 10020
For information about special discounts for bulk purchases, please
contact Simon & Schuster Special Sales at 1-866-506-1949 or
business@simonandschuster.com
The Simon & Schuster Speakers Bureau can bring authors to your live
event. For more information or to book an event, contact the Simon &
Schuster Speakers Bureau at 1-866-248-3049 or visit our website at
www.simonspeakers.com.
Book design by Sonia Chaghatzbanian and Irene Metaxatos
The text for this book is set in Adobe Jenson Pro.
Manufactured in the United States of America
10 9 8 7 6 5 4 3 2 1
Library of Congress Cataloging-in-Publication Data
Castner, K. D.
Daughters of ruin / K. D. Castner.
p. cm.
Summary: As a war begins, four princesses of enemy kingdoms who were
raised as sisters must decide where their loyalties lie: to their kingdoms,
or to each other.
ISBN 978-1-4814-3665-6 (hardcover)
ISBN 978-1-4814-3667-0 (eBook)
[1. Princesses—Fiction. 2. Sisters—Fiction. 3. War—Fiction.
4. Loyalty—Fiction.] I. Title.
PZ7.1.C45Dau 2016
2015003949

FIRST
EDITION

Dedicated to anyone looking
for the reliable truth,
especially the truth in their
own lives.

Atton
Corent
Usabat Basin
Lake Eshen
Mahzarin Foothills
Gindir Mountains
Takh-e-Malin
Meridan
Lake Perdine
Findain
Estarchus

Tasan

Sinchan

Bituin Sea

Cisra

Three little queens went riding into Meridan
Three little queens who won't ride out
The price of war makes a strange inheritance
Four little puppets all pretty and proud.
—Children's nursery rhyme

THE KINGDOM OF MERIDAN,
TWO YEARS PAST THE TREATY OF SISTER QUEENS

The royal carriage tilted on two wheels as it careened onto the dirt path behind a pair of panic-stricken horses. Flames blew out from the suitcases tied to the back of the coach and ruffled in the wind like torn skirts.

The driver was long gone—thrown to the ground by the two bandits sitting in his seat.

One of them—the one missing both of his ears—leaned over the harnesses, trying to reach the reins, which were dragging at the horses' feet. The other bandit had a permanently broken nose. He held his partner's belt to keep him from falling.

Doors on either side of the carriage flapped open and shut.

A five-year-old girl with pigtails sat on the floor of the

coach and cried. She held a dagger with two hands and whacked it at the cushioned seats for no reason. Suki.

Three older girls waited for the carriage to topple back onto four wheels, then began climbing out.

The bandits didn't notice at first.

A girl with blond hair pulled back by a green and black sash—the colors of Findain—climbed out first, holding her dagger in her teeth. She was athletic and nimble, as if she had experience moving on a lurching vessel. Cadis.

On the opposite side of the coach, another girl exited. This one had short black hair cropped in the Corentine style and held her dagger backward along her forearm, in the way of assassins. She was lithe and made the least noise as she scrambled to the forward section of the carriage. Iren.

The earless bandit cursed as the reins dangled just out of reach. The broken-nosed bandit, holding him by the belt, looked back and shouted, "Hey! Get inside!"

The girls didn't listen.

As Cadis reached the luggage racks on top of the carriage, the last girl followed tentatively behind her, staying a bit too close. Like the others, she wore the light leather vest and vambrace of dragoon scouts made especially for one so small. Her chestpiece bore the royal seal of Meridan. Rhea. Her eyes flitted in too many directions. Her long curls flew in her face. The hand that should have held her weapon was used to keep the locks out of her eyes. The knife remained strapped to her calf.

The horses crashed through a hedge.

The carriage ramped over it.

For a second everyone was airborne.

The flames licked at the bags on the top rack.

The carriage landed with a crunch on the rear axle.

Cadis of Findain, with the green and black sash, landed on her stomach atop the coach. Iren of Corent had disappeared by climbing down the side of the coach to the undercarriage.

Rhea of Meridan lost her footing and held on to the top rack. Below her, the dirt lot sped past. If she fell it would scrape for bone and mangle what it found.

The broken-nosed bandit let go of his partner and grabbed the driver's whip.

"Back now," he said. He whipped at Cadis. She kept her knife in her mouth and held up a forearm. The vambrace took the lashes with no harm.

"Get back!"

The horses raced madly toward a rounded wall.

Cadis ground her teeth on the dagger and coiled her body, ready to lunge at the bandit.

He whipped at her arm again.

The back wheel of the carriage wobbled.

Its axle broke.

The Findainer planted her feet, just as the wagon jerked.

She heard a scream coming from behind her. Someone shouting her name, "Cadis!" but she paid no attention.

She had stepped on fingers as she launched herself at the broken-nosed bandit.

The two of them tumbled from the carriage and smashed into the dirt—the bandit taking the brunt of the fall.

Rhea wrenched back her crunched hand and fell. She hit the ground and curled in a ball as she skidded across the lot.

The one inside the coach, little Suki, had been strapped to the seats. She kept crying and slapping the sideboards with the flat side of her dagger.

The horses continued the blind stampede to the wall.

The earless bandit finally grabbed the reins.

Before he could straighten himself and yank the reins to stop the horses, a face appeared right below his.

"Hello," she said.

Iren of Corent had climbed the undercarriage and now lay upside down, a foot above the dirt lot and even less distance from the pounding hooves of the horses. She held herself like a plank, her feet wedged on the front axle braces.

The bandit yelped in surprise.

The girl smiled. In one backhand motion, she swung the dagger and cut the reins. There would be no stopping. Iren closed her eyes and let herself fall. The carriage sailed over her. She hit the ground flat and spread her arms and legs to scatter the impact. When the horses noticed the impending wall, they whinnied and twisted a sharp turn to the right, planting the broken rear axle into the dirt.

The flaming carriage toppled over.

The little one shrieked from inside the coach.

The earless bandit lost his footing, and the carriage's motion sent him flying.

The horses wailed and fell sideways.

Burning satchels bounced in every direction.

A cloud of dirt poured over the crash like a yellow fog.

As the dust settled in the Royal Coliseum, the five-year-old from Tasan sat on the dirt floor, where she had landed after falling from the coach, and continued to cry. The other three princesses circled around her, swinging their daggers at one another's faces.

No elegance. No showmanship. Not even the prudence to stab the blades at the exposed wrists, where any damage would cripple further attack. No love for the craft.

Just the pure hate of children forced to live together.

Hiram Kinmegistus watched from the conductor's trench, unamused and overheated in his academy robes. His shinhound sat beside him, licking a paw.

The tutor, Marta, shouted instructions to the girls.

"Suki, get up! It's okay, darling. No need to cry."

"Rhea, close your position."

"Like Iren. Look at her lead foot. Her *left* one."

"Her *other* left one."

"Too aggressive, Cadis."

"Suki, for the love of anything holy, please get up."

The girls only ever seemed to aim for the eyes, but had no sense of the length of the blades, or even their arms. They flailed at one another like flustered geese.

Near them, a broken carriage lay on its side, one wheel spinning in the breeze. Two horses, still attached by the harnesses, struggled to free themselves. Two men lay dead beside them.

The tutor glanced at Hiram, the king's man, standing in the trench with his arms crossed under his magisterial robes. He would report back to King Declan—from the look on his face, it wouldn't be positive.

The servants preparing the stadium for the upcoming Revels—washing the seats and hanging banners—quietly watched the princesses from the grandstands.

Marta shouted, "Suki, please, stop crying."

Perhaps it was unjust to pick on Suki, the youngest, when she and Cadis and Iren were taken from their parents only six months ago. They were driven—each from their homes, their own families, their own countries—to Meridan as "wards" of King Declan. Suki was five now, while the others were on either side of seven. They were to be raised as sisters, equal to Declan's own flesh-and-blood daughter, Rhea, as if such a thing were possible.

Half the court of Meridan couldn't tell if the Sisterhood of Queens was a gesture of ludicrous optimism, or a cruel joke that only Declan appreciated.

Six months ago, when Hiram Kinmegistus had appeared at Marta's garden fence and hired her to instruct the young queens, she had asked him exactly that. "Is this a political farce, Magister? Am I a tutor or a prison guard?"

The magister loomed above her tomato plants like the specter of a reaping angel and smiled crookedly. "If you'd ever attended the Corentine Academy, Marta, you would know they are roughly the same job."

Rhea was the one to pull the first knife. Even before the wheels stopped turning on the wrecked carriage, she screamed, "You did it on purpose!" And she charged Cadis. "You crushed my hand on purpose!"

Cadis was tallest and strongest already. She had sailed on ships back in Findain, with pirates. She blocked Rhea's downward swing easily with her own knife and slashed quickly to counter.

"Ow! You cut me, you *bestiola*!" Rhea dropped her blade and grabbed the bleeding slash on her forearm, just above the vambrace.

"Yeah," said Cadis. "That was the *point*."

"Actually, I don't think that was the point of this exercise," said Iren, tossing her knife aside, uninterested in explaining herself.

"Besides, my boots slipped," muttered Rhea. She let the words die off, disgusted with her own excuse.

Cadis didn't even bother to reply. She turned to Iren instead. "Do you think they just want us to make her look good?"

Iren shrugged. She nodded at the king's adviser in the conductor's trench. "I think they want us to show off, to dance in front of them, make them feel safe."

Cadis held her knife in her teeth as she adjusted the green and black sash that held back her blond hair.

As Marta approached the girls, she waved at her son. "Endrit, go free those poor horses." The boy dashed from the far end of the grounds, where he had been using the maze of balance beams while the little queens didn't need them. "And be careful," said Marta.

The horses scuffed with rising panic.

"Now," said Marta, "what was that?" She put her arms on her hip guards, a gesture common in drill sergeants. As an aside she said, "At ease, gentlemen."

The two previously dead men, lying beside the carriage, sat up, dusted themselves, and stood at attention.

The girls were none too eager to explain.

"Suki, please shut up," said Rhea.

"No!" said Suki, kicking dust.

"Don't worry about her," said Cadis.

"Don't tell me what to do," snapped Rhea. "You're not the leader."

"None of you is the leader," said Marta, commanding their silence. From the corner of her vision, she spotted Hiram climbing out of the trench and marching toward them. She cursed under her breath. "Now stop bickering and tell me what happened."

"Cadis cut me," said Rhea. She glared at the three girls who had been thrust into her life. Marta drew up Rhea's arm. She gently pulled Rhea's hand off the wound and examined it. Rhea winced.

"What did I tell you about that left foot?"

Rhea didn't answer.

"It was too far forward, throwing off her balance and hampering her ability to lunge or dodge tactically," said Iren without any hint of reproach, just stating facts. They didn't know her very well, but the other girls suspected that Iren spoke like a magister just to show off. She claimed she had an entire library back home in Corent. She'd read twice as many books as Rhea, which was about ten times as many as Cadis. They didn't know if Suki could even read—all she ever did was slap the books away.

"Very good, Iren," said Marta.

"Cadis was too aggressive," said Rhea.

"Only if my opponent could punish me for it," said Cadis. "So I'd say I was exactly aggressive enough."

In the silent moment, as Rhea boiled in her own resentment, they could hear only Suki's droning wail, the cleaning crews in the stands, and Hiram's footfalls as he approached. His hound had no leash or bell and made very little noise as it trotted behind the magister.

Just before he arrived, Marta whispered, "Please, children. Behave."

The three older princesses turned and acknowledged the king's man with the customary half bow required of minors. Cadis was unaccustomed to the gesture. In Findain, the ruling earl was considered first among equals. A bow would be laughably formal to the ship captains and merchant lords of her father's court.

She bowed anyway.

Hiram's gaze was fixed on Cadis, perhaps for that

exact reason, to see if the Findish—daughter of nothing better than a "gold noble"—would ever civilize herself.

"Our queens," said Hiram. He bowed only to Rhea, which made Rhea beam and straighten her pose. "I see Marta is preparing quite a show for the Revels."

"Yes, sir," they muttered, finally embarrassed of their performance.

"Go away!" shouted Suki. She grabbed a fistful of dirt and threw it in his general direction. Rhea kicked Suki's foot, which only punctuated her sobs.

"Marta, would you care to tell me your aim with this particular . . . endeavor?"

Marta cleared her throat but remained stiff in her formal stance and salute.

"Ah. I always forget," said Hiram, grinning. "A good old soldier. At ease."

Marta widened her stance and put her hands behind her back. She had been a decorated officer of Meridan's old wars, before Declan's rise and conquest, but the king's man still outranked her by several titles. He hadn't won any of them on the battlefield, but Marta was trained too well to show any disdain.

"You may speak, soldier," said Hiram, waving with the back of his hand.

"Sir, we thought it would be appropriate to show the girls working together as sister queens."

"So you threw them from a moving carriage?"

Marta's mouth made a straight line. "Not exactly, sir," she said through gritted teeth.

Hiram was a man in his prime—too young for the magister robes. Underneath he carried a baton, which he knew how to wield in lethal combat, but which he used to instruct the dogs in his kennel. In the inner linings of the robes were dozens of pockets, where the young magister carried rolled parchments.

As Marta waited to explain herself, Hiram pulled out one of the parchments and checked to make sure it carried the note he intended. "Go on," he said.

"The king said he wanted something grand that showed unity among the queens."

Hiram raised an eyebrow. He knelt down and tucked the rolled sheaf into a canister hanging around the shinhound's neck.

"I don't know where the fire came from," said Marta.

Hiram whispered something into the hound's ear and sent it running toward the coliseum gate.

When he returned to his feet, he was no longer interested in anything Marta had to say. "You two. Soldiers, attend."

The broken-nosed and earless soldiers scrabbled forward and struck sloppy salutes.

"What've you got to say?" said Hiram.

The soldiers remained silent. Rage coiled in Hiram's brow. Were these men refusing to speak? Declan's army was always hunting for new insults to throw at Hiram behind his back. He could sense the cleaning crew, pretending to work as they watched his every action. "Very well," he said, ready to dismiss them both. "Latrine duty, now."

"WHAT'S THAT, SIR?" shouted the earless soldier.

Hiram stepped in front of the soldier and peered down his nose. "Could you hear me the first time?"

"SORRY, SIR. WAR WOUND AND ALL THAT." The soldier pointed to one of his missing ears. Hiram couldn't tell if this was a jab at his own war record. He glanced at the broken-nosed soldier, who was still staring into the distance.

"And what about him? Why didn't he answer me?"

"HE'S A LOWLANDER, SIR, BEGGIN' YER PARDON. HE DON'T EVEN SPEAK DOG."

"Does he know what a latrine is?" said Hiram.

"YESSIR," said Earless, "BUT IN THE LOWLANDS I THINK THEY CALL 'EM HOME SWEET HOME."

The broken-nosed soldier betrayed himself with a knowing smile. Hiram caught a glimpse of it before the soldier could go back to pretending he didn't speak the language. Hiram didn't have the time to wrestle respect out of two lowly footmen.

"Latrine duty, both of you, go."

Both soldiers knocked their heels, turned, and marched off to dig out the coliseum cesspits in time for the Revels.

Hiram sighed. He'd have to speak to the girls.

He entered their loose circle and cleared his throat. "Your highness queens, tell me, what—" Hiram stopped himself.

He refused to shout over the din of a wailing child.

Cadis knelt beside Suki and tried to console her with a story. "Suki, hey, Susu. Listen. Wanna hear about Miss Rusila? I'll tell you a story if you stop crying." Suki usually begged for Cadis's tales of Rusila, the Maid Marauder—one of the great pirate legends of Findain. This time she shook her head and wailed even louder.

Rhea stood with her arms crossed, exasperated.

She was suddenly plagued by sisters and felt as pleased by it as a dog with drill-nose ticks.

Iren observed, as she always did, as if the other girls were behind a museum glass.

Hiram Kinmegistus waved Cadis away with a reassuring nod and lowered himself to be eye-to-eye with the five-year-old Suki. The three older girls backed away. Aside from Rhea, none of them had ever spoken with the magister. And even Rhea had always been in her father's court, where the palace guards made her feel safe.

When he had enough space to whisper something that only Suki could hear, Hiram said, "Now, little one, tell me why you're crying."

Suki had already swallowed her louder sobs. She trembled.

"Did you hurt yourself in the crash?"

Suki shook her head, her chin tucked into her chest.

"No? Well, that's good. It's good, isn't it?"

Suki nodded. She even smiled a little at the man's obvious question.

Hiram looked around, then caught Suki's eye again. This time, he spoke in Tasanese, a language Suki hadn't heard since the day her parents sent her away. It filled her with such comfort, as if she'd caught the scent of her own mother.

"Do you remember those two soldiers I sent away? The one with missing ears and the one with the broken nose?"

Suki nodded again.

"What if I told you I'm a misfit, too? Look." The magister opened his mouth wide and poked a finger back to a space where the last tooth should have been on either side.

Suki giggled at the absurdity of the king's man shoving his giant hand into his own mouth. Hiram pretended to gag, and Suki laughed even harder. He had a warm smile. "And what if I told you," he said, "that I was starting a collection of misfits, and now I need a little girl, hopefully with swollen cheeks from crying all the time?"

Suki's eyes went wide.

"And that all the misfits get latrine duty or my job, and you'd probably rather the latrines?"

Suki thought about it for a moment. "I'll stop crying," she said.

Hiram wiped a tear from her cheek with his thumb. "That's a shame," he said. "We could have used your small hands for the really grimy crevices." Suki squished her face in grossed-out amusement.

Hiram stood up and faced them all once again. Marta had joined the other girls. Hiram reached into a pocket of his robes and pulled out a blank roll of parchment and a sharpened piece of graphite. "So then, let's begin at the moment in the exercise when our expertly trained soldiers, acting as common rogues, take over the carriage and somehow manage to snap the breaking lever, to drop the reins, and spook the horses."

Cadis and Rhea looked at their boots, unwilling to start. Iren finally spoke. "They didn't spook the horses. The fire in the baggage rack did, which we started."

"Why?" said Hiram.

"To spook the horses," said Iren, as if it were obvious.

"So your plan was to create havoc and hope that it would all come to rights?"

"We didn't *have* a plan," said Rhea.

"Yes, we did," said Cadis. "*We* did." She gestured at herself and Iren. "*You* wouldn't listen."

"Why should I listen?" shouted Rhea, shrugging off Marta's hand from her shoulder. "You keep acting like the boss, and you're not. You're a cheating Findainer."

"Rhea!" shouted the tutor.

But Rhea was already weeping. She whirled back on Marta, a whole world of confusion and pain darkening her expression. "Why are you defending her? She threw me from the carriage."

"Wait, what?" said Cadis.

"Don't lie! You stomped on my fingers."

"I didn't," said Cadis. "I swear."

"And you cut me!"

She held up her forearm, covered in a blood-soaked bandage.

"But you attacked me first," said Cadis to no avail.

Nothing would stem Rhea's fury when she felt small and weak. Even if they believed her, Rhea knew her father would say she was begging for pity.

Hiram scribbled notes onto the sheet of parchment in the palm of his hand. Marta reached out to calm Rhea, but the young queen pulled her arm away. "Don't," she grumbled. "We all know what the dirty Findish did."

For the first time that morning, Cadis's composure broke, her face reddened, and she took a step toward Rhea. Iren, who had been shaving the fine hairs on her arm with her exhibition dagger, snapped a hand out and held Cadis back with the flat of the blade.

From the ground came Suki's entreaty. "*I* don't know what the dirty Findish did."

Hiram looked down at the queen sitting at his feet, fiddling with his bootlaces, and smiled. "Very well," he said. "You're old enough for the truth."

He reached down and picked up Suki so she'd pay attention and so she wouldn't cut herself on the pincer sheathed in his boot.

"The war began when the treacherous Findish assassinated our own good King Kendrick and Queen Valda."

"Of Meridan," corrected Suki.

"Yes, the king and queen of Meridan. *Our* king and queen."

"I'm a queen too," said Suki.

"Of course, and we'll get to that," said Hiram. "King Kendrick was my friend. He was a good man. And those gold nobles, jumped-up merchants, had him slaughtered for commercial gain."

"That's not true!" said Cadis, her whole body trembling.

"I'm sorry, but I was there," said Hiram. He seemed genuinely torn at the idea and took no joy in hurting Cadis. All the wounds were fresh for everyone. Perhaps it was still too early for such ugly history.

"Fighting alongside the traitors were the Tasanese."

"I'm Tasanese," said Suki.

Hiram continued. "They seized the opportunity to rise up and steal the crops of the lowlands, belonging to Meridan, and the hill-country ranches belonging to Corent."

"My daddy doesn't steal. He's king of the world," said Suki.

Hiram laughed. "Ah, but he does invade and annex and put farmers who disagree into the trees."

Suki didn't understand what execution by hanging meant.

"But the Corentine—" continued Hiram, rounding on Iren, "were the most devious. The ever-aloof Corentine, Meridan's only true allies, refused to honor our treaties and enter the fray. They holed themselves in their spires."

Iren shrugged. She didn't particularly seem to care.

"Meridan was gravely wounded, without king or queen or heir—enemies in every direction and friends in none. So, Declan the Giver, a lowly noble, rose up and took back the country he loved."

Rhea beamed with pride for her father.

"At the Battle of Crimson Fog, he survived an assassination attempt by the Tasanese, who sent their own princess to turn the coward's knife."

"Tola," whispered Suki.

"But Declan was too clever. And though it broke his heart, he sounded the battle horn that very night. Meridan charged the field. More soldiers died in the battle than at the siege of Blantyre, or even by Rotter's Plague. Most were Tasanese farmers, conscripted by the emperor to take up their sickles for war. The Findish supply lines were also caught unawares. When the sun rose that day, the chroniclers say the dew on the grass was bloodred. The 'mourning fog,' they called it. Outside these walls, they say everyone was present at Crimson Fog, because everyone felt the loss of someone they knew.

"Only Declan could unite the kingdoms and make peace. He paid for the mass graves Findain caused. He sheltered the war orphans Tasan created, and Corent ignored. You three," said Hiram, nodding at Cadis, Iren, and Suki, "are lucky you've been allowed to live under his protection, here in Meridan. And you're lucky to grow up alongside his own daughter."

Hiram finished his account and put Suki down. Marta glared at him with open disgust. It had all been whispered before in the bathhouses and empty chambers of Meridan Keep, but it had never been said. And never to the girls— the future sister queens of the four empires.

A silence that follows thunder hung about them. None of the girls would look Rhea in the eye. Everything had shifted between them.

Suki looked from Cadis, who wiped a tear from her cheek as quickly as she could, to Iren, who clenched her jaw in silence, to Rhea, who finally understood why Marta was trying to stop her.

At that moment the little girl realized that all the pain in her short life—her sissy's death, her good-bye to her parents—the massive nightmare that she wished and wished she would wake from, all of it was supposedly her own fault.

A black shroud seemed to fall over Suki's vision.

The five-year-old shattered the silence.

"It's not our fault!"

She charged at Hiram, battering his legs with her useless fists.

Hiram didn't respond. Any response would have made it worse.

In the ensuing tumult, Rhea stood by and watched as Cadis and Iren ran up to grab Suki. She knew now they would never be truly sisters, the way her father wanted. They would never reign together and usher in a generation of peace among the four empires. His great dream of a Pax Regina—peace of the queens—would be a disappointment he would have to endure. And she would be to blame for it.

She watched Cadis, the natural leader, peel Suki away

from Hiram's leg. And she saw Iren quietly sidle next to Hiram, reach into his robe, which had fallen open, and steal a roll of parchment full of the magister's notes.

When everything had finally settled:

The carriage reset and doused of its flames.

The horses calmed by Endrit's soothing words and bribed with his apples.

Two new soldiers called to play the bandits.

Only then did the servants return to cleaning the coliseum as if they had seen nothing.

Hiram's shinhound returned from delivering his message. The king's man nodded at Marta and bade the sister queens farewell.

So the four girls from four countries found themselves again in a new royal carriage, riding peaceably along, awaiting an attack.

Rhea wished desperately that they could go back to the first run and work it out among themselves. She had never had siblings before and didn't know how permanent the damage could be.

She tried to break the silence.

"Maybe we could do the same plan again?"

It was the best olive branch she could offer, admitting that Cadis's idea had worked for the most part. Though, of course, it was doling out tasks that caused their fight in the first place.

Cadis stared straight at a button in the upholstery. She

shook from the intensity of her focus on that one point—a taut rope on a ship at storm.

Rhea added, "But this time I'll go on Iren's side, so we don't get in each other's way."

Iren glanced up, nodded silently at Rhea, and then returned to picking her nails with her dagger. Suki sniffled. Her job was to stay in the coach until the bandits were fought off. Then she would crawl over the rigging and saddle one of the horses to bring them to a stop. She had been raised on horseback and could do the job even while pouting.

The very first unveiling of the hitherto queens would make a glorious climax to the festivities of King Declan's Revels. The entire coliseum would marvel at the martial skill and cunning of the future rulers of the world. But most of all, the people would find comfort in the fact that the heirs to the four thrones and four armies loved one another like sisters.

Rhea tried to intercept Cadis's stare by leaning into it. "Cadis? Does that sound good?"

It was Cadis's plan. Of course it sounded good. Rhea realized too late that making Cadis speak wasn't an olive branch, but just another kind of knife.

Cadis snapped her gaze to Rhea. Her eyes shimmered but held strong.

"Yes," she said, unblinking. "That's fine."

THE KINGDOM
OF MERIDAN

TEN YEARS LATER

CHAPTER ONE

Rhea

First from the others was Meridan's own
Lost a mother when she won a crown
Her daddy jumped up and defended the throne
Dance little queen, but don't . . . fall . . . down.
—Children's nursery rhyme

Rhea put up her hair as Endrit took off his shirt in the chamber below the private bedrooms of the castle.

Her maids were sent away.

The candles lit the room with warm halos floating a-pixie in the dark.

Rhea's thick black curls took dozens of jeweled floral pins, stabbed in every direction, to stay aloft in the formal style.

As she fumbled in front of the full-length mirror, Rhea glanced at Endrit's reflection. The years of assisting his mother in their training had made him the envy of all the noble sons at court, who seemed to be made of lesser mettle. Where the young lords would call for water and stop their coddled sword work at the first pain, Endrit had been the sparring partner—and punching bag—to the sisters, without the luxury of raising two fingers and storming off.

He was seventeen and looked like the flattering portraits hanging in the royal hall. Shoulders broad and tapering down across a barrel chest, and a taut abdomen. Rhea knew he kept his light brown hair a medium length because it looked soft and sandy when he lay under the trees in the orchards, regaling the swoony village girls with tales of castle comforts. And he knew it looked menacing when it hung wet over his obsidian eyes, in the heat of a fight.

After he pulled the linen tunic over his head, Endrit reached up and ran a hand through his wet hair. The third reason he kept it that length was to reach up and flex his arms and his abs and catch the princesses watching him in their mirrors.

Endrit smiled with mischief.

Rhea flushed and looked away. "Put your shirt back on," she said.

"Excuse me, Princess, but it's stifling in here. Some of us aren't used to castle fineries."

"Like clothing?" said Rhea.

"Like indoor heating," said Endrit.

Rhea parried the jab with an unimpressed eyebrow. "Do you suffer a lot of cold nights, curled up with the old tabby cat?"

Endrit's romantic exploits were the subject of endless teasing from the sisters . . . and endless speculation.

"I don't know about that," said Endrit. "Mrs. Wigglefoots never scratched so hard."

Endrit turned to show a crosshatch of scars on his ribs stretching across the muscles of his back. Each was from Rhea, Cadis, Iren, or Suki missing their mark, swinging wildly, or losing control during their blade work over the years.

Rhea had no witty riposte.

The scars were deep and irregularly healed, as if some had been carved into already-scabbed tissue. Rhea remembered when she was first learning to throw her weighted knives, when she didn't know to aim at the smallest target possible and was easily distracted. Endrit provided the human prey.

And if he wasn't so skilled at diving clear, she would have skewered him a dozen times. As it was, she knew she was responsible for many of those graze marks along Endrit's ribs. "Don't feel bad, Princess," said Endrit as he walked about the room, lifting the wooden dummies back onto their stands. "Some of these I remember fondly." Endrit was the only one allowed to call the sisters "princess" in that puckish tone, and only in private. Rhea liked it when he did, because it made him feel like more than just the servant they had abused all these years so they could become masters of their arts. It made him feel like a friend.

Rhea finished with a last pin in her hair. Her head almost wobbled under the weight. Rhea didn't spend any more time in front of the glass, not to admire herself as Cadis did. She simply used the glass to make sure her hair was ready for a royal ball and turned away. Not in disgust. Though maybe when she was younger. No, not disgust. Duty. Drive.

She was too busy to fuss about her thick mane or her inelegant posture. She was beautiful enough—though not as lovely as Cadis. And elegant enough—though not as regal as Iren.

Rhea caught herself thinking such thoughts and asked herself, *And what about Suki? How do we measure against the youngest?* Her answer was a welcome joke. She was certainly brave enough, but she would *never* be as wild as Suki.

Rhea straightened her red silk ball gown and said, "Aren't you ready?"

"No," said Endrit, lifting the last wooden dummy. "And neither are you."

He threw a golden armband he had retrieved from the floor. Rhea caught it and clasped it around her left wrist.

It was a chunky piece of jewelry, made finer by delicate scrollwork patterns cut into the gold in the shape of a shining sun. It matched the elaborate necklace Rhea wore—the masterpiece of her family's crown jewels. The lavish necklace began as a black lacy choker, set with hundreds of white diamonds all around and a giant ruby the size of an apricot at its center. Radiating from the ruby's setting were long, thin, round black stones that tapered into impossibly sharp points.

When her father had first clasped the necklace around her neck on her thirteenth birthday, he'd told her they were the teeth of the crest-beast of their house—the onyx wyrm.

It had been that evening after the shared birthday ceremony for all four sisters. Of course Rhea knew there were no dragons in the world, but she liked that her father told the tale as their ancestors would have, the way he had done when she was very young—before the war, before he had to treat her like her sisters, with no public sign of favor—like a bedtime story.

He looked at her in the mirror and she knew it must have been difficult for him, too. To pretend he had four daughters. To raise four queens—to pick up the burden their families had so recklessly dropped. She looked at him and saw a widower, a father, a great king. He was almost teary when he said, "You look a bit like your mother."

As Rhea remembered the moment and stared into the same mirror as that evening, she touched the eight black diamond spikes that lay across her bare neck, reminding Rhea never to look down.

She was dressed for a coronation in full regalia. Nothing in the basement chamber shined as brightly as the crested sun-shaped ring on her right hand or the pointed dragon-shaped ring on her left.

Only Endrit and her father had seen her in ceremonial dress.

The wooden dummies stood around the open space in haphazard groups as if they were revelers at the grand ball. The walls of the basement space glimmered with weapon racks. A few punching bags hung in the corners. A replica of the throne of Meridan had been shoved to one side.

No windows.

No hearth.

Each of the sisters had her own private training room. It was Declan's gift, a secret entrance leading down into a chamber below each of their bedrooms. Among the only things they didn't share. Rhea was certain he had built the best room for her, though she couldn't be sure. The sisters kept their rooms private. But she knew. She just knew. The girls had all run up to be the first to hug Declan. And as he hugged them back, Rhea had looked up, and her father had winked a conspiratorial wink. A sly and warm expression that said, *We'll keep the little secret between us.* Of course, was it such a shocking secret that a father loved his daughter more than others? Rhea was sixteen now, and knew they were unlike any other father and daughter in the kingdom. And so, perhaps, their secrets were uncommon too.

Rhea stepped forward and bowed a very slight bow to Endrit.

He had put his shirt back on. He was dressed no better than a stable hand. He *was* no better than a stable hand. But, oh, terrible hells could he dance.

He stood tall and bowed deep, watching her the entire time. Rhea felt a shudder that rattled her earrings. Endrit opened his arms, holding them in the formal waltz position. It was an invitation every woman in Meridan would accept.

"Care for a dance, highness?" said Endrit.

The room was silent but for their breathing. Rhea imagined the royal musicians playing as they would the following night in the grand hall at the banquet of the Revels. She steadied her hands. It had to be perfect tomorrow.

Endrit laughed. "Oh, come now. The marquis isn't worth a fright, is he? Should I slouch down, maybe snaggle up my face like he does?"

Rhea smiled, which threw off her concentration. Endrit swung his knees out into a bowlegged stance and twisted his lips into a sleazy grin. He made gross chupping noises with his lips. "Come now, my little sweet. Let me swing you around the room as only lovers do."

"Ew! Geez!" said Rhea. "Does he say stuff like that?"

"I dunno." Endrit shrugged. "Never met a prince before." He continued to make awful smoochie faces. As she giggled at Endrit's hideous caricature, Rhea felt her muscles relax. She breathed out and stepped into his arms, placed her hands into his.

Rhea looked up at Endrit's dark eyes and said, "I have to kill you, you know."

Endrit nodded. "And what if I kill you first?"

"Then you'll ruin the Revels and they'll probably hang you instead."

"That is too bad," he said. "I was beginning to like it here."

Only twelve women in the world were capable of training in the grimwaltz of the high style, because it required two exceptionally rare traits. First, it required a country—or in the case of Maria Fermosa, a criminal cartel secretly running a country. Second, and more specifically, it required one of the twelve sets of crown jewels, crafted generations ago by a master of the extinct Grimlaw Smithy.

Legend had it that each of the weaponsmiths of the great guild created one set—manipulating precious metals and gems into deadly jewelry worthy of queens and weapons worthy of assassins. Rings with poison caps, necklaces with hidden garrote wires, bracelets suited as much for shielding against sabers as for displaying the elegant wrists of nobility. The empress of Tasan was known for a crown that folded inward into a buckler. Maria Fermosa's corset was famously lined with diamond mail. "The better to help me sleep on the bed of knives my lieutenants like to set for me," she'd say.

Each set hid its own secrets. "Surprise is the only weapon they all share," said the master Grimlaw before he killed the eleven masters of his smithy and then himself.

The twelve crown arsenals passed down in the noble families, as did the martial art that governed their use. Just as monks of the steppe had created the art of wielding farm equipment to ward off mounted raiders and the magisters of Corent developed hand-to-hand warfare for the close quarters of the Academy spires, the grimwaltz, too, had a razor-sharp purpose. In formal state ceremonies, diplomatic parleys, and events of public address, the royals were the most exposed and the least armored. Born of the necessity to marry statecraft and spycraft, the tactical core of grimwaltz was defense of political assassination and preemptive murder.

The battlegrounds arose from the familiar settings: a throne, a feast, a dance.

Rhea held Endrit as they waltzed around the candlelit chamber.

Only queens trained with the crown jewels. But other forms of the martial art had spread among the commoners. Mothers would slip their daughters a razor bracelet before they went riding with a suitor. "Be happy, my love, but always take a bit of grim," they'd say. "Just in case."

The high style prized elegance and discretion over explicit warfare. Hundreds of years ago, the emira of Corent—Iren's ancestor—was said to have kissed a would-be assassin on his cheek and injected a paralyzing toxin with the hand draped behind his neck. She sat him down. The musicians played on. No one saw him stiffen.

Rhea's toe clipped over Endrit's foot and she stumbled the next step. She cursed her own clumsiness.

"It's okay," said Endrit.

It wasn't okay. Tomorrow was the Revels, when each of the sisters would perform for the crowds to showcase their training for the year. Cadis would fight like a typhoon and astonish them. Iren would flow as subtle and sublime as a zephyr, and Suki would shine like a wildfire.

As they traced an intricate pattern around the wooden dummies, Rhea asked, "Has Cadis polished her routine?"

They twirled a figure eight around two dummies that Endrit had arranged to look like a quarreling couple. Endrit smirked and looked away, as if sharing some joke with another partygoer. He was always the one that other men tried to impress—even if he was below them.

"Come on, now, Rhea," he said.

"Come on, what?"

Endrit didn't respond.

Rhea hated that. When he expected her to know things. And the knowing was somehow being grown-up enough to see things as he did. She hated it even more that she *did* know in this case. She knew he would have said, "I keep *your* secrets, Princess." Meaning he'd keep the others', as well.

Endrit lifted his arm to let Rhea take the inside turn under it. As her back was turned, Endrit reached behind him and pulled a thin filleting knife—of the kind Findish sailors used to cut rope and clean fish.

When Rhea whirled around to face him, Endrit kept the knife behind his back. With his other hand, he pulled her into his chest. He smelled like barn hay, sweat, and horse liniment.

This part of the dance was an intimate struggle between them. Rhea wanted to see what he held behind him, but Endrit thwarted the attempt. She stepped forward into the space that Endrit's foot vacated. He held her in a cross-body lead, so that she faced in the same direction.

Her shoulders nested across his chest. She craned her neck upward to keep eye contact. She felt his breath waft over her lips.

They turned around the room. Any audience would see

the blade glisten behind Endrit. But only sparring dummies shared the floor.

They stepped and cross-stepped, back and forth, feint and parry. With his firm hand on her lower back, Endrit always managed to turn Rhea before she could see the knife. They tangled and clutched, until finally the moment they both knew was coming, when the flautist would stand for a trilling climactic solo, and Endrit sent Rhea into a wild free spin toward the middle of the floor.

Rhea twirled at the center of the chamber hall with one arm above her head like an automaton in a music box. Her other hand rested on the ruby brocade hanging from her neck. She felt her skirt billow and corrected her balance for the weight of the sparkling jewels she wore. Her back arched. She spun on the ball of her foot and felt graceful for the first time all night.

And more than anything, she felt watched.

As Rhea straightened out of the spin, she lowered her arm. Endrit extended his hand and she took it. They knew the flautist would hit a note at this point that sounded like a goldfinch being crushed in a doorjamb.

Endrit reeled her in. She spun toward him. As she did so, Endrit lifted the knife and stabbed just as Rhea turned in to his arms.

The knife whistled downward.

It clanged on the ruby brocade, nestled in Rhea's palm. The delicate gold chains strapped it around her fingers so that it held firm—and armored the inside of her left hand.

The tip of the fillet knife found a socket in the brocade to stick itself.

She stared at Endrit.

He whispered, "You've got this. Fight speed."

Rhea's hand shook, holding off the pressure, until she wrenched her hand and sent the blade scudding across the stone floor of the chamber.

In the same motion, she pivoted her hips and dug a right hook into Endrit's ribs.

He grunted and let go.

Rhea dashed away, to a safe distance.

In the moment's reprieve, Rhea made a formal ready position and inserted the point of the dragon ring on her right hand into the well of the sun-shaped ring on her left. With a twist, the head of the dragon punctured into a compartment of the sun ring and coated the tip in corkspider poison.

Endrit bored down on her with clenched fists. He opened with a left. Rhea smacked it down with the brocade in her open palm. He winced as his knuckles cracked on the stone. He swung with a heavy right. Rhea ducked under and punched twice on the same rib as before. This time she pulled short before stabbing him with the poisoned ring.

Endrit staggered back.

But not long.

He lunged with a vertical knee and caught Rhea's chin in her crouched position. Rhea's eyes flashed white. This part always hurt at full-contact fight speed.

Rhea moved with the impact and hit the ground at a midroll.

She scrambled behind a dummy to buy time to regain her footing and to reach for a hairpin. As Endrit approached, she flicked her hand and launched two of the weighted pins at his face. Endrit lurched sideways.

The darts planted into the face of the dummy.

The audience would understand the dummy was a stand-in for the attacker. Already, between the poison ring and the darts, she had killed two would-be assassins.

Endrit strode forward, reached down, and grabbed a broadsword from the belt of a dummy. Without hesitation, he marched toward her, raised his sword, and struck down across her body.

Rhea dove under the angled blade. She followed the motion into a sideways somersault. She ended in an alleyway formed by dummies standing in two rows. Endrit pressed the attack. He dashed around the dummies to one end of the rows.

His heavy blade would be carried only by soldiers or royal guards attempting to kill her, a simulation of the ultimate betrayal and a grim reality—the possibility of her own bodyguards turning coat of arms.

Her father used to whisper, "Even our men. Even Endrit or Marta. If they turn, you put them down like rabid dogs."

She couldn't blame him for worrying. It was betrayal and assassination that had taken the last king and queen of Meridan. She knew he was determined never to let that happen again. In the advent of such a paranoid outcome, Rhea would be woefully disadvantaged, just as she was now, with Endrit approaching.

Rhea gave ground and reached for more throwing blades. More and more locks of her hair tumbled onto her shoulders as she pulled the pins and sent them flying at Endrit.

He marched inexorably forward.

She showed off her precision. It had gotten even better over the last year.

Dummies on either side of Endrit sprouted gems between their eyes as he approached.

A whole unit of blackguards, dead.

Rhea stood at the end of the row.

Endrit closed the distance and swung again.

This time she caught it up high, early in the swing, with the side of her thick bracelet. A delicate shield for hacking blades.

Endrit slashed down again and again.

One.

Two.

Three.

Rhea counted in her head.

High block.

Step back.

Low block.

Step back.

The blows made her entire arm jolt. On the last step, she had a disarm maneuver that was new to the routine, the one that could maim both of them if she failed.

Don't falter. Don't falter, she thought.

Endrit swung the sword sideways at her neck, like a scythe cutting the heads of wheat. Instead of deflecting the strike, Rhea stepped to meet it. She blocked with her inner forearm—bless the smith for making her bracelet strong. When the sword clanged on her bracelet, Rhea followed it with her left hand and hit the blade up by the hilt with the brocade in her open palm.

The sword twisted between the two opposing forces and wrenched out of Endrit's grip. The blade caught Endrit's shoulder, slicing the tunic as it flew off, clattering on the stones.

Endrit winced, but he didn't drop a step.

He grabbed Rhea around the neck, just above her choker.

She pulled two of the black stone sunrays from her necklace and made the motion of stabbing just inside his collarbone on either side.

Endrit let go, as any assailant would have been dead by then.

They moved into the big finish: a series of sparring drills where Endrit attacked from every direction—swinging wildly, changing forms from the Corentine ridge-hand to Tasanese grappling. Rhea exhausted the rays of her sun necklace, cutting off kicks at the knee, meeting "vicious with vicious," as her father would say.

She was an exhibition of cold, efficient, and most of all, lethal control. That was the heart of grimwaltz and the heart of a ruler, after all—control.

The dummies in the dark room each found a new way to die.

The wound on Endrit's shoulder bled.

The left side of his tunic was nearly soaked.

The final stunt was a subtle routine that began with Endrit grabbing Rhea's wrists. Some of Marta's best choreography. Rhea stepped out to break Endrit's balance and twisted her hands around to grab his wrists. They struggled for leverage.

The music the next day would swell—every stringed instrument in full volume. Then, just as abruptly, the music would drop.

Rhea and Endrit straightened, hand in hand.

They were back in waltz position as if nothing had happened.

Except now Rhea's curls were untamed and unbearably hot. Her hands still shook, twitch reflexes still set to caution. Endrit's tunic was a sopping rag—sweat and blood. He said, "Well done," but his grimace gave him away. He was hurt.

The chamber was a slaughterhouse strewn with two-dozen dummies—stabbed, poisoned, or crippled.

They each stepped back, bowed, turned, and bowed again to the pretend audience.

Rhea instinctively angled her bow in the direction where her father would be sitting—the king's balcony of the Royal Coliseum.

The instant they finished, Rhea rushed to Endrit's side. "I'm so sorry," she said, helping him take a seat.

Endrit took the help, but didn't seem to need it.

"Don't worry. That was perfect."

"I cut your shoulder open."

"They want realism. Your dad would have loved it."

Rhea paused a moment from examining the shirt.

"You think?"

"I'm telling you, Princess, it was perfect."

Rhea took a moment to relish the idea of gaining back the honor she had lost after the Revels of the previous year. No one told her she had lost it, but she saw it in the eyes of the king and in the way Marta patted her on the shoulder and said, "Good work. Learn from this and you've won."

She only ever said that to the loser.

Rhea had certainly lost her sparring exposition to Cadis. In front of all the nobles of Meridan, Rhea had dropped to a knee before the future queen of Findain. It may as well have been surrender—a banner that read THE BLOOD RUNS THIN IN MERIDAN KEEP. The entire crowd had been stunned. Her father, who loved her—she knew he loved her—still couldn't hide his disappointment.

It wasn't his fault. Rhea knew she had caused him endless jibes in the court of public opinion. Rhea had subordinated the house of Declan to a bunch of treacherous Findish merchants in one clumsy step.

She heard a voice.

Endrit's.

Rhea snapped out of her memory to see his obsidian eyes peering at her.

"Where'd you go, Rhea?"

"Nothing," said Rhea. "Take your shirt off."

Endrit laughed. Rhea added, "So I can see your cut, you dandified peacock."

"Of course," said Endrit. "And anyway, to the victor go the spoils." He gave a cheeky grin.

Rhea rolled her eyes and helped him pull the sleeve so he didn't have to move his left shoulder. The cut was shallow. It would be scabbed by tomorrow.

"We have bandages in the outer hall," said Rhea.

"We're done? Are you saying all I had to do was stab myself?"

Rhea pressed down on Endrit's shoulder. He howled with laughter and pain.

"You're lucky we got it perfect," said Rhea, standing. "Otherwise I'd make you go until you bled out."

"A noble way to die. I'm sure there'd be a royal funeral."

"A royal funeral? Ha! We'd flop you down behind the barn," teased Rhea. She left the jewels scattered around the private chamber: the pins stuck in the dummies, the blades of the sun necklace embedded in several wooden posts. She'd return the next morning.

"I suppose that's fair enough," said Endrit. "That happens to plenty of royals too."

When Rhea and Endrit walked into the common hall that connected the rooms of the four queens, Rhea was disappointed to find her sisters and Marta there, thus ending her privacy with Endrit. And Rhea's sisters seemed disappointed to see a shirtless Endrit—not because of his partial nudity, but because he was in that state with Rhea.

The six-sided room had one door on every wall—four leading to the queens' rooms, one coming from the throne room, and one for the servants to use coming from the kitchen.

At the center of the room sat a giant round oaken table large enough to seat fifteen and sturdy enough to stage a Tasanese circus. The sisters ate their meals at the table, studied there for Hiram's exams, and on nights such as these, when they couldn't sleep, they convened around it to while away the hours.

Cadis had been regaling them with an improvised tale of Rusila, the Maid Marauder, something about winning a race to a treasure by lashing her ship to the back of a sea dragon. Only Suki had been listening, as she lay on her back in the middle of the giant table, throwing an iron ring up to the vaulted ceiling between the segments of the chandeliers and catching it on her feet.

Iren and Marta sat together on the far side. Before them were several sheets of stained glass. Iren used a long steel cutter that looked like a fountain pen, with a diamond tip, to cut intricate shapes into the glass. Marta used Iren's nippers to snap the cut pieces out of the sheets.

At first blush, it looked like she was making an elaborate set of wind chimes in the old Corentine style. The spires of her home were famous for decorative glasswork, situated as they were in the windy mountains, above the cloud line. The Corentines admired the elegant and delicate work. Many of the balconies of the Academy spires were hued of colored glass.

When Rhea and Endrit entered from the bedroom, everyone stopped—the storytelling, the juggling, the glass-work.

In that short instant, as Rhea weighed all the disappointment in the room, she couldn't help but feel hurt. Hers was not malicious. She just wanted more time with Endrit. *Why shouldn't she?* But theirs, well, their disappointment was because they wanted to spend *less* time with her.

Marta stood up when she saw Endrit bleeding. The pliers in her hand fell to the table. Just as quickly Marta controlled herself, as she always did. She wouldn't embarrass him by doting over it. But for the slightest of moments—every time one of them injured her son—they would see the shadow of outrage pass over her.

"What happened?" said Marta in a controlled voice.

Only then did Rhea realize she was in bigger trouble than she'd thought. She had summoned Endrit to her chamber after-hours. She had continued to train at full contact, though they all knew that Marta forbade training the day before the Revels, to give them time to mentally prepare. And she had cut a bleeding gash into her son's shoulder.

Rhea's answer caught in her throat.

To her eternal gratitude, Endrit stepped forward. "This? This is nothing," he said.

"How did it happen?" said Marta.

"Game of checkers," said Endrit, grinning brighter than a three-tiered candelabrum. "You should teach these girls how to lose gracefully."

The ludicrousness of the excuse, and the sheer confidence it took to expect the others to believe it, made Marta finally crack a smile. Endrit glanced back at Rhea and winked.

"You will address them as 'queen,' or 'highness,' or 'princess,'" said Marta as she sat, but the bite in her tone was already gone.

"Yes, ma'am," said Endrit.

Suki rolled over, sprang off the table, and walked with Endrit toward a hutch in the corner. At fifteen, she was one year younger than Rhea and two years younger than Cadis and Iren. Somehow the divide seemed even wider. She still wore her hair in two pigtails.

"Hey, Endrit!" she chirped.

Endrit guided her over to his right side so he could put his good arm around her shoulder. "Hey, Susu. How's my favorite acrobat?" he said.

Even from behind, Rhea could tell that Suki was blushing.

She couldn't help but envy his easy air and his ability to make friends with them all. *How can any one person like four such different girls? And how do they all like him?*

It was a mystery to Rhea. She suspected the world outside of Meridan Keep, outside of the Protectorate, had plenty of easygoing friends, whereas the four queens could never be so casual and could never escape the fact that they were in constant competition.

For instance, in the competition for Endrit's attention, Suki had clearly just won. She took him to the hutch, grabbed several bandages, and was already helping him tend to the wound. Meanwhile, Rhea was standing in the space between her door and the table, with nothing for her arms to do but dangle.

"How was the game of . . . checkers?" asked Iren, as she cut a long line across an azure sheet. The glass sang a high, grating pitch.

"Uh, good," said Rhea. She sidled into a high-back chair at the table. Marta's disapproval soured the air.

Iren, of course, didn't notice, or pretended not to.

She has such slender fingers, thought Rhea as she watched Iren inlay a razor-thin shard of glass onto a tableau. Iren's exhibition last year was an obscure juniper tea ceremony from the Corentine dale country. The year before that, she'd played her harp—all thousand veils of the *Falconer's Dream* by PilanPilan.

It was as if Iren wanted to prove how advanced the Corentines were, how cultured, how smug.

Rhea's father didn't mind it as much as he did Cadis with her athletic exploits. Hiram lapped it up as if it were the first time anyone had played PilanPilan in Meridan Keep. Though to be fair, it might have been.

Rhea couldn't keep her eyes off of Endrit and Suki in the corner. Endrit's rakish grin was all she could see and Suki's obvious tittering all she could hear.

"We were just saying it should be nice weather tomorrow," said Cadis.

Rhea doubted that they were sitting together and discussing some almanac. She recognized halfhearted court conversation when she heard it.

"Oh?" she said. "Should we switch to plate leather?"

Marta looked up from her study of Iren's glasswork. "Of course not. Full armor if you plan to go full speed."

Rhea knew it. She just had nothing else to say. It was getting harder and harder to be around them. To force herself where she was obviously not wanted. Where she halted all sisterly conversation and sucked the warmth from the room. Rhea was about to excuse herself back to her bedroom when she heard the unmistakable scraping of a shinhound's paws on castle stone.

When they all turned to the outer door, Rhea used the opportunity to steal a gaze at Cadis. She had tied her long blond hair into many thin braids that became dreadlocks—the common tradition of the Findish marauding parties. Bits of shell, coin, and other precious stones where woven into each braid and clinked musically when she turned her head. The green and gold sash that wrapped the braids back accentuated her resolute jawline and sharp-hewn nose. She was a queen already—although of a different sort from Iren. She was a war general, a queen by no right other than that she was stronger, more charismatic, and deadlier that anyone else.

Rhea made sure to look away before anyone caught her

staring—"stewing in her own jealousy" as Suki had put it once. Rhea swore she wasn't jealous. What was she to be jealous of? Meridan had beaten Findain. No, she preferred to think of their relationship as an early distancing of Meridan and its subjects.

The truth was that she and Cadis had been avoiding each other ever since the last Revels, their last match, a full year ago.

Marta wouldn't allow them to spar anymore. "Not until you can stand as sisters again," she'd said. Rhea wasn't sure they had *ever* been sisters.

The shinhound scrabbled into the hall—a welcome distraction for everyone but Suki. Without looking up from her glasswork, Iren reached out a finger, pointed to a square of marble on the floor, and said, "Ismata, sit!"

The massive beast lowered its head, marched directly to the square, and sat awaiting further orders.

Cadis exclaimed with surprise, "Ha!" No one had ever dared order a shinhound before.

"You can tell them what to do?" said Endrit.

"And you named him Ismata?" added Suki.

Iren continued to work, but she smiled and nodded. After making them wait a moment, she said, "I'm counter-training them."

"Without Hiram's knowledge?" said Marta, scandalized by such an impertinent idea.

"I had to name them so my commands could override his. Come here, Ismata." The shinhound bounded forward and let Iren scratch him under the chin. To Iren, this was just another project. But if Hiram found out, the magister would put the entire kennel to the sword.

Iren reached into her sleeve, drew out a strip of salted beef, and held it out. The shinhound snapped it up.

"Now you're showing off," said Cadis.

"Wouldn't you?" said Iren.

"Oh, of course," said Cadis. "I'd teach the dog your tea ceremony and present him at the Revels wearing laces and a petticoat."

Endrit laughed.

Marta sucked her teeth. For such an embarrassment, the magister would kill the dogs and burn the stadium with all the revelers still in it.

"I think it's hilarious," said Suki, eyeing Endrit to make sure he agreed.

"You shouldn't have done this," said Marta as she approached the hound and pulled the rolled parchment from the holster around its neck.

The beast, even while sitting, was nearly as tall as she was and twice as thick. Rhea imagined her teacher during the Battle of Epiphany Rising, fending off war dogs with a long-handled bident, which the soldiers called "shin guards."

Marta never talked about the bite marks on her forearms, just as she never discussed the war.

She unrolled the parchment and read, "By the word of good King Declan, Protector and Preserver of the Pax Regina."

Rhea let go of the lock of hair she had been nervously twirling around her finger. She tried not to tense in front of the others, but rarely did her father speak to them through the magister's hands.

Marta continued. "Regarding the Revels, tenth of their kind. In light of the ever-present threat of attacks and sub-terfuge by Findish radicals—"

Rhea knew what would happen next. Marta paused, as if to give Cadis time to act righteously indignant. Cadis stood erect and jutted her chin to take the insult with public dignity. To Rhea, the show was overwrought. Her father had expressly written "radicals." No one was saying the perfect princess had anything to do with it. But that didn't matter to Cadis. She wore her victimhood proudly.

"Go on," said Rhea.

"—to protect against such treason against the four crowns, the midnight ball will be reserved to the noble families of Meridan, royal guests, and guardian hands of the high court."

"That's not fair," said Suki.

"None others shall be permitted into Meridan Keep," said Marta, finishing the message. "So spake the king."

Rhea held her breathing. Of course her father would be cautious. He was the only one with the burden of protecting the Keep from attack. Hiram's spies must have uncovered a plot of some kind. But none of the girls were interested in spycraft. They just knew Endrit and the other performers couldn't come to the celebratory dance. After all his work.

Rhea was heartbroken too. But she knew the others would blame her for the whole thing.

And she had the least to complain about. She'd be dancing with Endrit anyway, at the exhibitions. Even so, she *had* hoped to dance with him later, when fewer eyes would be upon them and they weren't trying to kill each other, when—maybe—she could close her eyes, feel warm hands about her, and calm her anxious thoughts for just a short while. Rhea bemoaned the loss quietly, to herself.

"It'll be just us and a bunch of inbred nobles?" said Suki with a pout.

"They don't inbreed in Meridan," said Iren.

"Then why are they so scrawny and weird?" said Suki.

"Because they're pampered and boring," said Iren.

"Well, I'm not touching any of them," said Suki. Sometimes she still sounded like the five-year-old brat who had been spoiled rotten back in the court of Tasan. The high emperor had five children. The sycophant Tasanese nobles treated all of them like a pantheon of insolent gods.

As soon as Rhea rolled her eyes, she regretted it. Suki—of course—had been watching Rhea as she insulted Meridan, to measure the success of her needling.

"I hope there is a Findish revolt. Then we can finally go home."

"Suki!" said Marta. Rhea bit back the obvious retort, as she always did with their baby sister. If Findain instigated all-out war, the last thing the girls would be doing was going home. But if Rhea said it—even though Iren and Cadis already knew—it would destroy the last vestige of their relationship. They stabbed and stabbed the dragon, but if Rhea ever breathed her fire, they would act shocked and claim they always knew dragons to be so vicious.

"What?" said Suki. "How long do we have to do this? I have my own little siblings to condescend to." She cast unsubtle glances at Rhea as she spoke.

Is she foolish or delusional? Even if she returns after ten years, which of her siblings would even recognize her? In such a formal court, would they ever bow to a Meridan-raised queen, even if she is the oldest now?

For a tense moment only the shinhound made any noise, chomping on some other treat that Iren must have given from a hidden fold in her sleeve.

Endrit—*thank the gods for him*—finally broke the silence by giving Suki exactly what she seemed to be mewling for. He reached out, put a hand on her waist, and pulled her back from her battlefield. He wrapped his arms around her shoulders—so obviously as a big brother would, though Suki wouldn't know it—and said, "There won't be anything so exciting as a revolt. The Findish have their future queen to fight for them at court."

The stable hand is no diplomat, thought Rhea. Cadis had no sway in the Meridan court. It would only make them feel like hostages. But Rhea was tired of caring how her sisters felt all the time.

"Come on, girls," said Marta. "To bed. You'll be up all night tomorrow."

"Not if those Findish radicals attack," said Cadis bitterly. The barb wasn't as funny as she might have expected.

"And not if I have to dance with nobles," said Suki.

Rhea felt them all avoid her gaze. They blamed her, though they would never say it. She was the daughter of the man who'd conceived of the Protectorate—the nature of their entire relationship. Their captor—if they wanted to think of it so ungenerously. Rhea was certain that Cadis felt so. She had a seafarer's wanderlust, always consulting maps and travelers' accounts of the wider world. She was the one already fit to rule—the only one among them rightly called a woman. But here she sat. Of all of them, Cadis seemed the most shackled, the most caged. Rhea would happily open the cage, if she could, and wish good riddance of her so-called sister.

At least she would not be treated as their constant villain, even though she was their sister and friend and advocate.

"I could speak to the king," offered Rhea. "Maybe we can bring guests."

Suki scoffed, "If I wanted your dad to listen to someone, I would have asked Cadis." It was Rhea's mistake to ever hold out an olive branch.

"Has anyone considered that maybe I'm not so keen on dancing with a bunch of termagants who do nothing but abuse and boss me around?" said Endrit.

"Endrit!" said Marta, the only one still horrified by his familiarity with the queens.

Suki laughed, turned around, and slapped Endrit's shoulder where she had just bandaged his cut.

"Are we toilsome prey compared to your handmaidens?" said Cadis. The look she received from Endrit, which both Rhea and Suki observed, was a raised brow, an impressed smirk, and a mischievous sparkle of the eye.

The shinhound shuffled nervously and barked to remind Marta that the parchment needed to be returned.

"Oh, they're not maidens," said Endrit. "Does the captain of Findain not approve?"

Cadis made a playful show of turning her back to him. Rhea always suspected that Cadis could have him if she wanted.

"All right. To bed with all of you," said Marta, clapping her hands.

Iren continued to gather her glasswork into the oilcloth, and that was signal enough for all of them to disperse. Suki griped and demanded a kiss on the cheek from Endrit, who obliged.

Cadis marched straight to her room. The precaution for their personal safety was still a personal insult, apparently.

Endrit slung his arm around his mother as if she were another sister and leaned down to kiss her sincerely on the temple. As he walked Marta out, he said over his shoulder, "Good night, my queens," as a jester might say it, with too much gravitas, to make it sound foolish.

Suki chirped, "Good night!" and ran off, leaving Rhea and Iren sitting across from each other at the oaken round table.

Iren collected her glass-cutting tools in silence. Rhea sat

for a short while, listening to her heart, still pounding from her training.

Rhea suddenly felt the overwhelming desire for a sister—a true sister—in whom she could confide, one whose only loyalty was to her, and not the others. She wished she could tell Iren about her training and ask if Iren felt as she did about Endrit in moments of such intense and terrifying desire that she imagined herself pinning him down, kissing him, pressing herself to him, but found herself at a loss for what to do after.

The image would turn murky and dreamlike. Rhea would feel embarrassed, as if Endrit could tell that she was childlike and ill versed in the details of love.

When they were younger, Iren had showed them an illuminated page from the poems of the ribald monk Hakan. In the corner, a couple sat entwined, one kissing the other's nape, the other openmouthed like a baby bird, begging the gods to transfix them, just as they were, onto the parchment of a book, so that they could remain in their embrace forever.

The girls had giggled at the lewd painting and teased one another.

Cadis had elbowed Suki and said, "That'll be you and Cooky Cogburn," the greasy old kitchen master.

"No! *Akh*. I wanna be the girl who rides the gryphon across the sea," she'd said, pointing to another illuminated page.

That was a particularly nice memory for Rhea, a time

when they were four sisters sneaking together—not three and the king's daughter.

"Something wrong?" said Iren.

Rhea returned from her memory to the table, the central chamber, midnight before the Revels Ten. The candles guttering outside. The guards clapping their heels on the stone.

"No," she said.

"You were staring at me," said Iren.

"Sorry," said Rhea.

"Nervous?"

"No," said Rhea. She hated them to know her weaknesses.

"We could have Cooky send up mulled cocoa."

"No, thanks," said Rhea, smiling at the coincidence of old Cogburn in her musing.

"After the last time, it's natural to be nervous," said Iren. She paused from her packing to look up. It wasn't a warm expression, but it might have been the best Iren could muster. Only she could be so blunt in her caregiving. Rhea didn't respond.

"You missed one," said Iren. She pointed with a glass grinder at Rhea's left ear. Rhea reached up and felt a hairpin still in her hair.

"Thanks," she said. *Will I forever feel like the sloppy pig slumped before the emira of Corent?*

"I was serious about speaking to the king about admitting Endrit," said Rhea. Iren stacked the glass pieces from largest to smallest, arranged by color.

Finally, she said, "Ismata, go kiss the future queen."

The shinhound sprang around the table and licked Rhea's outraised palms. Rhea laughed. It felt wonderful to laugh. It was a small gesture, but Iren's favor came in tiny doses, and Rhea was relieved to have it.

"For your kindness, Your Majesty," said Iren.

Rhea walked down the wide stone corridor of Meridan Keep as she always did—as her father taught her—with a weapon hidden in her palm. The hairpin was sharp enough to suture a crocodile's maw. "Pray you never need it," her father had whispered, "but some in the castle will never love us. Some think I killed my friend Kendrick and hid his heir in the dungeons."

But such was always the way—Rhea knew—with royal clamor. Rumor and conspiracy rarely bothered with the truth. Rhea had watched her father weep for good King Kendrick, his bosom friend, every year. She had seen the dungeons, which Declan had emptied of prisoners and showed to disbelieving nobles.

"All this room," he had said, standing in the basement floor. "I suppose Meridan Keep will boast the largest wine cellar in all of Pelgard."

He had no heart for dungeons and no interest in rumors.

"Meet rumors with quiet, my love."

When Rhea was younger and felt her sisters hush whenever she entered a chamber, that was his coda. *Meet rumor with quiet.* But he was no fool, for as she got older, he told her of the discontented nobles who would fare better under some mocked-up heir to Kendrick—a puppet they would name Taylin, after Kendrick's misbegotten babe. He told her of the Findish rebels. And he added to their code: "Meet rumor with quiet, treason with cunning."

Rhea followed the shinhound Iren had secretly named Ismata toward Hiram's study, where she would likely find her father as well. The magister was cunning enough for all of them.

His shinhounds carried secret messages throughout the palace and the spy networks of Meridan.

No treason would match the young magister's cunning.

Rhea wondered if he knew of Iren naming the hounds and training them to her command.

As she climbed the tower to the magister's study, matching the hound's pace, Rhea noted the soreness in her thighs. Perhaps she'd worked too hard before the Revels.

She paused on the landing, outside the candlelight of the study to compose her breath. From the room, she heard Hiram's voice. "Ah. Good boy, Ismata."

Rhea smiled. *Of course the magister knows.* Perhaps he was charmed by her childish attempt to give pet names to war dogs.

"Is there a return message?"

The voice was her father's.

A rustle of parchment.

"No. The king commands. The children listen."

Her father made a mocking sound. *Do they know I am here?*

The scrabbling of the shinhound must have covered her footfalls. Rhea felt a momentary thrill at the illicit idea of spying on the two great men of Meridan.

Iren, in all her properness, would have surely disapproved of queens skulking in dark hallways.

Rhea eased forward along the wall to the edge of the entry and listened.

"Very well, then. They're likely cursing my name," said Declan.

"Good," said Hiram. "Those who complain for want of handsome dancing partners lack real dangers to speak of."

"I've heard that Taylin is handsome," said her father in a playful tone.

"Oh, I'm sure he's quite the beauty. Grown ten feet in every direction."

Her father laughed. It must have been great relief, when every day the nobles spread rumors against him, as if the dead heir would arise to take the throne and give them back their ill-gotten lands.

Her father sighed heavily.

"Old friend, I fear the Findish use the myth to court our own banners away from us. They claim he captains a galleon and a crew of rivermen who pledge his return."

"Rumormongering to stir discord. The Findish revolt isn't nearly so illustrious," said Hiram.

"I know. The poor child is dead. But these river rats pirated far too inland for my liking. I think we'll have to buy their loyalty."

Rhea had never heard her father speak of corruption. She thought of retracing her steps back down but feared the shinhound would hear and reveal her.

"Oh?" said Hiram. "But they have money."

"And I hear they eat scum snails dredged from the river," said Declan. "The only choice is to give them a bride."

"Pity the bride to such beasts," said Hiram.

"Pity my daughter, then," said Declan. "I've given them Rhea."

Rhea bit back a gasp. *Will he really? Are the Findish rivermen so important? Am I? Has he lost so much faith in me after the last Revels? Has he given me up? Really?*

She gripped the jewel of the bladed hairpin so hard that it imprinted into her palm. She imagined guards charging up the stairs at that very moment to deliver her into the grasp of ravenous pirates.

Rhea's mind raced with improbable thoughts as she stood with her back to the stone wall, until she heard the giggling of the two men in the study.

"You may enter now, daughter mine."

I should have known. Rhea stood frozen for a second longer, feeling sheep-headed for having been taken in by the foolishness. She knew she would have to show herself—a child pulled from a hiding place.

Hiram cleared his throat and the shinhound trotted out into the hall to herd her in. It was cruel to threaten her life with a joke, but she deserved no better for spying, she supposed.

Rhea patted the dog, exhaled, and stepped into the doorway. Both men wore insufferable grins. Rhea knew they could read the credulity on her face.

"Check her teeth," said Hiram. "The river rats will want a deck maid who can bite through the scum line if it gets caught."

He barely finished before both of them broke off into peals of laughter. Rhea was once again a child. But even so, seeing her father smile—rare as it was these past ten years—was a welcome joy.

Hiram's private study was warmly lit by sconces inset into stone, caged to keep sparks from the many shelves of scrolls and codices. Cabinets full of curiosities—natural and unnatural—lined the back wall.

Declan and Hiram sat in pinned leather chairs. The reading table between them held a map of the four kingdoms of Pelgard, a few volumes of poetry, and a snifter of plum brandy from Tasan's plantation archipelago.

Both had cups in hand.

Her father had a tin box of ice, which must have been raced upstairs by shinhound from the sunken domes along the outer wall of Meridan Keep.

Rhea waited.

"Tell me, good spy, what did you hear?" said her father.

"Nothing but doddering and foolishness, Father." The insult had the opposite intended effect. Rhea continued. "I've come about the ball."

"Of course you have," said Declan.

"The Findain threat is real, domina. Don't let our joking numb you."

"I know," said Rhea, "but we'd like to bring guests, at least."

Her father sat up and placed his cup on the table. "Marta and her son?" he said, his face familiarly grave.

"Yes. Not only them," said Rhea. "Other servants, the cadets competing in the Revel games."

"Boys," said Hiram.

"Kings and magisters, practically, compared to the river rats."

Hiram gave a conceding bow and smiled. He liked a sharp riposte.

Her father stared at the figurines situated on the map. She could see his concerns. What if some cadets were Findain sympathizers? What if they attacked at the ball? All the "what if" possibilities that necessitated her training in the grimwaltz.

Rhea added to her cause. "It would mean a great deal to us, especially to Suki. . . ."

Her father turned his attention. "And why especially for the little queen?"

"You've seen it. She's still learning her charms on Endrit."

Is it any less so for myself? If anything, it might have been more so.

"She talks of going home," said Rhea, "and seems distant, heartsick."

Her father seemed genuinely grieved by the notion.

"Very well," he said. "I know this . . . arrangement is difficult."

Rhea wished she could dash across the room and hug her father.

"Wise, my lord," said Hiram. "We don't want Suki to end like her sister."

Declan acknowledged with a joyless smirk. "Anything else, my blood daughter?"

Rhea shook her head, no. "Thank you."

"Have you prepared this time for the Revels?"

Rhea was not defending for such a stab.

She knew he referred to her surrendered loss to Cadis.

Perhaps it was the reference to Suki's ignoble sister, Tola, that sent him edge-ward. Tola the soldier who had attempted to murder Declan during peace talks. Tola, who singlehandedly forced Declan's hand into the Battle of Crimson Fog. Tola, who had inadvertently given Declan his greatest victory at such great cost of lives.

"Yes, Father," said Rhea. "I've trained."

"I've heard you train as one who wants only to survive," he said, still testing her.

"I meet such silly rumors with quiet, Father, as I was taught. I train only for victory."

Her father nodded. "Very well. Let the cadets and the servants dance. If they mean us treachery, then I can always throw Hiram at their feet and run away."

Rhea was thankful and ashamed, as she often felt around her father. At once swaggering as heir of the house of Declan and horrified to be its weakest in generations.

She took the downward stairs in leaps, hoping her sisters would credit her for the news. Knowing them, they would see it as yet another show of favoritism.

Even though she risked her father's safety for it, Suki would likely act suspicious and look to Iren and Cadis for some reaction to parrot. Iren, of course, would remain conveniently silent and Cadis, annoyingly pleasant.

No matter. Endrit would be at the ball.

She didn't need sisters of such disloyal quality. She didn't know if the rumor her father had mentioned had been spoken by one of them, but she knew the sentiment was theirs.

And she knew what to do.

Meet rumor with quiet, treason with cunning, and vicious with vicious.

CHAPTER TWO

Cadis

Next came the Fin who dealt everyone false
Smiled at the others as she plotted their deaths
Hasty and brutish were just some of her faults
Broken nose . . . hideous . . . mackerel breath.

—Children's nursery rhyme

The Royal Coliseum roared, like a great beast—hungry for more spectacle. Cadis knew the story by heart.

The people of Meridan wanted blood. They lived for it. They reveled in it. But they did not want to see themselves wanting blood. Not they who were so just.

So they told themselves the little story of a festival—a celebration of martial talents—when really, in their hearts, all they truly wanted was to see an accident, a slip and stab in the gut, a cloven hoof and upturned chariot.

They cheered for sport, but Cadis had stood before an audience since her name-day, and she could see it in their eyes. They wanted death and waste and violence.

Back in Findain, their celebrations revolved around the

grand delivery of histories and the debate of philosophy. Masters each stood on the bows of ships at port—each their own stage—and bellowed into the harbor. Bad bargain comedies, tragic lovelorn tales of the sea, orations on the dignity of man, mummery, puppetry, even shadow plays projected on the unfurled sails of the ships—art, the true human art of stories and performances and song.

But here in the Revels, Cadis would be lucky to hear a mealymouthed official mumble a few words for the opening ceremony and a few blaring trumpets to announce the next contest.

And that was all right. Cadis wouldn't crash against the rocks of their desire. No good salesman or storyteller would. She would be like water—flowing and unstoppable. She would read her audience, and she would give them what they wanted—for a price, even if that price was something as begrudging as their respect. Or, at least, the inability for them to hold their noses up and claim their queen superior, as they always did.

Cadis was Findish, after all. And if she told the right story, she had to believe they would listen.

A cadet cut herself on her shield, taking the blowback from an opponent's mace. The crowd roared its approval once again.

Cadis watched from the conductor's pit as she waited for her archery exhibition. She had warmed up already. By herself, speaking the words that calm, breathing the rhythm she had long ago established to steady herself—the rhythm of a ship at sea, a metered verse, an even fight. The war drum in her chest pounded.

Cadis felt the beads of sweat forming at the nape of her neck, under her long dreads, the droplets pooling and finally sliding down her back, under the leather breastplate armor.

She wore crimson and gold, the colors of Meridan, a gesture—maybe futile—toward unity . . . or at the very least, an evasion of the previous year's insult, when she defeated Meridan's future queen wearing Findish green.

Cadis had no intention of being any less proud of her skills, but it might appease the crowd that she salute them in this way, not to mentioned the convenient fact that there would be no rematch with Rhea.

On the coliseum floor, only two cadets remained standing in the open melee—one lumbering she-bear with double clubs, the other a scout with several open wounds and nothing but a trapper's knife.

The people of Meridan cheered on the giant, the obvious favorite. They had no sense of good drama.

Cadis adjusted the greaves on her forearms, which protected her from the recoil of her bow. She should have had Hannah—her maid—help her tighten the straps, but Cadis had dismissed her a few days ago, when she'd caught Hannah rifling through her private drawers.

There was nothing to find. Cadis had no part in any Findish rebellion—if such a conspiracy even existed. She was loyal to Declan, though no one believed it. But she wouldn't tolerate maids spying. It was too close to mutiny to be overlooked. She put the seal of her father's guild on a promissory banknote and gave it to Hannah before sending her away. Any merchant of Findain would redeem it for a small fortune in dry goods. At least the maid wouldn't go around claiming the Findish were as pinch-purse as people said.

Cadis felt a gruff hand clasp her shoulder and another pull at the strap.

"Where's Hannah?" said Marta as she adjusted Cadis's armor.

"I set her adrift," said Cadis. And then she added, "Thank you. What are you doing down here?"

"I came to help," said Marta. "You need a squire." She looked up from the harnesses long enough to catch Cadis's eye.

"So you knew," said Cadis.

"Of course," said Marta.

"Why'd you ask?"

"I knew that part. Now tell me something else. *Why* you sent her away."

Cadis clenched a bit. It was vaguely shameful to admit. "She was spying on me."

"Did she find anything good?" said Marta.

"No," said Cadis quickly.

Marta patted the armor plates. They were secure.

"Too bad," said Marta. "When I suspected people were searching my goods, I used to leave a dagger with their name engraved into the blade for them to find."

Cadis laughed. "Really? A knife? Really?"

Marta nodded. Cadis laughed again.

"They'd run out of my tent, wet in the pants."

The giant made short work of the scout. A club to the jaw. A splatter of blood and teeth. Cheering and ecstasy. Blood-mad frenzy.

Cadis watched the cart drivers take away the scout.

She mouthed the calming words and breathed the steady rhythm.

Her bow was ready to sing.

As the attendants set up three billboards at the center of the coliseum, Cadis stepped out of the dark trench and into the sunlight. When the crowd saw her, there was a mixture of halfhearted claps, a few hisses and curses, and an entire orchestra of full-throated cheers from the oblivious children who had no sense of politics and knew her only as the warrior queen.

Cadis waved as she walked to her opening position. She thought she heard someone shout, "Rebel!" from the grandstands, but she wasn't flustered. Cadis was born on a stage—so they said—or rather, a ship deck at a captain's side, which was nearly the same thing.

Marta stood at the horse gate. She nodded when Cadis caught her eye, and shifted her stance to cover the magister's box sitting at her feet, which was filled with bandages, poultices, and various other emergency materials, in case of a horrible accident. Cadis needed no such coddling of insecurities.

She smiled at her mentor and made the gestures of an arrow hitting her chest. She dangled her tongue from the side of her mouth, as if it were a kill shot. Marta's eyes narrowed, and she tried to scowl. She made a motion indicating the crowd, who probably thought the gesture was some code to her fellow rebels.

"Don't worry so much," shouted Cadis to her lifelong tutor.

"Pay attention," said Marta. "You'll be great."

"I know!" said Cadis. "Tell me something else."

Marta laughed. They were the most alike, it seemed. When Marta would tell little stories of her military service—never much, but short anecdotes or aphorisms she remembered— everyone agreed they sounded like the cocksure bravado that Cadis, more than the others, exhibited. Cadis—who had not known her own mother nearly long enough—was most proud of the comparison.

Cadis breathed the rhythm, spoke the calming words, and marched across the stadium as a captain would march across her deck.

Cadis turned to the king's balcony, where Declan sat on the throne, with Hiram standing beside him. Cadis bowed, then bowed to the people. The crowd went silent.

Several attendants trotted from the auxiliary gate with iron, grated buckets filled with arrows. They placed three in the dirt, situated a hundred yards from each of the wooden billboards. They placed a fourth bucket farther back, unassociated with a billboard.

"People of Meridan," shouted Cadis in a booming voice. She held her bow out to the side theatrically, to present herself dressed conspicuously in crimson and gold. "You have taken me into your home. Today I am one of you."

Cadis bowed again to the people. They cheered, but only after Declan accepted the offering with a nod. When she rose again, Cadis could see Marta rolling her eyes, amused by the melodrama. At former Revels, Marta would have admonished her for grandstanding, but now, Cadis had noticed, her speeches were built into the schedule.

Enough pomp.

Cadis approached the first station and pulled an arrow from the metal quiver staked into the ground. The fletching was bloodred, the color of the Tasanese flag. Cadis nocked the arrow, squinted at the billboard all the way across the arena, whispered the calming words, breathed the steady rhythm, pulled back the bowstring, and let go. . . .

It flew.

It was the truest thing in all of Meridan.

Not a crook or a bend.

Not a turn or a flinch.

Tok!

It stuck the board at center mast and dug the entire arrowhead into the grain with a satisfying stocky sound.

Behind it flew a dozen more arrows, all perfectly spaced, each driving into the board until the fletchings formed the perfect replica of the Tasanese crest, the bituin tree.

Cadis didn't pause once the performance began. She

stepped sideways to the next station, nocked an arrow with a fletching the color of Corentine blue, and let it fly. One after another. Blindingly fast, impossibly precise. Soon the second billboard showed a constellation of blue fletching shaped like the spires of the crest of Corent.

Iren herself couldn't have stitched a more accurate rendering.

Cadis moved on to the last station. The fletching, green. Findain. Home.

She sent the first arrow toward the center of the board to make the crow's nest. She knew this crest by heart. She could have shot it into the side of a kite flapping in the wind, three hundred yards in the air.

The Findish clipper ship.

Fern green.

Full sail.

The arrows hit their marks as if they were blooming out of the board.

The last one shuddered into place to form the prow.

Cadis was breathing heavily.

Her fingers burned.

Her shoulder throbbed.

But it was perfect.

Three constellations as faultless as the night sky.

Several children lost themselves in the wonder and clapped hysterically.

But the rest of the crowd murmured their suspicions. It was an insult to have left out Meridan. There were no more billboards. Surely this proved the allegiance of the faithless Findish queen.

Cadis let the murmuring grow into a dissatisfied rumble. A few men booed from the balcony. It was the climax. A good story always needs some uncertainty, some tension. Cadis stepped to the last quiver of arrows, their feathers crimson and gold.

The crowd was not appeased. There was no billboard for them.

Cadis nocked the first arrow.

She raised the bow upward. The crowd shrieked and flinched away when it pointed in their direction, but Cadis lifted the bow until it aimed straight up into the sky. She aimed by aligning it to the flagpoles at the top of the mezzanine.

She let go.

The people gasped.

It could land anywhere.

Mothers and fathers covered their children.

Cadis didn't wait for it to land, but sent another and another.

They were lost in the noon light. Cadis continued to shoot, straight up, adjusting by imperceptible degrees. And soon the first arrow whistled back down, and a rain of others followed, stabbing into the dirt floor of the arena.

Not a single stray drop—all around her. Cadis shot as if to put out the sun.

And it rained as if to mock human ambition.

Soon the mothers and fathers realized they were safe,

and the children finally wrestled out of their grip to get a better look.

The arrows planted into the coliseum floor all around Cadis to form the dragon on the Meridan crest. A gigantic wyrm. The mezzanine noticed it first, and the roar began. Cadis grinned as she launched the last arrow into the air.

She had choreographed the climax for the better part of the year.

A bow to the king.

Declan, well pleased, nodded.

A bow to the people, who laughed in astonishment and continued to grow in volume as the arrows fell into place to detail the image.

And finally, as the best Findish bards knew, Cadis left them wanting more. She turned and strode toward the horse gate, even as the arrows plummeted around her. By the time the last arrow hit the ground, forming the eye of the dragon, the entire coliseum was on its feet, and Cadis had disappeared into the shadow of the gate.

"Well done," said Marta, as she reached out to take the bow.

"Well done? That's it?" said Cadis. She threw the bow aside, grabbed Marta in a bear hug, and lifted the shorter woman off the ground. "I did it!"

"Of course you did, darling."

"Why aren't you more surprised? Be more surprised."

"Okay, okay. I'm surprised," said Marta, laughing and straightening her uniform.

"Well, you shouldn't be," said Cadis, pretending to scoff. "There was never any doubt."

They both burst into giggling until the attendants came to fetch Cadis for her next event.

They walked to the other side of the arena using the custodial tunnels so that they could prepare. Marta peeled the shooting bracers from Cadis's forearms and replaced them with hard-plate armor.

Cadis caught her eye. "Any words of wisdom, squire-girl?"

Marta would have punished her for such a comment in training. Instead she grinned—there was time yet for a punishment.

"Yeah," said Marta. "Don't be so sure of yourself. This next opponent hits back."

"Her kicks may flick and punches sting," said Cadis. "But *hits* and *hurts* are different things."

An attendant handed her the curved cutlass used by Findish corsairs. Cadis swung it in circles as she walked, to loosen her wrists. Her every muscle vibrated with the thrill of her performance, with the sheer glorious excitement of being great at something, truly great, and reveling in that blessing.

Marta forced her to stop for a moment in order to strap her shin guards. Cadis bounced on her toes and made it difficult, until Marta took a pinch out of her calf.

"Ah!" said Cadis.

Marta straightened. She looked Cadis in the eye—the

bravura all gone, leaving only the professional soldier. "You should be careful. You hit your marks. You go fight speed, full contact. And you don't get hurt."

Cadis matched her stare. Deadly serious. "Marta. Marta. I know that stuff already. Tell me something else."

Marta let slip one last giggle.

"You're a splendid braggart. Just don't kill each other, please. It's just a dumb circus."

Cadis nodded and let out a whooping holler, as corsairs do before boarding enemy ships.

None of them knew why Iren insisted on a melee show-case; she wasn't very good at them. It might have been her mother's command—the emira of Corent. The two were always writing letters, as if Iren were away in the country, as opposed to an unwilling ward of their enemy.

Cadis begged and pleaded once, years ago, to read one of the letters. It had been a testament to their friendship—and the offer of three favors to be named later—that finally swayed Iren. Immediately after snatching the letter from Iren's hand, Cadis knew she had given away the favors too easily. Iren and her mother would write entire letters dedicated to the intimate details of a single supper. In one Iren spent three pages explaining her plans for a tapestry. Cadis had handed back the papers, astounded by the Corentine's affinity for all things logistical and untheatrical.

Iren took her letters and called in her first favor imme-diately—Cadis's favorite practice bow. Iren had no use for it. Cadis imagined it was her way of raising the price on snooping into her affairs. Cadis handed over the bow. She had never paid so much for so little a story.

And she let Iren alone to write her letters.

To his credit, King Declan allowed all the correspondence. He had no desire to cut them off from their loved ones. It anchored them to their homes. "You are to go back and rule, after all," Declan would say.

As Cadis walked down the stairs to the undervault of the coliseum, she thought of Jesper Terzi—her own anchor. Jesper who had once kissed her in the crow's nest of her father's ship—when they were barely pups. Jesper who held her hand when they heard her father's ship had gone down—and she was orphaned to the world. Jesper who remained her friend, when all others seemed to give her up for dead. He was the only one to visit her—five times in the last ten years—when his caravan came within a hundred leagues of Meridan Keep.

Cadis smiled as she recalled Jesper and Endrit meeting like two young bucks, squeezing each other's hands and puffing out their chests without meaning to. He acted like an overprotective brother—sizing up Endrit. It was sweet that he assumed any boy would have his sights on Cadis.

She hadn't seen Jesper in two years, not since the rumors of a Findish rebel group had created a state of constant suspicion around her. And in the outland villages, the dangers were even worse.

A Findish caravan would be a target for Meridan scouting regiments, or even local mobs who knew they could attack with impunity. As a result, only one of every three letters ever made it to Cadis. But when they did, they came in great sheaves, wrapped in old sailcloth. They smelled of the open sea and read like he was sitting right beside her in jovial conversation.

He detailed all the drama between the captains' guild and the caravaneers, but made no mention of a rebellion or the secret rebel group that had taken over all of Meridan's society gossip. They called themselves the Munnur Myrath. To the imagination of Meridan nobles, they were demons and fiends—which led to the artless insult leveled at her people, the "Fiendish." But he would have surely told her if anything so climactic was afoot.

His letters avoided such politics. He wrote less and less of Cousin Denarius, Cadis's caretaker and mentor. The kind old man had raised her when her parents were lost to the sea. He sat in her stead as archon now. She missed Denarius most of all. But Jesper would only bring more suspicion if he spoke of the archon.

Cadis's eyes were not yet used to the undervault of the coliseum when a gauntlet swung out of the darkness and hit her in the stomach—knocking the air out of her lungs and the daydreams out of her mind.

"*Ooph,*" she said, doubling over and catching the iron glove.

A calm, quiet voice spoke from the shadow behind a pillar. "You don't seem prepared."

Iren.

Cadis took a deep breath and fit the gauntlet over her left hand. Above them, the attendants were clearing the arrows and the crowd distracted itself with the intermission carnival. Hawkers sold skewers of dried beef and crackled rice.

"A cheaty move," said Cadis.

"I could hear you jangling all the way from the stairs," said Iren, stepping into the uneven light from the braziers, dressed in Corentine-blue light armor, with short rapiers sheeted in an X on her back.

"We can wait till you're ready," she added.

Cadis had to smile. She was easily twice Iren's size. One solid swing of her cutlass would break any of Iren's blocks, and yet there her diminutive sister stood, as bold as a mountain flower.

Iren tossed Cadis her cutlass.

"Oh, sister mine," said Cadis, playing coy, "has this summer heat melted your resolve? Are you melancholic to be down among the poorly cultured and ill read?"

"We all suffer," said Iren. "Your dreadful braids must itch with parasites, for instance."

"Ha!" said Cadis. "There are easier ways to kill yourself, sister."

They each stood on a wooden platform facing each other. Attendants in the corner began turning giant cranks to open the trapdoors in the coliseum floor.

As light poured into the vault, Cadis winked at Iren. "That was it?" she said. "That's all you've got to goad me?"

"I suppose you smell funny," said Iren with a shrug.

"Besides, who needs head games when I've got such perfect odds?"

"No gambler in their right mind would bet on you against me. I'm the champion."

"Only because Rhea can't keep her feet under her."

The reference to the previous year raised Cadis's hackles even though she knew it was coming.

It had been a close match until Rhea had become distracted and stumbled. Cadis pounced as any fighter would. But to the people of Meridan, it was a disgrace. A dishonorable victory. Another treachery from the Findish.

"All I have to do is fight you to a draw," said Iren, "and they'll love me. They don't care if I lose. They just don't want you to win."

It was true. Even if Cadis *was* wearing Meridan colors, even if she bowed and pledged a thousand times, she would never win them over. Iren was right. And she was smart enough to let Cadis come to the realization herself. They made a perfect pair in that regard. Cadis, eager to win back the Meridan people, their affection, their esteem for the Findish. Iren, always present, helping her remember the prizes that were simply too lofty. At best Meridan would give her begrudging respect. For Cadis—who wished desperately for everyone to love her as she loved them—this was a painfully difficult fact to remember.

Cadis reached up and unclasped her crimson and gold breastplate and let it fall to the ground beside her platform. Underneath was a light leather jerkin, unarmored, but at least unmarked by the sigil of Meridan. She would present herself—herself. She felt a wave of gratitude for Iren.

Their platforms began to rise. The dull roar of the crowd and a light rain of sand from the arena floor wafted down the open shafts.

"All right. You win," said Cadis. "I won't go easy."

She could see Iren's lips quiver, holding back a smirk. "You never have before."

"Have too," said Cadis, playful and petulant. "You don't even know how much."

Iren finally let the smile escape, like a bird from its cage. "Have not," she said.

The proxy sisters shared a moment of connection, beaming at each other with true affection, until the arena floor severed their eyeline and the platforms brought them out once again, onto the sunbright stage, where they would battle as hardened foes. "Did you see my arrows before?" said Cadis.

They bowed to each other.

"Of course," said Iren. "They were spectacular. But you look better now. Red and gold don't suit you."

A shinhound, seated somewhere near the king's balcony, saw Iren and barked. Iren drew her double rapiers and set position. Cadis waved her cutlass in a figure eight to loosen her wrist.

Without warning, she sprang forward and in one charging motion swung the heavy blade down toward Iren's head.

CHAPTER THREE

Suki

One came carried from Tasan's Imperium
A sister dead, in a black dress clad
Spoiled and twisted by a rank delirium
Slowly and surely she . . . went . . . mad.

—Children's nursery rhyme

S uki stood in the saddle of her horse (Helio (which was hers, even though Declan had named it)) to see Cadis and Iren sparring on the other side of a giant hedge (on the closer side to the king's box) while she warmed up for her ride (which was next) when she caught sight of Rhea (goodiegoodie queen witch) and Endrit (gods, he was beautiful) watching from the conductor's trench, standing extra close to each other (though that might have just been the angle of her view (because Endrit would have to be a wild pig idiot to want that mangy nag (and he wasn't (because he had a dozen options (like Cadis for one (and he could maybe even choose Suki (hopefully)))))))).

"Stay straight," she (Suki) said to herself, as Marta had

taught her. *Stay straight*. A kind of double meaning (old soldiers loved that sort of thing (training advice that doubled as life advice)). Suki kept the reins of Helio straight as he trotted along the wall of the arena. Some spectators said something (Suki ignored them). And she tried to keep her thoughts straight (not twisted in a thousand directions at once (but seeing Rhea (after what she said the night before) made it impossible)).

The night before.

The night before, when Endrit had whispered to her in the corner, "What would I do without you, Susu?" (after she'd patched up the sloppy cut from Rhea). He'd leaned forward to whisper it. Suki had craned her neck up. Almost a kiss. And she'd said, "I dunno, bleed I guess," (which was very clever for its double meaning (his cut, and his broken heart)).

They were almost alone in the corner together. Endrit had even said, "Yeah, you're probably right." He was comfortable around her (Suki could tell (more comfortable than around the others)), which meant they had something special.

Even when he danced with Rhea, Suki could tell he was uncomfortable with her clumsiness (they danced to Tasanese music (the best kind) and it was too subtle and elegant for Rhea).

In all the twisted scheming and court intrigue that swirled around Suki's head, Endrit was calm and honest and simple (which might have sounded like an insult, but it was love, love so deep (like a well) that it stayed still in all the turmoil of their lives).

Cadis would have described it in words, that it was like a water well in a brush fire. But Suki felt it as an unspoken musical sensation (like the ethereal connection she had with Helio when they rode). The word for it in Tasanese translated in the common tongue as "co-spirits" (meaning they shared a soul and could look at each other and know what the other was thinking (and be comfortable around each other even if one of you is a servant and the other a hostage queen)).

Tola had told her about being a "co-spirit" (she had it with a prince from an outer province (who got killed at the Battle of Crimson Fog (or maybe committed suicide when he heard about Tola (or maybe when your co-spirit dies, you just fall over dead too)))). Tola (dead).

Suki remembered a glorious sunny morning (years ago) in the Summer Palace, when Tola taught her trampoline somersaults (servants threw her into the air with a silk sheet). Nearby, another dozen servants threw Tola (who was trained by the Tasanese Royal Acrobats and had long legs that made her seem like a bird in flight). Tola would shout instructions (up and down (her memory was of bouncing up and down (seeing her sister's smile on every up (and feeling an invisible string connecting her to it (the smile), like her whole heart was tethered to Tola (and thinking that must have been how co-spirits felt all the time)))))).

But Tola was dead and the string in Suki had been dragging on the ground (until she found Endrit).

And even if the emperor (her father) of Tasan would

never allow his heir to marry a servant, Suki didn't care, because she would wear the key to the walled palace one day, and she would bring Endrit, and she would demand to see every guard who was there on the eve of Crimson Fog, and she would summon them before her, and they would be so afraid, they would tell her exactly what happened (Did Tola really betray the peace? (why?))(And if she did, how did the Meridan dragoons ever stop her?) (And (maybe she didn't want to know this part) what did they do to her?) (Why did they only return her sword (broken) and a lock of hair?) (Could she be . . . (no) alive? Could she be somewhere nearby (in Meridan Keep?)?) No. That was madness. Whatever happened, Suki would hear it from those guards when she was finally empress.

And then she would drag them behind horses through the badlands, until there was nothing left tugging on their ropes but a few red stains.

Suki circled back around and hopped up onto Helio's saddle, standing on her tiptoes to see above the hedge. They were still fighting (Cadis and Iren), and still in the trench (Endrit and Rhea) touching arms.

Rhea (smiling like a court fool) seemed to feel the heat of Suki's glare. Out of nowhere, she glanced at the hedge. Suki dropped down into the saddle (she probably didn't see (who cared if she did? (Suki cared, obviously, because spying made her seem childish))).

Rhea's opinion of her didn't matter (unless she told Endrit about it (which she probably would)).

Suki spurred Helio into a canter and then a gallop. The people on her side of the arena took notice and sat (they were standing before, to watch Cadis and Iren on the far side). There was a general murmur of confusion. Was the next exhibition starting before the other ended? (Who cared if it did?) Suki wasn't a puppet. She was a queen. She would ride whenever she wanted (and Rhea could deliver a dozen threats from her daddy—hang them all).

Suki slipped into the stirrups and raised her back for a full-tilted gallop, once, twice around the equestrian yard. The center was filled with hedged gates. Scattered across the course were bundles of bamboo stalks—a dozen tied together and pounded into the dirt to be as tall and as thick as a soldier in battle.

The arena erupted into applause. The sparring must have finished.

(*Hup, hup!* C'mon, Helio!)

Helio tore across the arena. Suki hopped out of the stirrups, into a tight crouch on the saddle. Before the audience could completely settle, Suki hit the starting gate—a massive three-tier jump. Helio launched into the air. Suki sprang off the saddle into a backflip. Together they careened over the gate. Suki vaulted through the backflip, extending her legs to point directly at the sky, and then swung around, spread, and hit the saddle just as Helio hit the ground. The crowd roared and turned fully toward the equestrian course.

(Declan didn't even get his bow, poor old man.)

Suki and Helio clipped around a flag at full speed. Suki

leaned all the way to the left, to snatch a Tasan̄ e long sword out of the ground. She came up and leaned to the right to grab another. Both swords had the long, thin, straight blade, double sharp, with pointed ends. The ornamented handles resembled the knotted branches of a bituin tree and were laced with tightly woven ribbons (bloodred (Tasan)) that fluttered behind her like tail feathers of a firebird.

From a seated position, Suki could point the blades down and carve into the dirt. She wondered if Rhea and Endrit had gone down into the undervault together, or if they were watching from some corner. She couldn't spare a glance (one false step, a loose stirrup, a missed swing, and she'd break every bone in her body (and embarrass herself)).

Helio threaded between a formation of bamboo stalks. Suki cut them down at angles that would have been ear to shoulder—through the neck. The severed heads of the bamboo bundles slid, then fell from their bodies.

She had embarrassed herself the previous night (after everyone had gone to bed). She had waited by the night kitchen (for Endrit) even though she had no reason to believe he would come. They hadn't said anything (but just in case, a fateful meeting, a chance connection). That was all she imagined. Maybe he would pass by and see her by the torchlight, and (it didn't matter) Rhea walked by instead, coming from the magister's tower (startled both of them).

"What're you doing here?"

"What're *you* doing here?"

"Don't be impertinent, Susu."

"Don't ever call me Susu."

(She sighed like it was such a strain on her patience.)

"I was just speaking to my—the king" (her daddy), "and Endrit can come to the ball."

"Good. The rebellion scare is stupid."

"Caution isn't stupid when lives are in danger." (Thanks, Mother.)

"Yes, everybody is out to get you, Rhea."

"Not me, him. Or have you forgotten?"

(She meant Tola. The one who broke the oath of peace and tried to assassinate Declan.)

"He cares about you like a daughter, you know," said Rhea, full of condescension and false sympathy. Suki almost lunged for the witch's throat.

I have a father. (Suki didn't say that (but thought it).) Though, in truth, she didn't remember him very well. The emperor would never send envoys to her (or any correspondence), because it would be like begging and admitting defeat over and over again.

"He just doesn't want you to end up like her," said Rhea.

"Just shut up."

Suki had run back to her room like a child.

Embarrassed that she couldn't hold them in (the tears) in front of Rhea.

Embarrassed that she had been found waiting for him (Endrit) when he didn't even know she was there.

Embarrassed when she should have been enraged. She knew Rhea was sheltered, but she had to have recognized a death threat when she delivered it (did it matter if she didn't?). What in the world were they doing here, if they weren't a bunch of girls held hostage under constant threat? And how could Rhea pretend otherwise? Was she willfully *this* deluded?

(Suki had said as much over breakfast that morning, before Rhea joined them (Iren, as usual, listened, ate her berries, offered nothing (and sweet Cadis, always appeasing, always trying to prove her loyalty, refused to believe that Rhea would ever threaten Suki's life, "it was late and you were on edge, I'm sure. It was just a misunderstanding and ... Let's just focus on today.")).)

Suki jumped another gate and lopped the heads off another set of bundles. Charging faster, riding around the arena. At times her off hand dragged the sword in the ground, cutting up a trail of dirt.

Suki seethed at the insults (and the threats (and the embarrassment)).

She missed everything she remembered about home (which was little), the PilanPilan orchestra, the red tapestried city, the painted walls. She didn't remember many people, though, and feared more than anything that they didn't remember her.

When she finished with a final acrobatic handstand into a sidesaddle (and a two-handed cut on a full phalanx of bamboo stalks), she didn't even acknowledge the king's balcony as the crowd cheered (and she didn't bother to stop as the cheering faded uncomfortably (when they realized she had carved the name "Tola" into the arena floor)).

From her mount, Suki threw her long swords like javelins (each lanced into the ground on either side of her sister's infamous name (Rhea could shove her threats)).

She trotted to the horse gate (Good boy, Helio), slid off the saddle, and marched out, glancing back only once over her shoulder (looking for Endrit), which she shouldn't have done, because it would have looked much more regal if she had been flawless and focused (and not distracted by anything (and didn't care about anybody)).

CHAPTER FOUR

Iren

The last condescended from Academy spires
Pretended at life with a cold, dead heart
Face like a crypt, from a family of liars
Quietly, quietly played . . . her . . . part.
—Children's nursery rhyme

Cadis always stared at the point she would attack.
An archer's habit.

A bad one in melee.

Too earnest.

She brought her cutlass down at Iren's head.

Iren stepped left and struck the side of Cadis's heavy blade with her light daggers.

Cadis hid her stumble with a quick-footed turn back to guard.

Iren didn't bother to lunge.

The daggers were short and thin.

Good for tight quarters, like the stairs of a mountain pass.

In the open Iren was disadvantaged.

On paper anyway.

To the amateur eye.

Iren waited.

Cadis would press the fight.

She was trying too hard to give them a show.

Her swings were bombastic.

Giant broad strokes.

She wanted the peons in the mezzanine to feel it.

But they both knew combat was a game of inches.

A killing blow was most often subtle, unromantic, even banal.

Iren crossed the daggers and blocked another overhead swing.

Her wrists took the impact.

She sprang back, and the falchion continued down to the ground.

From the leaning position, Cadis would try to fake one way and go another.

It worked on Endrit far too many times.

He was too concerned with their well-being.

If you were watching her hips or feet or shoulders, she'd have you swiping at air.

But Iren watched the belly button.

Cadis feinted left. Shimmied right with her shoulders. Then struck left.

Her waist never faltered.

In a real fight, Iren would have stepped in and stabbed

her dagger up through Cadis's chin, through her mouth, into her mind.

But then in a real fight Cadis wouldn't have been so sloppy.

She wanted something.

Respect.

Or if not respect, at least forgiveness for humiliating Rhea in front of them.

Wanting something like that, in a full-contact fight speed match, was a weakness too obvious for Iren.

Cadis thrust forward.

Iren stepped in and punched Cadis in the face.

The dagger hilt weighted her fist.

It crunched Cadis's nose.

Blood spray.

A roar from the crowd louder than any all day.

Cadis's head snapped back.

Iren hammered the hilts of her daggers down onto Cadis's shoulder.

She screamed and dropped guard.

Iren swung again and smashed her in the eye socket.

Cadis stumbled.

Iren pounced forward.

Iren swept the hilts down and scooped under the back of Cadis's knees.

Cadis fell back and hit the dirt.

The crowd stood and leaned over the railing.

Even Declan.

They wanted more blood.

They wanted her broken for all the crimes of Findain.

For their lost king.

Iren kicked her in the ribs so hard the peons in the mezzanine heard a crack.

A cheaty thing to do.

They would have expected it out of the Fin.

Cadis was hurt, but didn't stay down.

She somersaulted backward and got to her feet.

Her eye was swelling. Nearly shut.

Her teeth were bloody.

Some in the crowd cheered.

A good show.

The Fin had grit.

They had to give her that.

Cadis wobbled, but held her cutlass in front.

Iren let them drink in the sight of Findain bleeding.

She closed one eye against the sun.

Then Iren threw a knife.

A little boy screamed.

Right before all of Meridan, at the Revels of the Pax Regina, the princess of Corent took a kill shot at the archana of Findain.

Gasps and whispers.

It was not a declaration of war.

It was an assassination.

Cadis flinched and lifted the flat face of her cutlass just in time.

An audible sigh of relief.

Iren had gone too far.

A dead queen would mean war.

Iren made an effort to grunt.

A frustrated sound for people to hear.

She was down to one dagger.

Cadis's nose was broken.

The blood loss had her dizzy.

Her swollen eye blinded her on the left side.

Iren shifted the dagger to her right hand, where Cadis couldn't see it.

A little boy in the fourth row shouted, "You can do it, Caddy!"

His mother quickly pulled him away from the railing.

It was forbidden to be so casual with a queen.

Cadis caught her breath and swung again.

The crowd erupted, this time in admiration.

She was brave.

And she could take punishment.

Iren ducked the blade.

Cadis wheeled around with a kick.

Iren took the boot on the chin.

She heard a pop as she fell.

The pain was more of a numbing sensation all along her neck and cheek.

Iren rolled over.

The sky was cerulean blue.

The color of Corent.

The sun was summer white.

Here in Meridan, it felt impossibly far away.

The shadow of Cadis blotted out the sky.

Iren tried to lash out with her dagger, but her arm was pinned under a knee.

She dropped her weapon.

Before Cadis could strike, Iren put up two fingers in surrender.

The roar was deafening.

Iren closed her eyes.

She thought of her room in the high spire of Corent.

She missed her mother.

When they arrived back at the great hall at the center of all their private chambers, Cadis and Iren released the maids.

Cadis collapsed onto a couch by the wall. Iren poured water from a carafe on the center table into two glass cups.

"Here," she said, and handed one to Cadis.

Cadis looked out from under the wet towel she held over her swollen eye. She took the glass. "Thanks."

"You're welcome."

Cadis laughed, then winced.

It must have been funny to say, "You're welcome," in that moment.

"You've been practicing," said Cadis.

Iren shrugged.

Cadis lay back on the couch and covered her face. "You're dodging me."

"All day."

"Was that a joke? From silent Iren?"

"I thought we were being funny."

"Truly, when did you become so—"

"Good?"

"Vicious."

Iren drank her water.

"In the ring, I mean," said Cadis.

"I've been practicing," said Iren.

It would be sufficient excuse for the others—the king, the magister, the Meridan nobles. To them she was just lucky. A few landed strikes, some dishonorable play, no real evidence of greatness.

But Cadis had seen it up close. The speed of her punch, the control. When they grappled, only Cadis could know the taut-cord strength of Iren's lean frame. Only Cadis could know that Iren was nothing like she seemed.

"Fine," said Cadis. "Keep your secrets."

That was a hurtful thing to say, thought Iren. She put her glass on the table and walked toward her room. She would need her needlework for the next exhibition.

"Hey," said Cadis. "Hey, Iren."

When Iren turned, Cadis was sitting up. Her face was a mess, but she'd heal.

"Thank you," said Cadis. "I know what you did."

The mob of Meridan had better gristle to chew.

Iren nodded. She smiled for a short second.

It was nice to share some secrets.

The afternoon Revels took place on the palace green and had a convivial tone. Streamers hung from the trees. Cooks worked at fire pits. Flower dancers twirled to the tinkling of lutes. Only the court, the *homo nobilis*, and the patrician families were invited.

Even fewer would attend the ball that night.

The entire day was a thinning procession to the foot of Declan's throne.

Iren sat in a gilded tent crocheting the final corner of a bed-length tapestry as nobles paraded through.

Like animals in a menagerie.

They didn't realize that they, too, were being watched.

Iren preferred it so.

The tapestry depicted the scriptorium of the Academy, where initiates sat at tables and transcribed from the archives. Stitching every codex on the shelves in the background had taken her the better part of the year.

"Why can't she do a nice pastoral scene?"

"You know how the Corentine are—always declaring themselves the smartest in the room."

"Would it kill her to have some nymphs in a glade or something?"

The nobles had nothing interesting to say. Not even to one another.

A few admired her technical skills.

Most gossiped.

Some dared to poke fun.

"I suppose crochet will be an important skill when she's headmistress of the Academy."

"It's meant to show discipline, constancy, attention to laws and lives, no matter how small."

"Thanks, magister of all things obvious. This isn't our first Revels."

"I think she's the most talented one."

"Gave up pretty quickly in the melee. And fought dirty."

Iren kept her eyes down on the tapestry.

Suppressed a reaction.

On the far side of the green, the royal musicians began a waltz. The crowds began to migrate in that direction.

A susurration and applause.

Rhea must have presented herself in full regalia.

The newer patrician families would be pushing to the front, to gawk at the jewels of House Declan.

Iren hoped the routine would be perfect.

It would be easier for all of them if Rhea could shine brightest.

Endrit would make a good show of it.

Even if Rhea was too nervous to give it any panache.

Iren needed a new color thread.

Only a few spectators in her tent.

A glancing check to make sure none of them was watching.

She turned the tapestry over to tie off the old thread.

For a short instant it revealed a strip of parchment paper, pinned to the underside, jotted with her shorthand notes.

Iren quickly switched out threads.

Back to her first position.

She needed to hurry.

If Marta came to check on her performance, she would ferret it out immediately. Nothing passed her notice. It vexed Iren terribly. But their tutor had not yet arrived, and no one in the tent was near so trained as Marta.

Of the seven stragglers in her tent, one was the doyenne of House Sprolio—a great-grandmother much impressed with Iren's skill. She sat near enough to see. She was asleep.

Two were *homo nobilis*—not yet presented—thirteen or fourteen at most. They giggled at the far corner of the tent.

Playing at love.

Nothing of interest.

Another couple—middle-aged, unrecognized—walked with their daughter—ten years old, upset. A three-way disagreement.

The mother and father trying to remain discreet. The daughter using that to her advantage.

Domestic entanglement.

That left two targets for Iren's attention.

Don Fabiano Sprolio, watching after his mother.

General Hecuba, a three-star general of Declan's tribunal.

Sprolio—six hands high, fifteen stone, soft gut—was master of a small house, important for its location in the midland between Meridan and Findain.

Sprolio had the conciliatory charm of a man stuck between two warring factions.

And a facial tic when he lied.

Code name: Weasel.

General Hecuba stood beside him, half his size, twice his presence. A former dragoon knight, cut from the same cloth as Marta, now an officer. Cold. Hard. Small. She wore the formal uniform. Not on duty. Officially.

Code name: Stone.

Iren kept her head down.

She held a thin lead rod under the tapestry with her left hand and wrote on the parchment: *Stone met weasel.*

Above the tapestry, her right hand continued to crochet.

"Welcome to Meridan, Don Sprolio."

"Thank you, General. Always happy to return to . . . civilization."

"The king sends his regards."

"Oh? Goodness. An honor to be thought of. Such a little house. I can't imagine why."

"I think you can."

Hecuba had no patience for the dissembling that came with spycraft.

She paused.

To frighten Sprolio.

To check if anyone was in earshot.

Iren pretended to wrestle with a stubborn needle.

Hecuba continued. "We know Findish rebels have crossed the midland."

"Not through *my* lands," sputtered Sprolio.

Iren jotted another cryptogram: *Fish move on dragon.*

"As many as a full company."

"We—we—already told Magister Hiram we've seen nothing."

200—gorilla fish.

"Yes, you did. But it strikes me that falling asleep would be quite lucrative for House Sprolio, no?"

Hecuba nodded toward Fabiano's mother, snoring beside Iren.

"Are you—are you implying—?"

"Don Sprolio, I don't imply. I am asking if you have harbored Findish rebels. I ask if you have taken coin from the caravans to look away. I ask, Don Sprolio, because all of Meridan Keep is under mortal threat."

She paused.

"And if it is true, then I will let the rebels know that I have discovered their treason by trussing you up on the castle gate with all your inner workings exposed. They will recognize a gutted fish, Don Sprolio."

The don let out a cough.

Iren glanced at their reflection in a crystal pitcher of water sitting on a side table. She punched more code into her hidden parchment that translated into: *Weasel a sea dragon?*

Her mother would understand.

She'd given Iren the assignment herself.

Malin, the emira of Corent, had taught Iren much in the years before the Protectorate. Her childhood had been brief and productive.

Codes and ciphers.

Pictograms.

False ink made from the winoc root.

Nearly a dozen cryptic languages.

The symbols of flowers.

Of colors.

Of stained glass.

"If we can speak, we are not apart," she had said.

Iren would send the parchment with her assignments by carrier bird—through Magister Hiram, their constant overseer. But it would read to him like a young girl's trifling diary about the Revels.

Dull and predictable.

Iren's cloak-and-dagger.

That others thought her shy and gormless.

The snow-singer bird had a similar reputation.

Always wide-eyed and preoccupied.

A hare might not even notice as the bird bounced along the snow, distracted by every trick of light.

But the hare would be mistaken.

Even if the snow-singer had her back turned.

The poison's in the tail, after all.

And hares are tasty food.

Don Sprolio made a panicky defense of his innocence.

General Hecuba silenced him with a firm grip on his elbow.

"Don't clamor. We've known. Tell me something useful. Where. When."

Iren scribbled notes in the parchment.

"I don't know where. I don't. I swear. But tonight. The attack is tonight. Please don't tell my mother."

Hecuba pushed him toward the nearest exit with a disgusted grunt. Mother Sprolio's head lolled back, deep in slumber. The sweethearts in the corner continued their tickling.

Iren jotted one last word onto her parchment.

War.

Back in the central chamber, the girls were fighting.

Again.

The nobles streamed into Meridan Keep for the ball.

The lesser gentry loitered on the lawn.

"You shouldn't have done that," said Rhea.

She sat at the round table in front of a looking glass.

Her tired maid sat behind her, pinning the crown jewels back into her frizzy hair.

"Are you even talking to me?" said Suki.

Maids scurried around the hall—

Dressing Suki.

Dabbing gauze and jaro ointment on Cadis's black eye and busted lip.

Iren entered and set her crocheting on the table.

Cadis smiled at her. Iren raised a hand and waved.

A maid approached Iren.

Iren palmed the coded parchment and slipped it into her sleeve.

"My queen," said another maid, approaching with a corseted blue dress.

"No need," said Iren.

"But the ball," said the maid, confused.

"I won't be dancing," said Iren.

The maid only blinked.

"I don't need a corset," said Iren.

"A summer dress, then? It is a ball," stammered the maid.

Iren sighed. "Then make it two pieces, please. The one with the skirt that doesn't swish."

"Who else could I be talking to?" said Rhea, across the room.

"I don't know," said Suki. "You scold everyone. You scold constantly. If I were keeping track of your scolding, I'd be a magister by now."

Her maids tittered.

Suki shouldn't have allowed her maids such impudence. Rhea turned her head. "You practically accused the king of murder!"

Her maid gently coaxed her back toward the glass.

"And what is he going to do about it? Murder me, too?"

Rhea was stupefied.

It was obvious what Declan could do to them.

Suki should have known.

She was thrashing about in her own mind.

Cadis leaned around her maid and said, "Let's everyone settle down."

She was dressed already in a long beaded dress that

hugged her hips and exposed her shoulders.

The ballroom would hold its breath when she entered.

Then gasp to see her battered face.

"It was a good day today," Cadis continued.

"Hey, bootlicker," said Suki. "Your face looks like smashed fruit. Are you so desperate for their approval? They hate you and you're still begging pardon."

The maids all hushed. The conversation had become dangerous. Their presence was necessary, and yet unwelcome.

"Easy," said Cadis, through gritted teeth.

She glanced at Iren.

Iren folded her needlework into a drawstring bag and handed it to a maid.

She whispered a command, and the maids scattered from the hall.

"Why should I go easy? Will the whole country of Meridan give me a pat on the head and a pastry? Will they suddenly realize that a thousand-year-old empire in Tasan—that has created the dresses we're wearing and the music out there and the majority of the food and—and—and—will they suddenly realize they're a bunch of trumped-up barbarians and leave the governing to civilized nations? Is that your idea, Cadis? You fondle them while they call you traitor. With their boots so firmly on your neck, how do you stretch to kiss them so? Or are you playacting? Waiting for your rebel friends?"

"Enough," said Cadis.

She stood. Even from across the hall, she loomed over Suki.

"I'm the empress of Tasan and I'm not commanded by a shipyard wench."

"Suki," said Rhea.

"Nor a usurper's secondborn."

A sudden hush.

Suki knew where to cut.

No one ever referred to Rhys.

Declan's firstborn, who died during the War of Unification.

And for whom Rhea was a hollow replacement.

Rhea's eyes watered.

She stared at Suki.

"Why are you doing this? Did I do something to you?"

"Are you jesting?" said Suki.

"Just tell me."

"Are you truly jesting?"

"No. I'm sorry."

"You—if you—" Suki sputtered. Her eyes stabbed in too many directions. Iren observed as Suki became tangled in her own thoughts.

Her hatred for Declan.

Her sorrow for Tola.

Her pride.

The desire to win the current engagement and the possibility that Rhea was honestly confused.

The competing thoughts panicked across Suki's face.

She looked at Cadis.

Then Rhea.

"I'm not doing this," said Suki. She turned and ran to the door to her private chamber.

When she pushed it open, she hit a maid in the ear and screamed, "Get out!" The young maid stumbled into the central hall, looked about at everyone.

A mouse, fallen from a gunnysack.

She scurried toward the door to the kitchens, holding her ear.

Rhea had been crying.

She wiped tears from her cheek.

She said, "I didn't do anything to her."

Cadis sucked her teeth.

Rhea sighed. "Gods, what? What else have I done?"

"Don't playact, Rhea. You're no victim here. You're the *only* one, in fact."

"Are you *all* against me?"

"Against *you*? It has nothing to do with you."

"Yes, it does," said Rhea. "We're sisters."

They spoke at cross-purposes.

Cadis paused. "Are you blind? We're prisoners."

Cadis left.

The room was empty but for two.

Rhea turned to Iren. "Is that true?"

A stupid question.

Really, a beg for assurance.

Iren turned and walked out.

"Not all of us," she said, as she closed her door.

CHAPTER FIVE

Rhea

In the grand ballroom of Meridan Keep, lit by a thousand torches in sconces on the high columns of the vaulted ceiling, the high nobles and Endrit stood in a wide circle around the four queens as they spoke the pledge that closed the Revel ceremonies. And Rhea wondered, not for the first time, if her sisters conspired to kill her.

"Unto the throne of Meridan, the chair of Declan the Giver—" they said.

Suki struck a surly pose and mouthed the oath.

Is she even speaking?

"—on the occasion of the Treaty of Sister Queens—"

Did Suki scoff?

No one else seemed to notice but Rhea.

Iren murmured the words in her half-present monotone.

"—at the close of the War of Epiphany Rising and the unification of the four kingdoms of Pelgard—"

Of the three, only Cadis stood and declared as a queen and general ought to have done.

But is she playacting? Wouldn't anyone half as clever as Cadis insist on her loyalty if she intended to stab in the dark?

"—we queens pledge allegiance—"

And they stepped forward, one at a time, dressed in their colors, both hands on their hearts.

Suki, in a yellow summer gown embroidered with the roots of the bituin tree at the hem, up into branches that curled and twisted like flames. She had fought their seamstress like a banshee eel to have a red dress. "Red was the color of Tasan's empire before Meridan was even a wilderness post."

Of course, it had been such a grave insult to make her wear the *other* color of Tasan so that Rhea could wear red.

Suki gathered herself up, held her chin aloft. "I, Suki, empress-apparent of the ancient and glorious kingdom of Tasan, born third to Empress Reiko and Emperor Niran, first in line of succession before two who remain, crowned by the will of Ysvin, the creator, do so pledge."

Declan nodded from his throne, rose, and stepped down from the dais.

Suki flinched as he approached, but no one else seemed to notice.

A servant stood by, holding a jeweled case. Declan

reached into the case and took the ring of royal succession—Tasan's signet ring. This year the jewel-smith had socketed another ruby into the image of the bituin tree, making ten in total.

Declan presented the ring back to Suki.

Her hand shook as he placed it on her finger—a stark reminder that he, king of Meridan, had given her the right to rule. And each year at the Revels a new gem would be added, until the thirteenth year, when the signet rings would be whole again.

Three more years of this, thought Rhea.

Three more years of Suki inserting insults into her pledge. Rhea knew she had written in "ancient and glorious" to describe Tasan because she constantly called Meridan "upstart and artless" by comparison. It was a knife intended only for Rhea to notice.

Can we possibly make peace and become sisters in that time?

Is this a complete farce?

Iren stepped forth, stared at the floor mosaic, and spoke. The crowd leaned in to hear.

"I, emira-apparent of Corent, Iren, daughter of Malin, provost and first magister of the academy, and King Gamol, who set aside his crown to take his personal guards to the field and serve as wartime magister—who was slain—do so pledge."

Iren too?

Is she also conspiring to humiliate the king?

Did they write those vows together this year?

And was the purpose to lay all the dead of a tragic war at the feet of my father?

He was the architect of the treaty. Do they not credit him peace?

Iren never spoke of her father's foolhardy decision to enter the fray.

The Corentine hailed it as the magister's ultimate duty, to act as a medic for his people. But Hiram scoffed in private. "He was an idealistic old professor in love with an idea and surprised when the sword in his belly wouldn't yield the floor for a scholarly rebuttal."

Declan made no sign of disapproval as he reached into the box and retrieved the signet ring of Corent.

The socketed sapphires that formed the windows of the tower emblem glinted in the candlelight. Declan placed the ring on Iren's finger. A few noblewomen sighed at the sight. Many still aimed for the seat beside Declan. Widower since Rhea's birth. "A wifeless king is a motherless kingdom," prattled Doyenne Sprolio often. She had a granddaughter only five years Rhea's senior to present.

It was truthism, too obvious.

A king without a queen was a kingdom without a mother.

But is it also an appraisal?

Are motherless countries somehow less?

Rhea knew she would rule in converse—a maiden queen.

None of the noble boys—with their fancy pomade, house-proud regalia, and their petty hierarchies—interested her.

Rhea was certain they wanted her only for her crown. Actually, in truth, she wasn't certain they wanted her at all. But if they did, it would be for her power. Why else would they compliment her on paper but in person stare constantly at Cadis?

Rhea had decided long ago that she would share a bed, but she would never share a throne.

She was completely numb to their presence. Except for Endrit.

And he was no possibility.

She could keep him, perhaps, at court.

They could find some private arrangement, a secret affair.

If she could stave off the demands of the lower houses.

If she was strong enough.

"I, Cadis, next in line to sit in the first chair of the Archon Basileus, among the equals of the guildmasters of the Findain Mercantile Exchange, daughter of Hector and Agathe, both lost to the endless sea, do so pledge."

As always, a few nobles snickered at the humble titles of Findish traders. Cadis stood eye level to the king nonetheless.

Pantarelli, the jester, had been censured the previous winter for a song about Declan lusting after Cadis. Many a scandalous rumor passed between the eligible noblewomen of Meridan, that the king was grooming her to be his own—that the Protectorate itself was an elaborate mating ritual.

It was a disgusting idea for petty nobles to gossip about.

Rhea paid no attention to the whispering as Cadis

received her ring from Declan. It could have just as easily been about the carriage of her shoulders.

Did she hold them back to push out her chest?

Or her blue dress.

Would any Meridan lady wear something so plain? Or so fitted?

Her face was battered still. The makeup couldn't cover the swelling. But even so, the men had plenty else to admire. Her valiant show with Iren had worked. The people seemed impressed; some seemed to have forgiven her entirely. Rhea had a begrudging respect for such expert maneuvering.

To Rhea it proved only that she was a secret rebel and a dirty traitor.

But for good or for ill, Cadis was always the one they talked about.

Rhea glanced at Endrit and caught him staring at Cadis.

Is he, too, obsessed with her?

Rhea almost missed her cue. She stepped forth and spoke, "I, Rhea, daughter of Declan the Giver, king of Meridan, champion of the War of Epiphany Rising, hero of the Battle of Crimson Fog, author of the Treaty of Sister Queens, and creator of the peace for all Pelgard, do so pledge."

A raucous cheer erupted from the nobility and the king's guard, filling the vaulted ballroom. Rhea instinctively laughed—an expulsion of nerves, really.

And as her father approached with the signet ring of House Meridan, she could swear he smiled.

¤ ¤ ¤

Rhea almost skipped as she returned from the dais, past her sisters, and toward a grinning Endrit. Of course, she didn't.

Her armory of jewels would jangle. And, of course, she didn't leap into his arms, though she wanted to. Too many heads would turn.

As if he had read her mind or body language as she bounded toward him and then pulled up short, Endrit scooped Rhea into his arms and gave her a long hug.

Did he hug anyone else as he hugged me?

Rhea felt her neck and cheeks flush, as doyennes all around the grand ballroom cast their aspersions.

Does it matter?

He smelled like jasmine and bituin oil. His shirt was the coarsest leather in the room, but warmed by his skin and softened by age. Rhea breathed as if for the first time all day, first even in a fortnight.

The Revels were finally over.

The one previous was finally behind her—or at least, the long year of shame and disappointment could begin to scab.

"Well done, Princess," whispered Endrit.

Only a few hours ago, they had regaled everyone with the exhibition of the grimwaltz. No false steps and no misses.

They were a spectacle.

Their bodies moved in perfect motion together.

Rhea wondered if Endrit felt the connection as strongly as she did.

He must have.

It was as if they were two marionettes connected by the same strings.

Rhea wished for a god to turn them both into stone at that very moment. Instead Endrit put her down with a grunt. He rubbed his neck and said, "That necklace wasn't made for hugging." He nodded at the onyx sunrays, each a sharpened stake.

My very own chastity belt, thought Rhea. She turned and stood beside Endrit as her father gathered attention for the closing of the Revels.

"Good ladies, good men of Meridan, let us celebrate the end of our revelry."

He was a perfect king from the storybooks, a man of the prime age—not a boy king and not a graybeard. He had a soldier's bearing and a scholar's presence. Hair the color of tar, with feathery white streaks.

"And welcome also to the emissaries of Findain—"

Rhea looked around and for the first time noticed a group of sun-browned men and women, all blond and unfashionably dressed, standing behind Cadis.

A diplomatic envoy?

They seemed uncomfortable to hold the attention of the room. Behind them lurked Magister Hiram, no doubt already begun in his maneuvering and negotiations on behalf of her father.

Endrit leaned over and whispered, "Here to take her home?"

Rhea snapped around to face him. Their noses nearly

collided. She said, "What?" And then, with her volume under control, she added, "They can't take her. My father wouldn't let them."

Her father continued his speech about each of the girls' achievements over the course of the year. He began with Cadis, notably, either to please the envoy or because she had the longest list.

Endrit and Rhea stared ahead but conversed from the sides of their mouths like conspirators, or children at the temple.

"They'll petition for it, certainly," said Endrit.

"How would you know?"

"We low-living creatures all share a gutter—didn't you know?" He bumped her. His arm touched hers and made gooseflesh rise.

"I didn't mean that."

"I'm only guessing," said Endrit. "Word of a rebellion has spread. Everyone outside the keep is jumpy, and Findish caravans have diverted away from the midlands for fear of reprisals and mobs."

"All the more reason for Cadis to stay," whispered Rhea, "where the guards can protect her."

"The Meridan guards are the worry," said Endrit.

"Maybe they're here for another reason," said Rhea. Endrit laughed under his breath. Rhea hoped he would bump her again, but it didn't come. She ventured a look. He caught her eye and winked.

"Maybe they're here to choose her suitor," said Endrit.

"Can't be," said Rhea. "In Findain, they marry for love."

"Then maybe they're here to bring yours."

Fear struck at Rhea's chest. The conjecture felt true. She gazed at the envoy, searching for one who might be suitable.

Would my father really match me with a Dain?

Is there some truth to their joke the night before? She would prefer the noble Dain to the river rats, but just barely.

Endrit's snickering told her she had been played a fool.

Of course, he would never.

"I hate you," said Rhea.

He didn't respond. *Does he think I meant it? Of course not. It was an obvious joke.*

Her father commended Iren for her domestic arts and calligraphy. Rhea felt a hand push her to the side, away from Endrit. It was Suki, wedging herself between them. "Hi, Endrit!"

Doyenne Sprolio turned to give them a silencing glare. Next to her stood Don Sprolio, and beside him, Lazlo Sesquitaine, a pauncy young lord from the neighboring lands to House Sprolio. He had proposed once to Rhea, when they were nine years old, playing chase on the outer walls of the keep. She had laughed in his face. He had called Rhea's father a usurper. She'd slapped him. He'd pushed her. She'd demanded his head for her next birthday.

Her father only laughed, but House Sesquitaine had sent apologies by the wagonload.

Now Lazlo was as tall as a maypole, as thin, and with a beaky nose perfect for looking down. Surely he had come to court to ask her father a favor. *Could it be marriage again? Does he remember our fight so long ago?*

Endrit made room for Suki and said, "Hey, Susu. Quite the tribute fire you blazed with Helio."

Suki laughed a bit too loudly. "You saw it! I thought you were in the conductor's pit." Her whispering was just a bit too loud for a ballroom full of nobles and a king midspeech. Endrit leaned over her so she would bring her voice down. He whispered, "Wouldn't have missed it."

"Wanna dance later?"

"Yes. Yes. Shh," said Endrit.

Is she being rude on purpose?

People all around them shifted in discomfort. Rhea thought she saw her father's lips quiver in irritation. "Why are you shushing me? It's the final speech."

"Susu, please," said Endrit.

Does the selfish brat not realize what it took to secure an invitation for Endrit? Of course she doesn't. And she likely doesn't care anyway. Nor does she realize the jeopardy she is putting him in.

What made it worse was that her father was speaking of Suki at the moment, drawing even more attention to the fact that she was outwardly dismissing the king. "No one cares, Endrit. We already put on their precious show."

Has she stolen into the wine cellar again?

Endrit was visibly agitated. Magister Hiram moved from behind the Findish envoy, toward them, with murder in his eyes behind the placid exterior.

Rhea grabbed Suki's elbow. "Stop it," she hissed.

Suki wrenched away. "Don't touch me."

The entire ballroom quieted as if a page had shattered a tray of goblets. Rhea was stunned by the scorn in Suki's expression. Hiram emerged behind them and intoned, in a deep whisper meant only for them, "This is not the place."

"—and blessed be Anant." The king finished his speech and the nobles clapped. From the dais, the royal musicians began directly with a song, and the crowd split off into pairs. Rhea had missed her father's account of her own accomplishments. Out of all the damage, this was the one Rhea felt most deeply.

As quickly as he'd appeared, Hiram disappeared into the crowd, perhaps to find the envoy again. Rhea could finally speak aloud. "What is your crisis?"

"Nothing," said Suki. "Come on, Endrit. Let's dance."

Both of the future queens rounded on Endrit, who suddenly found himself the ham bone stuck between the clutches of two shinhounds.

Rhea entreated him with a look, that such petulance should not be rewarded. And if she were honest, she hoped he would choose her anyway. Couples danced around them. Iren approached, eating a mushroom-filled tart. "We could hear your squawking from across the room," she reported.

Cadis was still on the other side of the ballroom, with a half-moon of lords around her imagining the magnificent highborn children she could give them, even if she was a Dain with a swollen eye and a cut lip.

Endrit still hadn't made his choice.

Suki pulled at his hand. It was rare to see Endrit unsure of anything—especially in the field of love. *Is he worried for his position? For his mother's? Does he think so little of us, that we would punish him somehow?*

His sandy brown hair had been parted and combed. Rhea noticed his shoes. He must have borrowed them from Hiram. He knew no one else who could afford such clothes.

The stable boy with obsidian eyes.

He said, "Save me a waltz, yeah?" and then he let himself be dragged away by Suki, who glanced back over her shoulder to turn the knife.

Iren stood beside her and watched them dance. "Should have never put him in that position," said Iren as she chewed the last of her tart.

Rhea noticed Lazlo Sesquitaine walking toward her now that she was unattached in conversation. Before the young lord could say anything, she exhaled her frustration and marched out of the ballroom.

The air in the hallway was cool, not cycled a thousand times through the mouths of old drunk men. Rhea stepped on the hem of her dress in her haste to exit and tripped. She caught herself on a statue of King Kendrick and looked around to see if anyone noticed. Only the royal guardsmen stood in the long hall—at each of the doors to the ballroom and along windows—stiff suits of armor they were taught to ignore, much like the statues of the kings and queens of yore. They were part of the furniture of a castle keep. This night, her father had overdecorated.

Rhea straightened herself. Her necklace was beginning to press on her collarbone.

Should I go to my chamber? Will Endrit follow to have that dance he promised?

Maybe leaving is the power position—if by leaving, I can also take my prize with me.

But no, in the presence of the guards, he would never be allowed. And yet she couldn't go back in. Suki would love that. It would be as if she were pleading. Her father would scold with a look. Queens should not flit about like beetles.

She stood in the empty hall with mute guards all in a row, feeling silly. Maybe she could—

The door behind her opened, and the noise and the stale air of the ballroom lapped over her. Rhea spun around, hoping for Endrit but willing to settle for Marta, or even Iren. Perhaps Magister Hiram had come to draw her back, to introduce her to the Findish envoy, who were, after all, the ambassadors to her court.

It was not the magister.

"Hello, Father," said Rhea, with a curtsy.

Behind the king, she could see a roomful of eyes, glancing and pretending not to glance as he exited. He strode into the hall, waving back his personal guard. They stood facing each other, mostly alone, until the door closed behind him.

She could see in his face one half of her own features—the sharp nose, the high cheeks. By substitution, she knew the rest of her must have been her mother—the black curls, the hazel eyes—and she wondered if that half of her was what made him cringe.

Rhea didn't know what to do, and so she hugged him.

Is it too much?

She heard the clang of a guard's shoulder plate as he jolted from her sudden movement. He caught himself and stayed in position.

Thank the gods the king slackened and returned the embrace.

"Why did you leave?"

Because we sisters quarrel. Because I would not dance with Lazlo Sesquitaine. Because I've lost a fight so petty—a dance with a boy who is my servant—that I am more embarrassed to have lowered myself to Suki's jealous nattering than the fact that he did not choose me when given the opportunity.

"I needed a moment," said Rhea.

The king turned and walked down the hall. He opened the crook of his arm. Rhea took it and walked beside him.

"It's nice to be finished for a year," he said.

It's a giant's boot off my neck.

"Yes."

"Yours was the most praised," he noted.

Really?

Rhea could have shrieked with such riotous rejoicing that all of Meridan Keep would tremble. "Oh?"

"Indeed. The Findish envoy called it 'alarming,'" he said. "You nearly impaled the boy several times."

"We've been practicing."

"The disarming of his sword—"

"That part in particular."

Her father nodded. He was proud. She could tell. She felt such a rush in her blood that their strolling pace seemed suddenly excruciating.

"Hiram tells me a rematch next year would be unwise."

Hang Hiram and let him rot for his meddling.

"I could beat her this time. Didn't you see Iren outsmart her for most of the match? I didn't avoid it, if that's what you mean."

"I didn't mean that," said her father.

"Cadis and Iren requested to fight each other."

"The envoy thought it was to be charitable, to spare you embarrassment."

Hang them all. Even my victories are now charity from Cadis?

They walked in silence into the central chamber of the Protectorate, toward her room.

"Do they think I'm afraid of her?" whispered Rhea, so a guard wouldn't hear. Her father made an exhalation, a single laugh.

Is it so obvious to him?

He patted her on the arm. "Just . . . meet rumor with quiet, darling."

But it was no comfort to be silenced from defending herself.

Rhea's rejoicing seemed so long ago. The work of a year cast as nothing but a coward's refuge. They reached the door to her chamber. A guard standing by opened it. Her father stopped, as if he had been ushering her there to keep her from further shaming the family. Rhea stepped into her room and commanded herself not to cry until he was gone.

He took her hand and put it to his lips. Then he looked at the poisoned mouth of the dragon ring, with its ruby eyes that matched the centerpiece of her necklace. "It's a beautiful ring," he said. "Get some air. Have a rest."

Rhea's vision blurred.

"But come back later. They want to see the queen in full dress."

That was likely his way of comforting her. "There are three other queens for them to gawk at," said Rhea. She turned and walked into her room so she could wipe at her eyes without him seeing.

"Yes," he said, "but none of them are mine."

Her chamber wasn't nearly as cluttered as the others'. Iren had her embroidery and glasswork on separate tables. Cadis had her shelves of Findish plays. Suki had a menagerie of Tasanese art—paintings, miniatures, musical instruments.

Rhea had just the writing desk, her bed, and some bureaus. It had two doors—one to the balcony and one to her real home, the training room downstairs. Rhea spent most of her time down there anyway. She didn't need baubles and dolls.

The door closed. She walked to the looking glass beside her balcony and gave herself three full sobs—wet and twisted and ugly.

She swallowed the rest.

The breeze on the balcony was as cool as well water. The night was full of stars. The city below was full of torches and revelers. The full moon presided over them. Cicadas sang to accompany the minstrels. Laughter all around.

That night, even the orphans of Walltown would sleep with full bellies. Rhea could barely distinguish the fires on the distant city wall from the light of fireflies much closer on. Beyond them both was all of Pelgard—all the people of three kingdoms not her own.

It would be an easy and lasting peace if all the nights could be likewise beautiful. Rhea felt the gnaw of hunger. She hadn't eaten.

Perhaps she would swing by the kitchens for a secret meal. She hated for people to watch her chew. She would give Cooky a kiss on the cheek for his year's labor. His cheek would be greasy, but it would be everything he talked about until the next year's Revels. Then she would return to the ball. Without so much as a nod to Lazlo, she would have that dance with Endrit. She might even kiss two men in one night.

As she planned her course, Rhea half consciously noted the figures prowling across the bridge below. Some moved under it, across the gulley. They stayed away from the fire-light, noticeable only as darker shapes sliding in the shadows. Rhea thought, *Isn't it strange for revelers to sneak away from the festival grounds?*

She pushed off the balcony to return to her room with little more thought. *Is it a hiding game?* she mused as she crossed the Protectorate hall, around the oaken table, to the door that led to the kitchens. Rhea turned the knob and pulled. It stayed fast.

The door was never locked.

Rhea wasn't even certain who owned a key. She walked over to the other door, which led back to the ballroom, and pulled it open. The guardswoman stood before her, sword at the ready.

Rhea stated the obvious, "You're in my way."

With a hint of apology, the guard said, "Begging pardon, Majesty."

"Then get out of my way," said Rhea.

"The king said you might be crying in there and to ask you to—uh—"

It must have been awkward to deliver such patronizing commands. "—to clean yourself up, if necessary, so that others won't be—uh—"

"So others won't be what? Subjected to my emotions?"

"Satisfied by the sight of a weak queen, Your Majesty."

Rhea opened her eyes wide. "Look, no tears. I'm fine. Now stand aside or I'll put you down, guardswoman."

The guard seemed to like a queen willing to bloody her knuckles a bit. She bowed and stepped aside.

Rhea stepped through. They walked together, down the hall, back toward the ballroom.

"There is more to do tonight than babysit me, I hope," said Rhea.

"It's my honor," said the guard.

"Besides," said Rhea over her shoulder, "there are revelers playing a sneak game. They could drown in the gulley."

"What did you say?" said the guard. But before she could finish the question, Rhea opened the door to the banquet hall and an explosion shattered the west wall.

CHAPTER SIX

Cadis

C adis recognized the explosive ballista instantly, the signature cannonade of the Findain naval arsenal.

All around her were screams of nobles in utter chaos and guards shouting. Dust and smoke scratched at her eyes and burned her lungs. The smell of death—burnt hair, singed skin—already filled the giant hall.

Another explosion rocked the floor. The ballista must have arced downward and hit lower on the keep wall.

A moment ago she had been standing with a flock of suitors and the Findish envoy before her. They had contrived some political debate for her benefit, to impress, to cajole, to influence. She was used to the mixture—flirting, fawning, manipulation.

The marquis of an old Meridan outpost at the Tasan border clucked like a peacock about the need for the presence of troops in each of the three, ahem, *disorderly* kingdoms. Not only did the soldiers bring order, but also, they taught the locals all the latest techniques in farming.

A Findish merchant with long eyelashes and a habit of touching Cadis at the elbow replied, "Oh? Does the good marquis know much about—"

At that moment, the wall had erupted. A stone the size of a hillock melon smashed the young merchant in the back of the head. Cadis watched him crumple to the floor with his head crushed as the wave of smoke overtook them. For a rueful instant, Cadis thought, *Now we'll never know what the marquis knows about.* The marquis, too, was dead on the ground, a jagged rock sticking out of his back.

Cadis covered her mouth, squinted, and ran perpendicular to the direction of the blast. Running away would be panic. Running directly away would be exactly what the attacker would count on. Cadis ran to the north wall, toward the dais, where the royal musicians had left their instruments to join the roiling river of revelers, all screaming and rushing to the east exit.

Cadis mounted the stage to get a better view. A soldier had taken three pieces of shrapnel to the chest. She lay bleeding. Cadis kneeled and took the bow and arrows lying next to the dying guard.

"It'll be okay," she said to the guard. It was the best comfort she could think of. When the guard, heaving for breath, saw Cadis, she jerked back. She couldn't speak with her lungs full of blood, but Cadis knew the intention.

It's you who did this. The Findish rebel.

The guard pawed at Cadis, pushing her away, and Cadis complied. Neither of them had the time for Cadis's excuse.

A fresh chorus of terrified screaming came from the clogged door at the east wall. Cadis could see above their heads—a gang of masked assassins swinging curved blades, pirate blades, hacked their way into the room.

The herd of revelers now worked against itself. The nobles in the front turned back into the ballroom to escape the marauders and were met by the crowd farther back, still fearing for another explosion—pushing, pushing.

The mob churned. The killers had an easy harvest. The soft backs of horrified lords and ladies.

East to west, cutthroats and blood.

West to east, smoke and starlight.

Cadis took an instant to scan the battlefield. Thank Myrath, the goddess of all changes, death chief among them, that her sisters were not among the dead.

Iren was nowhere to be found. A good sign. If she wasn't lying dead on the floor, then perhaps she'd escaped to warn the king's guard. Rhea stood at the southern door, surrounded by the Meridan guard. Suki stood by the banquet table, out of the throng. She held her head. Blood had washed down her arm and soaked her yellow dress. She looked dizzy. A piece of the wall, or shrapnel from the ballista, must have grazed her scalp.

But she was fine. And she was well trained. She had grabbed a linen cloth from the table and wrapped it around her head.

The ballista had torn a giant smoldering gash into the side of the keep. More assassins climbed in through the hole. It seemed strange to Cadis that the Findain resistance could have possibly gained such a foothold, become such a powerful guerilla force. She'd thought they were nothing but a discontented few.

Cadis watched with ever-increasing horror as the rebels slaughtered men and women—knowing it was only the beginning of an inevitable war.

A masked man cut down Doyenne Sprolio where she stood and turned toward Suki. Her back was to him. Cadis thought to scream her name but remembered the weapon in her hand.

She nocked the arrow and loosed.

The assassin fell, grasping at the skewer in his neck. Cadis had spent a lifetime pulling back arrows, holding her breath, letting go in between two heartbeats, waiting for the arrow to fly and feeling the satisfying *thump* of hitting the wood billboards at dead center. The sound was an extension of the shot. If ever she missed and it sailed off, it felt incomplete, a hanging breath.

The sound of her first kill was like nothing Cadis had ever felt before, even in a ballroom full of mayhem and savagery. She'd punctured the assassin's neck with a wet, echoless *smack*. And he'd fallen. And Suki was alive. She whipped around, saw the man fall, and grabbed his sword. Suki would be fine.

Cadis had vantage on the rest of the field. She threw the strap of the quiver over her shoulder, jumped on a musician's stool to angle her shot line farther, and took aim at another assailant. An arrow sprouted in a rebel's chest.

He fell.

Smack. One in the thigh.

Smack. Another in her belly. The masked marauder looked down at the arrow as if surprised by a counterattack. She fell.

Some wore light armor, but most wore only hardened leather for stealth and ease of climbing the high walls of the keep. To be safe, Cadis aimed for the barest parts. She found she could punch an arrow down at the base of the neck, into the lungs or heart for instant kills. Like an avenging goddess, sending bolts of lightning from above. The collarbone made a morbid target zone, much bigger, actually, than the bull's-eye Marta set out for her. Even with the swollen eye and dizziness from her bout with Iren, Cadis could hit her marks.

A quick look around. Rhea had an arsenal dangling around her wrists and two remaining guards. Suki had pushed over a dining table and managed to round up a few nobles. She had them huddled behind it as she defended three sides from all comers.

They were raised for this, thought Cadis, horrible as it was.

"Cadis!"

Cadis looked around for whoever had screamed her name. "Cadis!" It was the chief officer of the Findish envoy, an older woman, rough-hewn from years of caravanning in the badlands. She was hobbled by a broken ankle. Two attendants helped her. Cadis jumped from the dais, pushed past a scrum of Meridan guards. She held an arrow by the shaft like a hunting knife. It was no other use in such close quarters.

When she reached the ambassador, Cadis asked, "Is this all that remain?"

The attendants nodded. Nearly a dozen in the Findish envoy slain by their own countrymen.

"Why would they do this?" said Cadis, swiveling her head so that no one took them by surprise.

"Who?" said the chief.

"The rebels."

"Rebels? These villains aren't rebels."

Cadis had no time to parse the distinctions. "Get behind me, then," said Cadis. "I can protect you."

The chief of the envoy stopped and turned around. She waited until Cadis looked her in the eye and said, "No. Archana, you misunderstand. We're here to protect you."

An old merchant woman with her two attendants? They were boys her age—probably heir to a guild in the mercantile exchange. Maybe they had come to woo her, but gods, neither could wield a butter knife. The chief put a hand to Cadis's shoulder. Cadis pulled back as a reflex but looked at the woman once again. She was serious. "You can't be here when this is over," said the chief.

"What are you—"

But the ambassador interrupted. "You'll become a prisoner of war. We can't fight if our queen is theirs."

Cadis reeled at the implication of total war and wondered suddenly if the purpose of the envoy all along had been to smuggle her out of Meridan.

"Did you plan this?" she said.

The ambassador shook her head. Before Cadis could ask any more, a pair of marauders rushed at the dais. Cadis dashed forward, hoping to distract both from the envoy, but the attendant boys threw themselves at the assailants. Cadis watched while she ducked under the swing of her attacker and stabbed her arrow into his shoulder, then pulled it out and then put it into his neck. She watched the first attendant run belly first into the attacker's blade and the second scratch at the attacker's face to nearly no effect. Cadis dragged her arrow across the neck and left it in the unstitched position. By then the other rebel had declawed the second attendant with a dagger.

As Cadis reached behind her and grabbed another arrow, the rebel pulled his cutlass out of the attendant on the ground and charged. Cadis had no time. She dropped the arrow and lifted the bow, hoping the wood could withstand the blow. The rebel shouted as he swung the sword down with both hands. The cutlass dug deep into the bow.

But the bow held.

Cadis kicked the rebel in the chest.

He stumbled back.

She reached up, took an arrow from her quiver, and shot in one smooth motion. The rebel fell with a feather in his left eye.

The chief ambassador sat on the ground, holding her broken ankle. Cadis bent to help her up, but the old woman grabbed her wrist. Cadis was once again staring into the green eyes of a Fin—strange and familiar all at once. "Leave," said the woman. "Tell no one where you're going and get home. Do it. Do it now."

"They'll think I'm a traitor," said Cadis.

"They already think it. This is their proof. Queen, if you don't go, Declan will stay our hand even as he murders your people."

Cadis knew it was true, that no matter what the reason, this attack would become yet another betrayal by the Findish. No matter the true identity of the killers.

Cadis pulled her hand out of the grip of the ambassador and kneeled over the masked man she had just killed. He was still warm. She pulled down the sweat-soaked mask that covered his mouth, exposing his neck. Emblazoned on his rough skin was a tattoo—in sailor's ink made of ship's pitch. It was the face of a woman with no features, no eyes, no nose. In the place of her mouth was a line of fish, arranged in a wicked smile. It was the sign of the Munnur Myrath. Cadis dropped the body and stood.

"What's your name?" said Cadis.

It took a second for the ambassador to understand the question.

"Birla," she said.

"Thank you, Ambassador Birla," said Cadis. "I will remember you to the scribes."

Cadis turned and ran into the havoc.

CHAPTER SEVEN

Suki

The killer used a sailor's cutlass (which was obviously Findish (and maybe even too obviously)), but she didn't know how to use it very well (her slashes were from the wrist and not the shoulder (which no sailor could get away with on any decent ship)), so they were either imposters who had never used slashing swords (Meridan soldiers maybe, who used short broadswords) or they were just incompetent pirates. Either way, it didn't really matter.

Suki had the weapon she needed finally (two chair legs) after trying to use a cutlass herself (too brutish, and needed a bigger swing than she could manage) and then a short sword she grabbed from a fallen Meridan guard (better, but didn't help her any with reach).

The chair legs, heavy and thick at the ends, reminded her of double clubs used by the night watch in Tasan (but those were beautiful and gnarled bituin branches (each a completely unique twist and curl)). These were just chair legs (she used one to knock the crummy pirate's sword aside (and the other to shatter her knee)). The pirate fell, screaming.

Suki was still bleeding (it wasn't sweat (the bandage was soaked through)). Her arm had a numb sensation.

Everyone screamed (peals of terror (angry roars (Cadis shouting, "Suki!" (Guards calling out orders to each other))))).

"Suki!" (This time Cadis's voice was much closer.) Suki turned. Cadis had a bow and some arrows (not useful).

"You tore your dress," said Suki. (Her legs were very exposed (Cadis had cut two long slits in her blue dress for better mobility (and tactical distraction for any boy with eyes))).

Suki looked around and added, "Have you seen Endrit?"

"No," said Cadis, grabbing Suki by the shoulders. "Suki, look at me. Are you okay?" (A dumb question.)

"Yes." (Endrit had to be around here somewhere.)

"Suki. Suki, pay attention. The rebels are starting another war."

"They're terrible with cutlasses."

Cadis was checking her over, like Marta after a training accident.

"You've bled a lot."

Suki looked down. The entire top of her dress was red now. "I stabbed two of them and hobbled that one," said Suki. (She didn't mean it as a brag (only that she felt the need to tell someone what she'd done (but it was in defense of innocent people (and if not innocent, then at least people who weren't blowing up parties (and interrupting dances)))).)

"Have you seen him?"

"Who?"

"Endrit!" (Why wasn't Cadis paying attention?)

"No. Listen to me, Suki. We have to get out of here."

"Not without Endrit," said Suki.

"I mean for good. We have to escape the castle and go back home."

(That would be crazy.)

"That's crazy," said Suki. "They'd think we had something to do with this." (Did Cadis plan something like this? (why wouldn't she tell them? (Iren and Suki—not Rhea, of course)).)

"Have you seen Iren?" said Cadis.

"I saw her go that way," said Suki (pointing at the south wall).

Suki interrupted the swing of a charging rebel (by hitting his elbow with a club and jabbing the other into his abdomen). An arrow whistled by her ear and lodged into the rebel's chest (he fell).

"Suki, he'll use this to declare war," (Declan) "to invade Findain, maybe Tasan," (he'd lose if he did) "and if he has us, they won't resist."

It sounded good (but maybe it was idiotic (maybe this was just a tavern brawl, and outside, everything was nice and orderly (and guards on the walls were waiting to catch them (and the next morning they'd be horrible queens who'd tried to use a little attack from local criminals to escape the Protectorate that was the only promise of peace for Pelgard (and even if that was naive—what if Tola was alive somewhere and Declan hurt her because of this (or if she wasn't alive, he would do the same to Suki (and the empire of Tasan would be ashamed of yet another empress))))))). Even Suki (who only ever wanted to leave) knew that they couldn't just leave and walk back home.

When Suki turned around to answer, Cadis was gone (run off to get Iren instead probably).

Suki looked for Endrit but couldn't see him (and couldn't stop thinking of the threat from Rhea, "You wouldn't want to end up like your sister." (Was this the battle?)). She found Rhea fighting amid her guards (only two left), but when Suki looked (really took a second to notice), she realized the assassins wouldn't target Rhea. (All her fighting was instigated by Rhea herself (assassin stabs at guard, Rhea bounces forward and punches his neck with poison ring (another one grappling with other guard, Rhea sneaks up and puts a necklace stake into his heart (Nobody seemed interested in Rhea))).)

It was all a lie. They were protecting her.

That was the final clue that brought it all together for Suki (the threat the day before, (the fact that no one attacked Rhea (the fight over Endrit—as if she were entitled to his affection))). Rhea always seemed so useless (and disappointing) to her father, but she had to know where they were hiding Tola. She knew. She had to know.

And Suki knew in that moment that Rhea was evil (to take everything she loved (Tola) and deserved (Endrit) for herself).

The anger made her numb arm tremble and her head spin. Suki ran toward Rhea (the nobles she had been protecting (a sweet old man who'd said, "You're a lucky man to be dancing with her," to Endrit (in the short time before the blast) and smiled at her like a nice dad, and his two daughters) shouted after her (but Suki couldn't hear them (or pretended not to))) until she reached one of Rhea's guards (looking the other way) and brained him with her club.

"What are you doing?" screamed Rhea. "He's with us."

"No, he's with you," said Suki. (It was the perfect thing to say and the perfect time to say it.)

A rebel preoccupied her other guard. Rhea couldn't even respond. She had only a look of terror (that her plot had been discovered?). Suki felt an icy tremor in her shoulder (had it bled out?). She looked down. The tip of a cutlass jutted out (her nose almost touched it (the blood was really flowing now (the room spun))). Rhea threw a pin from her hair, and Suki felt the weight of the cutlass release from her shoulder (the person holding it must have let go).

As Suki fell, she thought, *I hate her*. She hated that she

needed Rhea's help (and she thought that she should turn so she didn't fall onto the hilt of the sword (which would push it farther through)), and finally, as Suki blacked out— her arm cold, her sister Tola likely dead—her last thought was about Rhea (and it was one word (revenge)).

CHAPTER EIGHT

Iren

Time of the blast: Midnight.

Iren balanced on a rafter beam above the outer hallway.

King Declan stood below.

Four paces ahead.

He walked toward his chambers.

Iren found she could follow anyone in Meridan Keep using the beams of the lamplighters.

Sometimes people looked back.

They never looked up.

The explosion shook the beams and the walls.

Like an avalanche hitting a mountain spire.

Debris vomited from the ballroom and over them.

Screams and shouting.

Iren fell.

She reached out and caught the wood beam under her armpit. Her arm wasn't long enough to wrap around. She was a cat, scrabbling for purchase.

A long drop.

Below, guards rushed to the king's chamber.

She tried to swing her legs under the beam and up the other side.

Her finger slipped.

A tumbling fall.

She twisted around face forward.

Her left knee struck the stones.

A sound like clacking teeth.

Shooting pain.

She bit her tongue.

Blood filled her mouth.

But soundless otherwise, still undetected.

Iren searched for an alcove or unlit corner to hide herself.

She had lost sight of Declan in the fall.

Cloistered in his chamber, most probable, surrounded by guards.

Assignment fifty-three: incomplete.

Iren inspected her knee, no skin break, swollen.

"There she is!" A muffled shout from the end of the hallway.

Three men. Masked. Dressed to look piratical or outlander.

They ran toward Iren. Tactically untrained.

They ran shoulders square. Huge targets.

Iren had throwing blades in the bracers hidden under her sleeves—

"Princess Iren. Halt where you are."

They knew her name.

Couldn't be outlander.

Iren stood straight, to hide her injury.

Throbbing pain as her knee continued swelling.

She hid the fact that it couldn't hold any weight.

The three men approached and stood abreast instead of surrounding her.

Redundant positioning.

Useless in a fight.

They didn't think much of her.

Iren pretended to shake. She hugged herself and reached into her sleeves.

Two teardrop daggers, tied to the back of each arm.

"What are you doing so near the king's chambers?" said the man in the middle. His voice was distant behind the layers of black terry cloth.

"I was scared."

Tiny movements to untie each dagger. Kept eye contact to distract.

"Why aren't you in the ballroom?"

"There are villains in the ballroom," said Iren. She thought of starting to cry, but the men seemed unconcerned.

"You were following the king."

"Were you following me?"

A scoff. A familiar one.

"Take her back to the hall," said the leader.

The two men on either side finally approached. Too late now to surround the prey.

Iren pulled the two knives and jumped forward. A glancing blow at the leader and she could puncture their shoddy circle.

It would be a footrace. Vaspata, goddess of diligence, preserve her knee.

Iren cut at the leader's face.

The fabric sliced open as easily as the cheek underneath.

The leader cursed and grabbed his face. Iren ducked under and ran.

One step.

The pain bloomed in all directions.

Behind her, heavy footfalls.

Two. Three.

A rush to the crossway. She would turn left.

No choice. Had to plant on her good knee, or fall.

Crackles of white light with every step.

If she could make it downstairs, to her cache of tools in the kitchen, a loaded crossbow waited.

Maybe Cooky would help her.

Ten more steps to the crossway.

A left, a set of stairs.

Too far.

Her knee buckled.

Iren came up hobbling.

A rough hand clamped on her neck and pushed her face into the sidewall.

She squirmed around to see.

Her captor let her turn but held her by the throat, her back pressed into the stone.

The second man grabbed each wrist in turn and stripped away her knives. The leader approached, hand to cheek. Blood between the fingers. A nice cut. His mask unraveling.

"When this is over, the delegations from three nations will investigate the crime scene. And you, little thorn, will be dead with a Findish blade in your heart."

"You can let it fall, Magister."

The man holding her tightened his grip. The leader sighed and let the tattered mask fall away.

Hiram Kinmegistus.

Iren let the line of her lips become a smile.

It was good to see him bleed.

"I suppose our game of cat and mouse is over," said Hiram. "I've known of your sneaking all about the castle. And your little stash of weapons."

"Oh," said Iren, throat nearly clamped shut.

"Did you think you'd escape and run back to the mountains?"

Iren let out a choked laugh.

"Let her speak."

The man opened his palm. Iren gasped for more air. Her tongue still bled. Still, all she felt was relief.

He didn't know.

The spymaster of Meridan thought her intent was something as silly as running away. All this time he'd known she snuck about the castle, evading guards, fooling even his shinhounds, and yet he still looked at her and saw a little girl, scared and lost.

"Why do you smile?" said the magister.

"I have no weapon," said Iren. The men waited. "And so I pray to the daughter of Vaspata."

She was surrounded.

The grip on her throat was tight and the hand armored.

She could dislodge it, at a cost.

Maybe not even then.

Her knee ached.

Another race would be foolish.

Time—maybe time could save her, if someone arrived to see the men assassinating a future queen.

But the blast must have been part of a plot.

Screams could be heard coming from the ball.

Clanging.

War song.

No one would come.

"The goddess of diligence has many daughters," said Hiram.

Always a fool for correcting.

"The daughter untimely born, who built the first bridge in the Corentine snowcaps."

She had no weapon.

And neither did Hiram.

He would never again be so exposed.

"The daughter of diligence. Preparation," she added.

They were confused.

She must have been delirious.

But Hiram was a prideful man, eager to show his learning.

Weakening himself, by speaking too much.

"Ismata," said the magister. Preparation's true name.

A fool for correcting.

He must have kept his shinhounds near, in case he needed them.

He was unarmed.

And he had given over his only weapon.

"Ismata!" shouted Iren, just before the masked man's grip clenched around her throat. "Latch!"

The scrabbling sound of heavy paws on stone.

Hiram may have known of the name but not its meaning.

Just a little girl, naming beasts.

She had nurtured them for years with new names and alternate commands.

Ismata reared around the corner, growling.

Iren felt her body slacken.

She needed air.

The hound leaped at the man holding Iren, gnashing at the face.

The man went down.

He nearly pulled Iren down with him.

His glove burned as it tugged at her neck.

She wrenched back.

The man hit the stones, screaming.

The second man approached from the left.

Her mouth had filled with blood.

She had been saving it for him.

He jumped forward to grab her.

Iren spat a surge of blood at his eyes.

The man startled.

He was blinded for a short instant.

Iren dashed the other way.

A few steps.

Her knee held.

Then pain.

Lightning.

Fire.

Thunder.

Pain.

The sound of rushing water filled her ear.

Iren fell against a tapestry hanging on the wall.

She didn't think Hiram could move so quickly.

He had kicked her knee from the side just as she'd put her weight on it.

Iren panted.

Hiram grabbed the cuff of her shirt.

She gouged at his eye.

Quicker once again.

He caught her wrist.

Was he a wartime magister?

In all her investigating, had she missed some secret history?

Iren had never been assigned to investigate Hiram.

So many pressing matters.

Seemed he had his own secrets.

His grip crunched her bones together.

She wouldn't squeal. Never.

"What's this?" said Hiram. He roughly pulled back the sleeve. It revealed the leather bracer along her forearm. Tiny rolled-up parchments tucked into pockets. A lockpick set. A thief's kit.

The second man wiped away the blood on his face and joined them.

The first was losing to the hound atop him.

Iren pulled but couldn't free herself.

She feared for an instant that she'd die and wondered who would tell her mother.

Down the hall, around the corner, a figure approached.

Footfalls.

The clicking of braided seashells.

Blessed relief. Iren recognized the noise.

Hiram unstrapped the band with deft fingers and pulled it off her arm.

"You're a spy," he said. A statement and a question.

"And you're the mouse," said Iren.

Someone had finally come.

An arrow flew between them and struck the masked man in the collar. He reeled backward and fell. Frantic. Grasping at the feather.

Hiram retraced the shot.

Cadis stood at the end of the hall, another arrow nocked and ready.

Blood covered the lower half of her torn blue dress and splattered all the way up to her shoulders. A butcher's smock.

Hiram let go of Iren.

Cadis had made no sense of the scene.

The magister turned and ran.

"Take the shot," said Iren, her voice hoarse.

"What happened?"

The question was enough.

Hiram turned the corner. He still had her notes.

Seven assignments, lost.

Declan's schematics for new cannon. Diverted trade routes of Findish caravans. General Hecuba's rumor of war. Iren strained to remember them all.

She would transcribe them again. On the road.

She was found out.

Soon Declan would know.

Even a future queen could be executed for spycraft.

Her mind raced with an order of operations.

Cadis had run up to her.

Iren turned to her, and together they said, "We have to leave."

Cadis was surprised by their unison statements.

"I mean forever," said Cadis.

"I know," said Iren.

"They're killing everyone."

"Even Rhea?"

"I think so."

Iren doubted it. But Cadis didn't need to know to comply. Iren's mother always said that information should only ever be given to convince an ally or to kill an enemy. Otherwise it had been given away too freely.

She had already given Hiram too much.

Iren decided to keep her discovery to herself for now—that Hiram was behind the attack. And therefore Declan had orchestrated it all.

He'd blame the Findish rebels. Start another war. This time he had choked his enemies with unfair trade and built his own military in secret. A final war. A war of bloody unification.

But why, then, the Protectorate?

Killing them made sense, of course. But why such an elaborate charade for ten years? Why give them Marta and Hiram? Why teach them their own histories, give them books lent from the academy and sailing lessons in the king's own aqueduct? Why give them Rhea?

Was Declan ever so foolish as to think they would love him? What had he discovered that changed his mind?

Iren knew if she had the time to write to Queen Malin, this would be her next assignment.

Number 58.

Iren turned to Cadis. "Do you need anything from your chamber?"

"Clothes, better shoes."

"I mean family items, personal things."

Cadis shook her head no. Good. The chambers would be ransacked. If they had not been already. Tonight Declan meant to murder them all.

"I have a stash in the kitchens."

The two ran down the discreet set of stairs meant only for the servants. Two flights down.

Past the larder.

Past the triple hearth.

Coals glowing.

No one present.

Cooky must have been upstairs.

Poor old chef. He always relished a personal appearance. A bow to the guests. His theatrics probably killed him.

Into the dry-goods storage.

Iren pulled down a gunnysack of barley from a waist-high stack.

Cadis caught on and helped.

Behind the grain sacks, a loose stone in the wall.

Behind the stone, a hidey-hole.

A cache of spare travel clothes, riding pants, black cloaks.

Three travel packs of food, canteens, and bedrolls.

A red velvet purse full of Meridan coin.

Two others, a green with Findish doubloons and a yellow with Tasanese paper marks.

"Why isn't there a purse for Corent?" asked Cadis.

"I don't need money in Corent," said Iren.

Cadis looked on in disbelief.

Iren shoved a set of clothes into her arms.

"Dress. Now."

Iren checked each of the packs. The motions had been practiced a hundred times in her mind.

As Cadis changed out of her bloody dress, Iren reached deep into the hidden compartment and pulled out weapons.

To Cadis's pack, Iren slung a bow and quiver.

The grips were taped exactly as Cadis did it.

"Remember that time you wanted to read my letters?"

Cadis blinked, then understood.

It was her favorite practice bow. She'd given it as one of the favors she owed Iren.

Iren stuffed two Findish filleting knives into the straps of the pack and another into a hidden strap in a pair of boots.

She handed the boots to Cadis.

Iren's pack had another thief's kit and another armband.

She began to dress and was finished before Cadis.

She wrapped a scarf tightly around her swollen knee for support.

From her bag she dug out a ring of keys.

It had taken four years to assemble. She had lifted each one from the belt of a guard or the apron of a maid. She'd pressed it into hot wax, then returned the original. From the wax molds, she'd made duplicates. It was not very different from the metalwork frames she made for her stained glass. As far as Declan knew, the extra candles were only for late-night reading and the metal for her glasswork.

They were both dressed, armed, and packed for a long journey.

Cadis stared at the mouth of the secret cubby and asked, "Why do you have extra?"

In the compartment sat another pack, riding boots, another set of clothes, and two long swords.

"Those were for Suki."

Cadis was naive, but she was smart enough not to ask about Rhea.

Iren walked out.

Cadis pushed the loose stone to cover the secret cache.

"Leave it," said Iren.

When Cadis caught up, Iren handed her a thin bamboo vial, stoppered with heavy layers of wax.

"What's this?"

"Venom of the corkspider."

Cadis jolted, as if the vial had bitten her.

Iren led them through the back of the kitchens, to the greengrocer's loading gate.

"Iren, why do you have all this?"

Cadis had a commander's tone, which Iren admired.

"Aren't you glad I do?" said Iren.

"I'm serious."

"Good."

Iren opened the loading gate with a key from her ring. Cadis stopped. Iren checked the alley. No one there. Guards must have sounded the alarm. Everyone would be rushing to the ballroom.

"Come on."

"No."

Iren sighed. "I have the stash for lots of reasons."

"Name them," said Cadis, firm.

"If Suki went mad and stabbed Rhea. If you, eager sister, beat Rhea again and the people of Meridan demanded our heads. If Declan wished for royal concubines. If the missing heir of Kendrick returned to claim his throne. If a tree fell in the woods and crushed Declan's skull on one of his rides. If Queen Rhea hated her dearest sisters."

Iren continued.

"If Findish rebels attacked us at the ball. If there needed to be an assassination."

"Assassination of whom?" said Cadis.

Iren shrugged. "Declan. Rhea. Whomever."

"By whom?"

"Don't be silly. By me. Who else?"

"I would believe almost anyone else but you."

Iren laughed. She put up the cowl of her cloak and signaled Cadis to do the same. "Then you believe too much. Let's go," she said.

They stepped into the high-walled alley, careful not to turn their ankles in the grooves of the wagonway.

Shouting and tumult came from the front entrance.

They hugged the dark patches and moved toward the outer gate of Meridan Keep.

They could buy horses in Walltown. Or steal them from stables of the hillside farms.

Cadis's braided shells made more noise than a peddler's cart.

They avoided the main thoroughfare.

One of Iren's first assignments had been to map the route. When she ventured a look over her shoulder, she saw Cadis watching her as if she were a mermaid. She still held her vial.

"Put that away," said Iren.

"Was it meant for the king?"

Iren scoffed to herself. She still called him king. Still scandalized by the thought of putting the rabid dog down.

"No," said Iren.

If Iren were going to assassinate him, she would have done it in his sleep with a pickax. But that information wasn't necessary. Cadis still looked aghast.

She had killed for the first time tonight. She might have realized the lie they had been living. And she had discovered at least some of Iren's secrets.

Maybe she needed assurance of some kind.

Iren paused in a dark alcove before an open crossroad, below the guard tower at the outer wall. She waited for Cadis's skittering eyes to look into her own.

Now would be the time to tell her that at least for the time being, they were together. They would protect each other until they were home safe.

This would be difficult. Cadis would have had no trouble with it. She'd just speak. A gift Iren didn't have. She'd speak and say, "I'm with you, sister." Perhaps she'd add, "I love you."

And Iren did feel thus. But it was difficult to say, because the evidence was new that Iren had been hiding quite a lot from her dear sister. It would be difficult to explain the two together. That Iren cared more for Cadis than she ever imagined possible. That they were friends. Bosom friends, Cadis would say. But her assignments remained. Her obligation to Corent remained. Iren would have liked to explain this, the possibility for both to exist—sisterly love and sisterly lying—but they didn't have the time, and she didn't have the words.

Iren took her hand, the one that held the vial. She guided it to a hidden pocket inside the collar of her cloak, where the vial could be easily reached.

Cadis looked into her sister's eyes, waiting for whatever instruction she might have.

Before Iren turned and dashed across the torchlit crossway, to the final gate, she said, "Drink it if we get caught."

CHAPTER NINE

Rhea

It had never occurred to Rhea, even after years of training in the grimwaltz, that if she was ever caught up in an attack of some kind and she had to defend herself, it would be unlike stabbing dummies in three specific ways—the sound, the mess, and the fact that her knives would not be returned.

It was a small detail to dwell on. Maybe everyone's vision narrowed when the wider world became as horrific as the ballroom had become.

Meridan guards had rushed in and either killed the last of the Findish rebels or chased them as they ran off. Some even jumped back through the smoldering gap in the wall and grabbed the ropes they had used to climb in, to rush back out.

They left behind them a ruined battlefield. Banquet tables turned over. Broken chairs. Burning tapestry churning black smoke. Bodies. So many bodies. So many men and women—their own visions slowly narrowing into permanent darkness. They were afraid. They shouted for help, for their mothers, for anyone. Anyone living, please come and hold their hands. Be alive around them.

It surprised Rhea that so many didn't even bother to shout for magisters. They were beyond healing.

Rhea sat in the corner, pressing a patch of her dress onto Suki's shoulder. Suki remained unconscious. Rhea had removed the sword. The blood had poured out. A guard had run up some time ago—she had no idea how long—and said, "Highness, are you hurt?"

"Get Hiram. Go."

She expected the magister any moment now. Wherever he was, hopefully he was uninjured. He would come and help. He would know what to do and how to wake Suki.

In the meantime Rhea sat with Suki's head on her lap, pressing the cloth down and doing her best to ignore all the sounds. The mess she could not ignore, because she sat in the middle of it. A mess of gore, and sweat, and cinder.

Had I made so much of it?

Rhea could not close her eyes or she would see them. The rebels. The one she stuck in the chest with three of the radial stakes from her necklace. He had looked down in surprise, then back up at her, directly, as if wondering why she would ever do such a thing. Then he fell. Those stakes were still missing from the left side of her necklace.

It sat asymmetrically on her chest, making its presence known.

She would see the woman who killed one of her guards. A lithe, masked killer. Rhea had turned around in time to see the assassin unsheathe her blade from her guard's rib cage.

Rhea had punched her dragon ring into the woman's cheek. The corkspider venom had ripped through her. She lay now in front of the south gate, every limb crooked and her spine twisted.

Rhea kept her eyes open and hummed to keep the noises out.

Her hair hung down in odd places where she had pulled out her pins and thrown them. She would rather lose them forever than walk around the room dislodging them, plucking them like mushroom caps from a moldy tree trunk.

Maybe Endrit will collect them for me if I ask?

No one knew the secrets of the crown jewels of House Meridan but Rhea. A maid tasked with cleaning might just as easily prick herself on a hidden blade or touch a poison needle with bare skin. It never occurred to Rhea that they would need cleaning. *Why did so much never occur to me?*

Marta had once said, "Grimwaltz is a dance for one." Rhea thought she was warning her about lusting for Endrit—a veiled warning in the form of an aphorism that he was too much a gadfly to dance with her alone, or a reminder that he was below her in station. She realized now how silly it was to assume the veteran of two wars had decided to school her on puppy love.

It never occurred to Rhea.

She prayed, though she never prayed, to Anant, god of bounty, god of Meridan, that Endrit was not lying somewhere in the ballroom under the rubble.

Where is that guard with Hiram?

Where is my father?

The king was probably shut inside his chamber with his dragoons. They would never let him out with so many bandits unaccounted for. He would be screaming at them, demanding that they go and find his daughter.

But what if?

He wouldn't be dead. Impossible. If the Findish thought they would improve their situation, they would be as foolheaded as their carnival plays. She would call all her banner houses and conduct the coronation in a war tent at the vanguard of her infantry on the road to Findain. She would sink every last vessel in the Findain harbor if they killed him.

And what of my sisters? Rhea had not seen Iren since the pledging ceremony. *Has she gone to bed? Is she hiding in her room?*

Underneath her reserved and brusque exterior, Iren was a frightful and timid girl. Rhea had seen her cry when she read letters from home—and once, almost, when Cadis called her siren, a silly jest on her silent nature. She would be curled under her bed, no doubt, writing to her mother.

As for Cadis, Rhea preferred not to think of her. Finally,

after all the years of suspicion, Cadis had proven herself the treacherous *bestiola* that she was. She was probably riding back to Findain at the head of a gang, whatever remained of the raiding party, laughing at King Declan's naive trust in her. Rhea had known it all along. On a level deeper than bone and marrow, she felt the irregular vibration of a heart bent toward evil and chaos.

In Meridan, the soldiers would say, "A Fin's heart sings for gold of any color." It meant they were selfish and inconstant—pursuing random business opportunities. There was no principle, no oath, no sisterhood they would not betray. And now she'd finally done it. She had destroyed the Protectorate, killed innocents, killed Suki perhaps, pulled them all into war. And if she wanted war, then Rhea would . . .

"Rhea?"

It was Endrit. His voice came from across the ballroom. "Rhea!"

Blessed Anant, he is alive.

He ran across the room. Rhea cried out with relief, "It's you!"

An odd thing to shout. Her mind was too much alight with a thousand different thoughts. But suddenly only one. He was alive. His mouth and chin were bloody, but he smiled.

When he arrived, she noticed his formal clothes were wet. His upper arm had bled through the bandage and stained the outer jerkin. "Where were you?" said Rhea.

"Looking for you."

Is that really so? "You weren't in your chamber," he said.

"Why would I be there?"

"I saw you leave and took the long way around to catch you. After the blast, the fighting spilled out into the halls. I've been trying to—"

His eyes went to Suki, and he trailed off the subject. "What happened?"

He didn't wait for Rhea to respond to begin inspecting Suki's injuries.

"She attacked me. I think she panicked. A rebel got behind her and stabbed through her shoulder."

Was that a cruel thing to have done? She had presented Suki in the very worst light.

"You saved her," said Endrit, as he lifted her hand and looked under the bloody fabric.

"I killed the rebel. Yes."

Am I so disloyal as to claim all of Endrit's admiration for myself? Rhea quickly added, "But Suki was probably just confused. She protected lots of innocent people . . . before she lunged at me."

Endrit smiled at the unconscious Suki. "That's our Susu," he said. "Nothing if not unpredictable."

Rhea laughed a little. It was the right decision.

Endrit began to untie the silk laces at the front of his shirt. "When I tell you, remove the cloth and pull the strap of her dress out of the way."

Rhea nodded. He was still calm. All around, soldiers ran

and called to one another. Outside, the fighting continued.

"I was waiting for Hiram," Rhea explained, so he wouldn't think her useless. He pulled a silk string all the way out. His shirt fell open. Bruises lined his right side. Two ribs were swollen.

"You broke two ribs."

"Me?" said Endrit, grinning. "Why would I do such a silly thing to myself?"

Is he only so rakish when undressed?

"Now," he said. Rhea lifted the cloth from Suki's shoulder. The blood flow was slowing. *A good or a bad sign?* Rhea didn't know.

Endrit strapped the shirt lace around Suki's shoulder above the wound and made a tight knot.

He must have fought his way back to the ballroom. A spear handle or a club could have made such injuries, or two strikes from a gauntlet—but none of the rebels had such heavy armor.

Endrit tied off the lace and began to remove his shirt.

"Tell me what happened to your mouth, then."

Endrit tore off the clean sleeve of his shirt and began wrapping Suki's shoulder. With a free hand, he touched his mouth and looked at his fingers. The blood seemed to surprise him. "A beautiful Fin found me in the hall looking for you. One of those brutish women, probably a warlord from those islands on the North Coast. She grabbed me and tried to take me home to be her prize."

Endrit focused on pulling strips from his shirt and

wrapping the bandage. Rhea tried to excavate the truth with her searching looks.

"She grabbed you?"

"Like a love-struck knight, just scooped me up."

"What did you do?"

"I told her my body was hers, but my heart would always be in Meridan."

"Be serious."

"Then I kissed her ear."

"Stop jesting, Endrit."

Endrit looked up. The playful tone drained completely. "If you want to stop jesting, then we need to talk about leaving here right now. Anything else doesn't matter," he said.

Rhea was uncomfortable looking into his eyes. *Is he joking? Is he traumatized by battle? Why would we leave? My father and the magister will be coming for us.*

Rhea didn't follow the sudden turn and resented the lack of warning. "No," she said. "Tell me."

"I bit her. I bit the raider on the ear until she let me go."

Rhea had no response. *Why did he have to make me twist it out of him?* To punctuate the moment, Endrit looked at the body of the masked Fin nearby, reached over, and yanked the half-buried hairpin out of his head. It made a wet sound, like pulling a boot out of mud.

He tossed it back to Rhea. Then he rose. His own bandage was layered with three shades of crimson to brown.

He leaned over, gently lifted Suki's limp form off of Rhea's lap, and slung her over his good arm.

"Well?"

Rhea rose to her feet, but she shrugged with her hands. "What?"

"Time to go, Princess."

Is he annoyed with me? "Don't speak to me like that."

Why is he mad? She had done nothing. Rhea knew a fight would be childish. However she expressed it—that she wasn't weak for caring what had happened to him—it would seem like petulance, like a demand to be comforted. And this wasn't the time. She breathed, as her father had taught her, then spoke. "Hiram and the king will be here soon."

"No, they won't," said Endrit. "The rebels are pushing toward his chambers. We have no idea if a second wave is coming. Meridan troops are probably riding in from the garrison, leaving the outer gate shorthanded. What would you do if you had planned this?"

"You mean if I were Cadis?"

Endrit didn't give any hint of his opinion on Cadis. "What would you do?" he said.

Rhea sighed. "Obviously, I'd use this to divert attention from some larger goal. I'm not an idiot. And Marta taught me just as well as she taught you, so don't pretend you know everything."

"That's my point. We don't know. But we can't stay here."

He was right, and Rhea hated that he knew it.

"Fine."

It suddenly occurred to Rhea that she had done nothing

useful since the moment he'd arrived. He had seen her sitting, like some distressed maiden, waiting for others to help. He had bandaged Suki, found her a pin, and held her hand as he guided her thinking. And he was right.

Am I really so—

She didn't finish the thought.

Rhea flushed with shame. And she wished she could explain that he hadn't seen what she had seen. He hadn't been there when the slaughter started. And he hadn't fought or killed or seen someone he loved look at him as Suki had looked at her, with hate. And after all that, he had found her in a distracted moment. A lapse in judgment.

That didn't make her weak.

And he shouldn't have even thought so—not after knowing her for so long. He shouldn't have spoken to her like his fool.

As they ran out of the ballroom, Rhea didn't look back, but let the bloody hairpin fall from her hand. She didn't want to clean it. She was a queen, and she didn't have to.

"Get behind me," said Rhea as they approached a pair of guards at the petitioner's arch. They had fled down a long set of stairs that ran parallel to the massive grand entryway used for nobles and ceremonial processions. The stone-wrought stairs were for utilitarian use. When locals from Walltown arrived at court to plea for the king's favor, or families of criminals came to beg clemency, they used the petitioner's arch. Rhea and Endrit used it now, as they knew the garrison soldiers would pour into the grand staircase.

The guards at the door were king's dragoons, not castle guard.

"What're they doing here?" said Endrit as they approached. The hall was undecorated stone wide enough only for three men abreast. It was intended to make one feel like a mouse, skittering into the veins of a giant stone colossus.

On closer inspection, Rhea recognized them.

"It's Joram and Lackwood. Just get behind me. They're not supposed to be here," whispered Rhea. Endrit stopped. She shouldered her way past him, putting her hand on Suki's limp form as if she were a sack of potatoes.

The two soldiers must have been promoted to king's guard recently. Up until then, they'd barely ranked as castle guardsmen. Joram had lost his nose more than a decade ago—in the War of Unification. Lackwood had lost both ears.

The wounds were no longer fresh and pink, and their faces no longer seemed to miss them. They had hardened and wrinkled into somewhat grotesque, mildly comical appearances. Her father wouldn't have had them in the king's guard for their looks alone. They were grunts.

"Stop," barked Joram when they drew within a spear's length. "Turn around and go back."

Do they recognize me? If so, they made no bow to royal courtesy.

Rhea looked down. She was still wearing half a dozen royal seals—on her signet ring, in the embroidery of her dress, and on her house jewels. Even if she was tussled and splattered, they should have known.

"Turn around and go back," said Joram, looking completely unfit in his crimson dragoon gear.

"Yes, we heard you," said Rhea. The oddness of it still confused her. The dragoons were a small cadre of king's guard. *Is my father nearby? Is he hurt?*

"If you heard him, then do what he says." Lackwood stepped forward with his spear tilted. It was the wrong weapon for such tight quarters. Rhea corrected her thinking. A spear was only the wrong weapon if they were guarding against enemies coming from outside. It was the perfect weapon to hold extended in a narrow hallway, to keep people protected—or trapped—inside.

"We ain't saying it again. Turn back now, Princess, and go to your chambers," said Joram. His noseless face puckered when he sneered.

"Then you know who I am?"

"'Course," said Joram. "Been wiping after you since you was weaning."

"What are you doing, Joram? Is this some kind of jest?"

Are they seizing this opportunity for some kind of petty revenge?

Rhea had never been challenged. Both dragoons would be dead by morning if she chose. The men leveled their spears at Rhea and stepped forward. Endrit whispered, "This is no dance, Rhea. They're not jesting."

Is he saying we should turn back? Can he find another

way out? Rhea hesitated. The situation had torn apart so quickly—the guards' treasonous aggression, Endrit's uncharacteristic timidity.

"Return now."

Their spear tips advanced toward Rhea's chest. She still couldn't believe it. She had given Joram a gold piece once, for Penance Day. She knew Lackwood was a lowlander—she had seen his kids in the Walltown Market.

"I order you to stand aside," said Rhea, gathering the remains of her dignity.

"No. *We* order *you* to turn back."

"Fight speed, Rhea," said Endrit. "Make a move."

Rhea looked back at Endrit, then at Suki. She had her plan. She whispered, "When I say the word, throw Suki."

Endrit took a moment to understand.

Does he think me callous? It doesn't matter.

He nodded.

Rhea turned back. The spears glinted, like a shutting iron maiden.

"Go," said Joram.

"No!" said Rhea. "You—"

"We'll hurt you if we need to," said Lackwood, interrupting.

"Duck!" said Endrit.

She had no time to duck. Over her head, Rhea felt the brush of something pass. It was Suki, still unconscious. Endrit had thrown her like a sandbag onto the spear shafts. Suki's deadweight took the soldiers by surprise and pushed their spear tips down to the stone floor. Rhea was trained all her life for these moments, even for the possibility of treason.

But it never looked like this in her imagining, never so clumsy and closeted. She was shoved aside before she could react to Suki's landing. Endrit dashed past the lowered spears before the soldiers could pull them out from under Suki and smashed his fist directly at Lackwood's face. His nose made a sound like an acorn under a boot. He fell.

Rhea regained her composure when she saw Joram let his spear fall and drew a knife from his belt. He lunged at her. Rhea grabbed the hand holding the blade before it could stab her stomach.

The two wrestled for control of the hand. Rhea shouted, "Get Suki!"

Joram began to bend her arm backward, but Marta had taught them both: Determine the battlefield, determine the victory. It meant the one who controlled the terms of the fight would likely win it.

The hardened dragoon would happily play a simple brutish game of arm wrestle with the winner stabbing the other in the chest. Rhea was too smart for that.

She put a knee in the man's groin. The man groaned. Rhea twisted and kicked the side of the guard's knee. It bent under him. She let go of the knife-wielding hand in the moment her opponent lost balance and used both hands to grab the guard's head. She smashed it into the stone wall like a coconut. The guard dropped the knife as he collapsed to the ground. When she looked up, Endrit had lifted Suki and pulled the wooden door open.

"Come on. Come on."

Rhea stepped over the fallen guards. Outside, signal fires burned bright, in high alert. Otherwise the night was starless and black. Had clouds rolled in so quickly since she had been on the balcony, admiring the moon?

"They'll be after us soon," said Endrit as they ran down the ramp toward the courtyard.

"You didn't kill yours?" said Rhea.

"Why in the world would I kill him?" The way he said it seemed to accuse Rhea of murder. *How am I supposed to guess at all these lunatic situations? What is appropriate and what is murder?*

"I don't know," she said, sounding like a child, even to herself. "Why in the world did you throw Suki at them before I said the word?"

Endrit didn't respond. There was no response. Her plan had worked. Rhea ran alongside him. Somehow she was even more irritated by his nonresponse.

Is he dismissing me entirely? Of course not. It was a stupid question.

Still.

She wondered if Joram would survive having his skull smashed into the stone. If not, she wondered what Lackwood would do without his decades-old partner. She told herself this was the price of treason. She tried to remember them both as sneering ogres. Then she wondered if Endrit had seen how hard she had hit Joram.

Rhea knew she was doing it. She watched herself as if through a glass. Watched as she twisted herself into contortions—wanting his approval, pestering him for it, all the while fearing she didn't deserve it and lashing at him when he didn't realize the impossibly heavy portent that each of his silences carried.

And worse, the Rhea who watched herself and knew all this made constant alternate appraisals—disgusted with her own need and at the same time desperate for the need to be met.

She should have acted differently in the hallway.

When they crossed the courtyard and entered the torch-lit half-moon around the gate to the inner city, they heard a shouted voice from a guard tower above them. "There! At the beggar's ramp!"

They were spotted.

Rhea looked over her shoulder. The door to petitioner's arch had been thrown open. Joram still lay on the ground, bleeding from his skull. Lackwood leaned on the doorframe, holding his bloody nose and pointing at them. Two more soldiers had arrived. They raced down the ramp toward Rhea and Endrit.

Endrit kicked at the door. It didn't budge.

Rhea ran around him before he kicked again.

"I got it. I got it."

She lifted the latch and opened the gate inward.

"It's a pull," she said.

¤ ¤ ¤

They stumbled into the inner-city maze, where nobles built their banks and ateliers cheek to jowl—jostling one another for real estate, pushing into the narrow streets. The inner city was abuzz with private parties from the Revels, spilled out drunkenly into the cobblestone streets. The blast must have been nothing but a loud festival noise to them.

Nearer to the castle, the merchants had heard the alarm calls. They had run out with their apprentices, boarding up their storefronts in case of riot. The soldiers chased Rhea and Endrit through the crowds. Rhea followed Endrit, who knew nearly every inch of the inner city. He took sharp turns off hidden corners.

He and Marta had a small street-level apartment, even though they were below the *homo nobilis*. Her father had given it to them so that they could come to the castle every day without the hours of waiting at the outer walls, where customs officers inspected every cart and person before allowing entrance.

Endrit had grown up in those streets, delivering parcels to the homes of the nobles, and later, playing kick-n-stick with the noble children. The soldiers kept up for only a little while, pushing people out of the way. But Endrit knew the little ways, and soon they were clear.

They had wended through two mercantile districts, around the *mercato centrale*, down to the lowest corner of the inner city.

The streets were empty and dark in the shadows of the

giant outer wall. Rhea knew this was a shifty neighborhood, because the buildings didn't have stone crests over the doors, indicating the lower houses of the Meridan banner men. Not even the crests a merchant family could purchase, marked with three coins on their left hemisphere, where swords, sigils, or scrolls usually went.

These buildings were for other uses.

Gamblers halls, courtesan guilds, even syrup dens for the opium eaters—but all of the highest order. Any tavern in Walltown had gamblers, but inside the walls, in the inner city, the *homo nobilis* expected a carpeted affair, among fellow high rollers, attended by well-dressed croupiers. The men and women of the guild were companions as well as lovers. Some had even ensorcelled a noble into marriage and jumped "from the bed to the banquet."

Does Endrit know any of those women? Rhea had only ever seen them on the arms of horse-nobles—knights who saved a duke in battle and won a title.

They were always beautiful, brazenly so, and smiled as if they knew exactly what the world wanted. Rhea sensed them speaking a thousand secret languages—the sway and turn of their hips, the looks and flutters of the eyelashes, the subtle touches, the sordid laughs—each as foreign and mysterious to Rhea as ancient Tasanese.

Have they tested their skills on Endrit? Is he friends with the sellswords who guard the doors of the gambers halls—or worse, the leachers of the opium dens? Is he so low?

Rhea looked up at the shuttered windows with candle

lights of every color shining behind them and wondered about the people inside.

Endrit stopped in front of a nondescript door in the back of an alley. "Here we are," he said.

Rhea had never been to Endrit's home before. It was only one story, with old reed thatching. Rhea's chamber was easily thrice the size of the entire building.

Endrit knocked three times, paused, and then twice more.

"I thought Marta liked to garden," said Rhea. There was no spot of ground in front of the apartment. It butted up to the gutter.

"She does," said Endrit.

Does Father know that? Surely he would have given them a cottage with some acreage in the back?

The door of the apartment opened without a noise. Marta was dressed in full armor.

Had she returned so quickly from the ball?

She took Suki from Endrit. "Come in. Come in."

Rhea ducked into the low doorway. Marta closed it quickly behind her. "Where are the others?" said Marta. *Does she mean Cadis and Iren?*

"Couldn't find them," said Endrit.

"Are they together at least?" She lay Suki down on a cot as she spoke.

Endrit shrugged. "I don't know."

"They'll find each other," said Marta. She examined Suki's bandages as efficiently as a battlefield magister. She lifted Suki's eyelids, then looked at the inside of her bottom lip.

Rhea noticed a purple streak spread across Suki's gums.

Marta touched it. She extended her hand behind her, at Endrit. Endrit reached into his pocket and handed her a small leather pouch.

"What is that?" said Rhea.

"Paste of the poppy," said Marta. She stuck a finger in the pouch and spread a bit more inside Suki's lip. "It will help her sleep."

Endrit must have applied it when he bandaged her, thought Rhea. Before she could ask, Marta stood up. She placed the pouch back into Endrit's hand with a nod. He had done well. Endrit seemed to stand a little straighter as he gave his report. "Insurgents are fighting up the main corridors to the king's chamber. The king's guard have sealed the exits to the castle."

"The dragoons?" said Marta.

Endrit nodded.

"Did you engage?" said Marta, alarm in her voice.

"Yes."

Marta clicked her teeth. Endrit spoke over it. "They attacked us. And no one died."

Rhea didn't offer a rebuttal.

"Did they follow?"

"Yes, but we lost them."

"Did they know you?"

"Yes."

"It was Joram and Lackwood," said Rhea.

Marta clicked her teeth again and paced. The apartment

was a small flat made up almost entirely of two cots, with a bureau beside each, a weapons rack big enough to outfit a full garrison, an alcove with a chamber pot, another across the way with shelves for pickles, cheeses, and bread. On Marta's bureau sat a row of books—military histories. On Endrit's was a mess of animal figurines and what must have been a dozen tokens of favor—a silken scarf, a sachet full of lavender, even a few letters sealed with the rouge from a kiss. They were scattered among the toys of his childhood as if all part of a boyish game.

Is this really Endrit's home? Suki had bigger stables for Helio.

It took Marta no more than three paces to resolve her plan. She marched to the door and pulled the iron pin on two of the three hinges. Rhea had no idea why.

As she did so, Marta said, "We don't have time. Endrit, get Suki. Rhea, push my bureau aside."

Rhea didn't understand, but she knew better than to question Marta. She walked to Marta's bureau and examined the side. It moved easily—Rhea assumed because it was nearly empty and was made of cheap wood. After removing the hinges, Marta strode over to the weapons rack and grabbed a black bag.

Endrit lifted Suki again and joined Rhea. The bureau was pushed all the way to the side, revealing only a smooth stucco wall.

Is there some sort of secret trapdoor? If so, how did they hide the seam so well?

Endrit bumped Rhea's shoulder so she'd look at him. He pointed up. Rhea looked. Above the bureau was a patch of reed thatching lashed together into a small square.

"No one ever looks up," said Endrit, grinning.

Marta had returned to the front door and begun pouring iron caltrops, sharp enough to pierce horse hooves, across the doorway. Rhea thought for a moment, *Won't the door sweep the caltrops aside?*

"Go to the safe house," said Marta.

"Wait. You're staying?" said Rhea.

"I have to find Cadis and Iren. I'll meet you at dawn either way."

Endrit opened the drawers of the bureau into stair steps and nudged her. Rhea complied out of a lifelong habit of obeying Marta's orders. She stepped onto the bureau, onto the books, and pushed at the patch in the roof. It lifted easily. Rhea slid it sideways, to rest on the roof, then hoisted herself out again, into the dark night.

The air was cold on her bare skin. The run through the city had made her sweat, and the dress was not made to be warm. Rhea braced her feet on two wooden beams and turned to pull Suki up. While she struggled to lift Suki out, Rhea saw Marta down in the apartment. She held Endrit's face in her palms and kissed his forehead. Rhea could tell she was saying something to him. He nodded, with a look of seriousness in his eyes that Rhea had never seen.

A heavy gauntlet banged on the front door and rattled its lone hinge.

Marta pushed Endrit toward the bureau and whirled around.

"Go," she said. "Do as I said."

Endrit bounded up the bureau and out onto the roof. He whispered, "Shhh," to Rhea. They could hear the soldiers, just over the side of the low thatched roof.

Another banging knock.

"Let us in, by order of the king."

Marta pushed the bureau back in its place and shut the drawers. She looked up at Rhea and Endrit one last time, then ran to the door. Endrit slid the patch over the roof, but Rhea held his hand. They let a sliver remain open to see through.

Marta moved across the room like a stalking cat and waited by the door for the third set of knocks.

The door rattled.

"Open or we break the door," said the officer.

On the last knock, Marta went to work. She leaned over the razor-sharp caltrops and silently pulled out the door latch and the last hinge.

The door now stood completely untethered to the frame. If the soldier knocked again, it would simply topple inward. Marta squared herself in front of the door, took a step back, and lunged forward. Her push-kick had all the form she had always taught them. *Chamber the knee. Push with the hip. Explode out.*

Her boot smashed into the door. The door smashed into the soldier's chin and went down with him.

Rhea heard a clamor of guards, shouting, charging over the fallen door.

Marta unsheathed two short swords and stepped back into the room. She clanged them against each other and shouted, "Hiya, hiya!" as if to rile them further.

Rhea realized it was to keep their attention while she stepped gingerly backward, over the caltrops. The first two guards crippled themselves on the spikes the moment they jumped into the room.

They fell to the ground, howling.

"Come on," said Endrit.

He put his hand on Rhea's shoulder.

Doesn't he want to see what happens?

It occurred to Rhea that more than anyone, Endrit would not.

The rest of the soldiers stepped into the room carefully. Marta took the opening while one soldier had her eyes down. She lunged forward and stabbed a short sword into the soldier's throat. A difficult target, hard to skewer with a wriggling opponent. Marta's hand was steady. She buried it to the hilt, then bounced back. The soldier went down gurgling.

More guards rushed into the room.

Had they sent so many for Rhea alone? Were they Findish sympathizers? Were they part of some coup planned by a lesser house of Meridan? All or none could be true.

They spread into a half circle around Marta.

"Get out!" she screamed.

Endrit pulled Rhea's shoulder. "She's talking to us," he said.

Rhea couldn't. She reached up and pulled a pin from her hair. She could help. Endrit grabbed her hand. "Don't," he said.

Marta clapped her swords together again. The soldiers flinched. "Get out now!"

They must have thought she was speaking to them.

A guard stepped forward and swung a mace. Marta blocked it high, exposing the unprotected area of the man's underarm. Marta thrust her other sword through his armpit, into his heart. He was dead before he lay down.

Rhea watched in horror and bedazzlement. She was beautiful. For the first time, Rhea saw her lifelong teacher as the woman she was decades ago, worthy of battle hymns and titles and a statue hewn into the rock face of the guardian hills.

She was in a category of legend compared to her attackers. But they were too many. Rhea wanted to wrench her arm away from Endrit and launch a dozen knives at the cowards slowly penning Marta in.

She hated them. And she hated the unfairness of a world that let someone like Marta fall to a bunch of traitor mercenaries. And she hated that it had taken her all this time to realize that what she needed from Marta—what she should have gone to her every day in training and asked for—was how to be brave when all she felt was paralyzing fear.

Marta felled another.

They closed in.

She turned to check behind her.

A club hit her at the cheekbone.

It broke her jaw and sent a clatter of bloody teeth.

Marta fell.

Rhea would have screamed, if she had the air to fill it.

Endrit pushed the hatch closed.

Rhea backed away and folded her arms around herself.

The night breeze was icy on her bare skin.

Endrit squatted down in front of her. When she turned away, he followed until she was forced to look at him. His eyes were the only things in the city blacker than black. He whispered, "We have our orders."

How can he go on?

Her vision started to blur and shake, and still he looked her in the eye—no jest or rakish grin, no playacting—he really was as strong as Marta had taught them to be. Rhea got up and followed him as they tiptoed in the darkness, from the back of the thatched roof to a jutting walkway built along the roofs of the alley, until they reached the massive face of the outer wall. It rose three hundred feet upward and was thick enough for two horse-drawn carriages to race along the top.

Endrit squatted down at the edge of the last building, which nearly butted up against the wall. There was just enough space between the two for Endrit to squeeze himself down to the ground. He left Suki on the edge of the roof. Rhea first lowered her down, then grabbed the ledge and dropped down herself.

She didn't need much explanation. Endrit had already opened a hidden porthole into the side of the wall. *A smuggler's gate?* Even knowing of such a thing without reporting it to the court of the king was punishable by shackling.

Rhea looked into the secret passage leading out of the proper city. She had never been to Walltown without an escort of king's guard and a retinue of attendants to speak with peddlers if she wished to perform charity by purchasing withered fruit or some crude pendant for Anant.

It occurred to Rhea that most of those attendants, her maids, her horsemen, were probably dead. Perhaps even Iren and Cadis, or Hiram and her father. She was now an orphan.

If not an orphan, then an exile.

After that night the kingdoms of Pelgard would descend once again into war. Whether they were alive or dead, the charge of the Protectorate was over.

"Time to go, Princess," said Endrit, nudging her forward. She would have to go first, so Endrit could walk backward, dragging Suki behind them by her underarms. Rhea gathered herself, then ducked into the secret door.

"Don't call me that," she said.

She was no longer a princess.

"What should I call you, then? Rhea?" he said, struggling to pull Suki, as he kept his head down in the low tunnel.

Rhea peered into the darkness as she said, "Queen. You should call me Queen. I'm likely all that Meridan has now."

A leaden silence.

Then she heard a sputter and a guffaw.

"Pfffft!" said Endrit. "Yeah, I'm not going to do that. Don't be so dramatic, Princess."

CHAPTER TEN

Cadis

"What do you think Rhea is doing right now?" said Cadis. She had been trying to win a smile from Iren for the past few hours to no avail. They rode on stolen horses from the unattended stables of a tavern in Walltown. Iren seemed to know of it already, as part of her escape plans.

"I'd say singing a chorus of 'Yes, Daddy, it was Cadis all along,' or if Declan's dead, weeping seductively in the shirtless arms of Endrit."

Nothing but a shrug from Iren. She was as dutiful and intractable as a millstone. *A little one*, thought Cadis, smiling to herself.

"Declan's not dead," said Iren. "But you're probably right about Endrit's shirts. They never seem to stay on, do they?"

Finally. A sign of life.

The horses needed a rest after their long sprint out of the stables to the outskirts of town and finally on to an obscure caravan route that made an arcing path toward Findain. They let the horses plod, but Iren wouldn't allow them to stop. Under different circumstances, it would have been an ideal country stroll. The birds had been uncaged recently from their winter nests and sang ballads to one another. The road wended through the hillocks of the midlands between Meridan and Findain—tree-covered hills, mild enough to farm, if the sanctions allowed.

Copses of trees dotted the hillside and a series of rivers streaked it.

It was midmorning. The sun shone and gave Cadis renewed hope that they would reach Findain—she would see Jesper and her cousin Denarius again—and the horrors of the previous night would recede, like a treacherous coastline from memory, as they sailed onward. If only they managed the long journey without getting captured.

"Do you think Don Sprolio has patrols in the area?" asked Cadis.

"No," said Iren.

"How do you know?" said Cadis. "A couple enterprising scouts could be over that hill, waiting to ambush."

"Sprolio brought his sons to the Revels," said Iren.

Cadis had been avoiding mention of the Revels.

"Were they handsome?" said Cadis.

"Not with soiled breeches and cut throats, no."

Cadis sighed. Iren had rebuffed every attempt at idle distraction, as if she had been constantly revisiting the events of the night—examining them like a dead bird—to expose the intricacy of their inner workings.

Cadis was no more interested in the Sprolio boys than Iren was. But she knew the value of a little chatter to pass the time, to examine shared experiences. "Fine," said Cadis, "be sour. I'll sing to myself."

"Don't sing."

"It's an expression. I wasn't actually going to sing."

Iren took a flitting glance over her shoulder as they crested a hill. "We're being followed," she said.

Cadis immediately hunched down in her seat. She acted as if she were pulling a stone from her boot as she looked behind them, but they were on the downward slope of the hill. Cadis waited and was rewarded some minutes later, when a lone figure rode into view. She was too far away for Cadis to learn much.

"Stop looking," said Iren.

"How do you know she's following us?"

"When we stopped at the last creek, she stopped so she wouldn't pass us."

"I knew it was suspicious that you wanted to pause for a drink."

"The horses were thirsty as well."

"Yeah, but that's not the Iren I'm beginning to know," said Cadis, hoping she'd take the barb in jest.

"I was also resting for you."

Cadis acted shocked by the insult but smiled through it. Iren betrayed the slightest smirk. "You don't need to worry about me, sweet sister," said Cadis.

"You took such a beating," said Iren. "I thought you could use some time."

Cadis gasped. "Are you referring to the black eye?"

"And split lip."

"And split lip that I got before besting you completely?"

"A technical victory."

Iren knew Cadis prized panache and style as much as technical victories. "All right, then," said Cadis, enjoying a bit of conversation for the first time that morning. "If that's how you want it."

Under her breath, Iren said, "Ready your bow."

Cadis did so by bending forward to pet her horse on the neck. She reached back and pulled her bow from her pack and placed it on her lap.

"And what about the ball?"

"Did you do something interesting at the ball?" said Iren. She goaded her horse into a quick trot.

Cadis followed. Iren continued. "You must have said some very clever things to keep the attention of all those boys."

"Do you have sociability lessons for me?" said Cadis.

"Not really," said Iren. "Maybe daub some powder on those bruises."

"Thank you, Governess."

"And the dress—"

"You said you liked my dress!"

"I lied," said Iren.

"I think you're lying now," said Cadis. "Don't be mean to my dress."

"I thought I saw one of the courtesans from Endrit's alley wearing one half as tight . . . and twice as long."

"Ha!" said Cadis. "Maybe she had less to be proud of. Besides, you wore that weird two-piece thing."

Iren shrugged.

"And I saved your life," said Cadis.

"Then we're even, since I spared yours in the melee."

"What? You did not let me win. Say you didn't let me win."

They pressed the horses until they passed a dense grouping of myrtles. Iren turned abruptly behind the trees and stopped. She jumped off her horse and ran up to a tree trunk. Cadis followed, pulling an arrow from her quiver as she hid.

They watched and waited as the figure of the lone rider grew closer and closer. She hadn't seen them stop.

Cadis whispered, even though she didn't yet need to whisper. "Do you think Hiram sent her?"

Iren nodded.

"Do you think he's conspiring with the old houses?"

"What?" said Iren, turning to look at Cadis.

"Who else would have the money to outfit a group and make them look like Findish rebels?"

"Why would they?"

"I don't know—to kill Declan. Hiram's from an old

house, and he's obsessed with the idea of Kendrick's heir."

"No, he's not."

"I'm surprised you didn't know that," said Cadis. She knew if she insulted Iren's intelligence, she would get her to talk.

The rider had sped up, perhaps feeling uncomfortable for having lost them for so long.

"They could all be in on it. Once they've assassinated Declan, they could put a puppet on the throne as the rightful heir and start a war with Findain at the same time."

Iren scoffed at the idea. "You're writing bad theater."

"How would you know?" said Cadis.

Iren could never suffer faulty logic. "The rider is a dragoon."

Before Cadis could ask, Iren said, "I know because she rides heavy in the saddle. She's used to cavalry armor. And she's terrible at this kind of pursuit. Hiram's spies aren't idiots and would never follow so close."

The rider was within arrow shot. She slowed and fumbled with something in her lap.

"So Declan sent her?"

Iren nodded. Cadis wasn't as naive as they all believed her to be. But she refused to blame Declan for every hangnail in their lives. Maybe Iren had been listening too much to Suki. "You think he'd try to kill us—?"

Before Cadis could answer, Iren cut her off and rose from her crouch.

"—the bird," said Iren. "Take the bird."

Cadis looked up just as the rider let fly a pigeon. It flapped up and up in their direction. Cadis took a knee and nocked her arrow. The bird scooped over the copse of trees and banked into a tight circle. The angle was terrible.

Iren was already up. She sprinted out of their hiding place, at the rider, who made a yelp of surprise. She kicked her horse and yanked the bridle to turn it around.

"Take the shot!" shouted Iren over her shoulder.

Cadis cursed and released the bowstring. The arrow flew. The pigeon shrieked as the arrow nicked its feather, but continued on.

Iren bore down on the rider. The horse began a gallop. Iren flung a knife hidden inside her sleeve. It planted into the woman's back.

The rider fell.

The horse galloped away.

The arrow landed twenty yards away.

The pigeon disappeared into the horizon. Cadis ran over to the body, which Iren had already begun looting.

"I missed," said Cadis, when she arrived.

"You didn't miss once yesterday," said Iren. Matter-of-fact.

"Well, I missed. I don't usually aim at birds or a woman's back."

"They're big targets," said Iren—her mouth tight at the corners.

Iren pocketed a coin purse and a ring bearing the dragoon coat of arms. "We have to change course," said Iren. "They'll have our location in a few hours."

Cadis wanted to ask how Iren had been so quick to identify the carrier pigeon, how she knew the spy would report her intel at that particular juncture, or if that had been a coincidence.

After seeing the rucksacks hidden in the kitchens, Cadis had begun to suspect that very little was coincidence where Iren was concerned.

Cadis watched as her sister rummaged through the clothes of the dead woman, checking the lining of her vest and the heel of her boots with the practiced efficiency of an undertaker.

Who is she? thought Cadis.

Little Iren who liked to embroider.

Quiet Iren who never fussed.

Cadis thought of a faraway evening, so many years ago, when they had just arrived in Meridan. Cadis lay in her chamber bed, ten times the size of her bed back at home, in a dark stone room, staring at the flickering light beneath her door and wondering if strange guards would steal inside to throttle her.

When the door finally opened, she clenched tight the dagger under her blanket. But no looming shadow filled the doorframe. Nothing did. It was as if the door had opened and closed. A mouse had stolen into her room. Cadis noticed only when her blanket rustled and Iren climbed in next to her.

For a long time, they lay without speaking, almost nose to nose. Cadis didn't know what to do with the knife. Or what to say. It had all been so new. They were strangers yet. Iren had been scolded already for acting sullen. Cadis was already the one Rhea hated most.

Iren stared at her for what seemed like half the night. When she spoke, Cadis almost mistook it for a sigh.

"Are you scared?" she said.

Cousin Denarius had not raised a dormouse.

"No," said Cadis. Her voice was loud. Anything above a whisper was like a scream. But Iren didn't wince. She didn't seem herself scared. She simply took the information in and considered it, like a thresher parsing through chaff.

After another interminable silence, she said, "Are you interested in being friends?"

Cadis had never met someone as peculiar as Iren. Back home, Jesper had become her friend after he flicked her ear really hard and she hit him in the face with a rotten peach.

"Okay," said Cadis.

Iren nodded, but didn't seem happier to know it.

"Have you had a friend before?" she asked.

Cadis nodded. "Yes."

"Good," said Iren. "Then you'll know what to do."

That seemed to conclude the subject as Iren settled herself into Cadis's pillow and closed her eyes.

Cadis stared at the peculiar girl from Corent. She seemed like an entirely different creature. After a while Iren broke the silence, when she whispered, "You can put that knife away. We're friends."

Cadis didn't know how she had known, but she tucked

the knife back under her mattress. For a long time she couldn't sleep with a stranger in her bed.

Eventually, she woke up with her friend curled up next to her.

And ever since, Cadis had been steering their relationship—reminding Iren when it might be appropriate to apologize, or seeking out her company when she buried herself too long in the archives.

She hadn't known quite the magnitude of the task she had accepted all those nights ago—to be friends with Iren.

As Cadis watched Iren outwit the king's spy, run her down, kill her, and immediately loot the body, she considered—for the first time since that night so long ago—that it had all been a calculated shadow play. That she had been used in the way that a puppeteer uses. Perhaps she had done it to avoid suspicion. That all those years of friendship were no different than a terra-cotta mask, a costume Iren could put on to seem the happy child, the docile princess, the queen with kitten teeth.

Maybe Cadis was as naive as they believed.

They rode in silence after that. Iren seemed as content as an engorged mantis, while Cadis wondered if Iren even noticed that Cadis was no longer putting forth the effort to speak with her.

With every mile, at every stop to rest, Cadis felt a mounting agitation that perhaps that night Iren would steal upon her in the darkness and kill her in her sleep.

¤ ¤ ¤

A full half day later Iren slowed her horse to come alongside Cadis and said, "I can tell you're mad at me, because you've spoken very little, and haven't sung anything either."

"I'm not mad," said Cadis. She refused to be read like a broadside.

"I can also tell you're mad because your tone is . . . curt. You're not usually curt."

"I'm not curt," said Cadis.

"You're also being contrary."

"How *else* would I disagree with you?"

"You usually avoid confrontation. You charm the situation. You're not charming, so you must be mad."

"You want me to charm you?"

Iren paused. She looked at the passing countryside. "Yes," she said finally.

"Ha! I'd have an easier go of it with a rootsnake."

Cadis laughed to herself, but it was the sort of laugh that betrayed—even more—that she was uncomfortable.

When Cadis looked at Iren a few moments later, she perceived in her silence, in the slight bend of her shoulders, in the way she squinted straight ahead at her horse's mane, that she was nearly ready to burst into tears.

Cadis sighed. "Oh, come on. I didn't mean that *you're* a rootsnake."

It had the opposite effect. Iren's eye glimmered. She would hold them back, but barely.

The road to Findain was beautiful this time of year.

The birds had no sense of wars or betrayal.

Iren tightened her composure once again and said, "Do you think I would harm my friend?"

"I spoke out of anger. You were right. I was angry. I don't think you're a rootsnake."

"I don't mind that you called me a rootsnake," said Iren. She spurred her horse back into a canter. "I mind that your dagger's unclasped."

The Findish playwright Jesiré Jesperdotter—for whom Jesper had been named—would have described the journey thus:

> They rode and rode and rode and rode
> Across the dale and under hill
> The wheel of days and nights unslowed
> Through keep and cloister, farm and mill
> From Meridan to Findain's shore
> A queen returned as ne'er before
> Riding at her heels a store
> Of rumors, rebels, raids, and war.

And so they arrived at the land gate of Findain's capital city, squeezed between the peddlers and returning caravans at noon hour of a sweltering early summer.

"They're certainly . . . boisterous," said Iren, as a swarm of children surrounded their horses to beg and hawk and busk and cajole.

Cadis found she had forgotten such details as the smell

of ripe fruit mixed with sweaty mules. The way in which old women winked to one another and the solicitous nod of the old men, a sort of rocking back and forth—as if the chin was a boat on the water—were distant memories to her. She had forgotten the murmur of the sea.

As they rode into the harbor and watched the fleets of merchant ships compete with the facing city for an audience, Cadis felt as much an outsider as Iren.

Jesper had tried to keep her informed of the constant ebb and flow of businesses that swept entire districts in and out of majority. He had mentioned the new amphitheater that towered above Cheapside, where the old fairgrounds used to be. And he had mentioned that the open-air market had been roofed, but he didn't mention the color—was it orange on purpose?

On the whole, he had done his best. Cousin Denarius had tried to keep her close by sending her transcripts of the broadside news reports—that told her all the latest market gossip and show times to theater she couldn't attend.

But neither could tell her the true happenings in the guildhalls for fear that Magister Hiram would steal the information. And none of it could have prepared her for the shock of returning.

"It's so small," she whispered to herself when they passed the rusted roof of the market. She had remembered it as a massive labyrinth to run through.

The streets were dirt in places.

No one made way for their horses.

The children didn't fear the guards, and the guards smiled at customers as they held the doors open to the shops.

Cadis imagined every sight from Iren's point of view and cringed a little. "Provincial" was the word that leaped to mind. "Provincial" and "frantic."

All around, the noise of commerce had a tense undertone that Cadis had never heard before. Hawkers seemed to press their wares with a desperate manner. Shopkeepers stuck to their negotiated sums, even past the usual friendly haggling.

"Is it really so bad?" said Cadis.

"What?" said Iren.

"The market. Commerce. It seems depressed. Jesper said the trade agreements with Meridan were crippling, but I didn't expect this."

"This?" said Iren. "You mean the bustling harbor full of goods?"

"No, but you don't understand. When I was a child, the traders were like dukes. You could find an elephant with diamond-studded ears if you wanted, fruits like you'd never seen, and some you did, but never so big or so sweet. I once saw a ship sail into the harbor with so much jade and silk and ambergris in its belly that it dredged the bottom."

"You remember with advantages," said Iren.

"What does that mean?"

"You were little."

"Just look—the stalls sell basic goods. There's no joy. People pay in copper."

Cadis sighed. The differences were enormous to her but likely indistinct to Iren, who had no use for the great theater of the marketplace. Iren saw only a great hubbub of people and animals, all shouting at once. To Cadis, the chorus was out of tune.

"Cadis? Oh, dear gods, Cadis! Is that you?"

They both turned toward the voice. Cadis nearly fell from her horse.

Iren said, "Whoa."

In the fourth cycle of *The Bones of Pelgard* symphony opera, the famed composer PilanPilan expresses the entrance of the legendary hero Khartik with an odd instrument. Not the lute, as he might have done if Khartik were a knavish flouncer on the stage. And not a dendo drum, as he would if Khartik were a gallant warrior. The genius PilanPilan signals the entrance of Khartik with a deep sultry tremor on the bass harp—a bawdy sound as the infamous rake enters the stage—and does as the liner notes specify in every performance of the symphony: he looks every woman in the audience in the eye with a hungry stare, as if she alone were his beloved Lia.

The casting for the part of Khartik was news for the broadsides. The role was more symbol than man—heat and youth and desire. Sex, even as it might live in the dreams of a virgin. A young man of endless appetite for Lia—lost Lia, whose witch mother hexed her into a lake flower and whose appearance magically shone onto the face of every woman

Khartik met. This was the role that drove the directors of Findish theater companies to drink.

When Cadis turned and saw Jesper Terzi in the market square, a bass harp seemed to play from somewhere deep inside her, and she thought the directors must have been throwing courtesans through his windows.

As he approached with a retinue Cadis had not yet even recognized, Iren leaned over and whispered, "Is he the one I met three years ago?"

"Mmm-hmm," said Cadis.

"What wonders grow on Findish soil," said Iren, quoting from PilanPilan's opera. Obviously, she saw the connection as well. He had the tawny hue of a sailor long at sea, taut as the rope, tall as the sail. He wore billowing white muslin trousers as thin as cheesecloth, with a matching half-open blouse. Both seemed to sway around him like sailcloth.

Cadis had no time to inspect him as he crossed the space between them and lifted her off her horse by the waist as if she weighed nothing.

"Let me look at you. What are you—?"

He cupped her face. Cadis had nothing—and a thousand things—to say.

To tell him of the attack.

To explain why she had snuck into her own city.

"You've changed," she spat out finally.

Jesper laughed—how very warm it was—and drew her in for a hug. Cadis felt a fortnight's worth of constant guarded travel, long nights keeping watch, and terse conversation release from her shoulders. Cadis closed her eyes for a brief moment. When she opened them, she saw the four others accompanying Jesper for the first time.

All four looked mildly familiar. All four stared at her over Jesper's shoulder. "Meridan Keep has been attacked," said Iren, not having bothered to dismount.

"By whom?" said a girl, roughly their age, from Jesper's group. Iren barely took notice of her. Cadis braced for the shock impact of Iren's reply—that the attacks were Findish rebels.

"We don't know," said Iren. "We killed three and twelve"— she nodded at Cadis for the twelve—"and escaped before battle's end."

She spoke in the clipped formal manner of a soldier reporting facts. After a pause, she added, "Your spies should have sent birds by now."

Cadis tried to catch Iren's gaze, to tell her to take it easy, but Iren's eyes flitted from one of Jesper's crew to another. Cadis realized she was studying their reactions to see who was surprised by the news and who already knew. *How does she know to do that?*

Once again Cadis wondered what inner workings of her sister had been kept hidden. Cadis turned and studied Jesper's face for clues. She quickly realized three things: She had spent her life under the optimistic delusion that people would simply speak their minds, she had developed no subtlety for reading thoughts, and by all the gods of theater and the spirits of the sails, he *was* Khartik incarnate.

Cadis had no category in her mind for him anymore—brotherly friend and playmate of all the years before the Protectorate and diligent messenger during. Now after, in her return to take up the mantle of the Archon Basileus—first among equals of the guildmasters—she had no idea what their relationship would be—though she had a budding notion for it.

It took a brief moment of introductions to remind Cadis of the identity of the others.

The imperious girl with short-cropped hair and well-used blade currently staring down Iren with open hatred was none other than Hypatia Terzi, Jesper's older cousin and daughter of Lieke Terzi, the master of the caravaneers' guild.

Cadis shook her hand, making sure to crush it equally. She knew the caravaneers were one of the three prime merchant guilds of Findain, beside the captains and the shipwrights.

But Lieke—and recently Hypatia—had spent the last ten years consolidating power almost equal to the other two combined.

Beside Hypatia slumped a whelpish hound of a boy—no more than fifteen, not yet lost of baby fat—who cast glances at Hypatia for approval of every breath. Timor Botros, son of Nicho, master of a lesser artisans' guild—textiles specifically. He actually waited for Hypatia to nod before shaking Cadis's hand.

Iren made an audible snort at the sight. Pentri Muto,

scion of the shipwrights' guild, stood farthest back and gave a slight bow as Jesper introduced him. He seemed wealthiest by clothing and demeanor, a short, thin, fashionable, uninterested young man who seemed like a male Iren to Cadis. Aloof but likely nowhere near as deadly.

Last, and standing farthest from Hypatia, was Arcadie Kallis, dressed in a sleeveless tunic to show off her captain's inking all along both arms. She had crossed the Pelgardian line, survived a shipwreck, and completed three cycles of the Grand Tour, by the look of the symbols on her brawny arms. She had a darker coloring than even Jesper, and her hair was a tinted mirror of Cadis's—black dreads with coral and shells woven throughout. She was the daughter of Genio Kallis, master of the captains' guild, rival to Lieke and the caravaneers. It seemed the daughters Hypatia and Arcadie continued the tradition.

Cadis nodded to Arcadie. Already, she liked her best.

These were the heirs of the first families of Findain. Cadis had vague memories of them all. Since birth, they were destined to sit at the table together. "And this is Iren," said Cadis, "of Corent."

She thought it would be a dramatic departure to offer no titles or histories. And she was right.

Iren gave a wry smile. The others offered a customary bow.

"Yes, of course," said Pentri from the back. "We gathered from the descriptions."

"Really?" said Iren, raising an eyebrow. "Have the

shipwrights of Findain written plays about us?"

"Why would shipwrights make plays? We build ships."

"Oh, who can tell what all these guilders do?" said Iren.

She was goading him, of course. And he seemed arrogant and brash enough to take the bait.

"We will excuse the mountain queen for not knowing the definition of the word 'shipwright.'"

Jesper looked at Cadis, half enjoying the volleys, half wondering if they should put an end to it. Cadis winked. She knew Iren was good in a fight of any sort.

"Thank you, sir, but I would no more assume that a shipwright makes ships than a boy named Pantry minds the kitchen."

Pentri's face turned the color of the flower in his collared jacket. "Pentri," he spat. "My name is Pentri."

"Beg your pardon," said Iren. "I meant a boy who minds the pig pens."

Arcadie Kallis laughed aloud, and the battle was won.

"I like her," she said, speaking to Cadis.

"You should see her cross-stitch," said Cadis.

They returned to the Odeon—seat of the guildmasters and the archonate castle—with rumors of the Archon Basileus spreading through the city, along with whispers of dead queens and a Meridan invasion.

Cadis found herself in the center of their party without meaning to, as if they too had been trained all their lives for their roles as guildmasters. They took archonate formation, Arcadie Kallis to her right—captain. Pentri

Muto riding before her—shipwright. Hypatia Terzi on her left—caravaneer.

Cadis noticed that Jesper had no position, and walked at her horse's flank along with Timor Botros of the textile guild. Iren brought up the rear, certainly by her own design.

By the time they reached the bridge to the island of the Odeon, it had been filled with Findish citizens. When they saw her, they shouted and began the chorus of "Rise Archana, Rise the Tide." Every man, woman, and child of Findain seemed to have the performer's gusto. Cadis turned in her saddle to smile at all of them. She wished she could embrace them. They all felt like family.

Jesper's voice was as deep as a jug's.

She could hear the smooth bass and turned to catch his eye. He bowed, and kept singing. Only Iren didn't know the words.

It was at that moment that Cadis felt—for the first time since she could remember—like she was home.

Then she saw the masters at the far end of the bridge, on the stairs of the Odeon, standing also in formation, faces as grim and rigid as the gargoyles. And she knew she was not entirely welcome. She wished to see with Iren's eyes—what insights she must have already gathered, what cynical appraisals had she made already of those they met?

After what they had been through, perhaps Iren's pessimism was not so useless as Cadis once believed. Or, better put, perhaps it was a good arrow to have in a quiver, for just the right moments.

They approached the steps of the Odeon castle, and the guildmasters sang their own chorus. Cadis bowed, waved to the people, and dismounted. An attendant reached for her saddle pack, but she thanked him and took it herself.

The people erupted.

It was a sign that the archana was of the people. Cadis blanched. For her, it was simply instinct. She did not think of herself as the great triumphant queen of a nation. All her life, she was the backwater gold noble for a bunch of oath-breakers. The story was a sad one. And Cadis was used to telling it. She was accustomed to admiration given begrudgingly, but never love, never willingly.

They were all a blur anyway.

She took the pack, waited for Iren, waved again, and walked through the giant doors with guildmasters and their scions in direct formation behind her.

Cadis leaned toward her friend, if only to touch someone, and whispered, "I think I preferred being the traitorous orphan."

Iren was helpful in her own way. "You're still an orphan," she said.

Cadis chuckled at the golem she had for a sister.

"You're right. Welcome to Findain."

"It's very quaint."

"We just walked over a bridge full of choral praise, to an island castle."

"Yes."

"Not fancy enough? Do they slaughter bulls in Corent?"

Iren proffered a nigh-imperceptible smile. "They slaughter only in Meridan," she said. "In Corent we'd just forgive everyone's library fines."

Cadis laughed. "A joke? You're becoming a regular jester."

"The archana returns. Excuse us for being giddy."

Cadis was genuinely touched by the effort.

Of course they both knew the Corentines did not go in for all that group singing. Nor for the mingling of class—though theirs was a system built on academy merits. And more than anything, they didn't encourage the folksy charm of a queen with a rucksack and a cadre of guildmasters daring to welcome her into her own house.

For the first time in a long while, Cadis knew what her sister was thinking.

She ushered Iren to the common room, as she remembered it from her childhood, and said, "That's just our way. It doesn't mean anything."

"If someone barred entry to the spire, no matter how gently, and waited for me to dismount before stepping aside, I would let my horse do the bowing and would ride over them like toadstools."

"Ha!" said Cadis. She had never heard language so florid come from Iren. Perhaps the sea air was making a poet of her. Cadis glanced to make sure no one had heard.

Iren was speaking of Lieke Terzi, of course. Hypatia's mother, master of the caravaneers, who had only begrudgingly stepped aside.

Perhaps Iren was right. But in the short exchange, Cadis

had already changed her mind about her sister's approach to such matters. She decided that perhaps she was better off without her sister's sharpened sense of others' weaknesses.

If she thought better of them—and let them know her high estimation—then Cadis believed sincerely that people would be elevated to higher purposes.

She knew exactly what Iren thought of her ideals. She had seen the eye rolls plenty enough in the past.

The common hall of the Odeon had little to do with its name, except for the general principle that both espoused—equity. In fact, it was a theater, perfectly round, and in the center was a perfectly round stage elevated only up to a man's knee. Every seat in the common hall was equal. Anyone who stood on the stage to address the assembly was equal, too, but afforded temporary advantage to honor the words and the attention given freely by the crowd.

So had the first Archon Basileus made it. Though he could have been king, he chose to be first among equals. And so had the guildmasters governed the country of Findain, with debate and political theater. This was the stage on which the Maid Marauder had been tried for her crimes—thrice. It was the stage Cadis had stood upon ten years ago with Cousin Denarius, to bid good-bye to the guilds before entering the Protectorate with an escort of armed Meridan guards.

She didn't know the guildmasters then—though Lieke Terzi and Genio Kallis had both been present. To the seven-year-old Cadis, they were just a bunch of adults who quarreled a lot, asked her too many questions, and voted on how she should be taught her sums.

Cadis always imagined that parents would have been fewer but no less troublesome. On the day of her departure, Cadis had cried for the first time in front of the guilds. She remembered it now as they filed into the aisles. She remembered Lieke Terzi clicking her tongue in disgust that Cadis couldn't finish the valediction without tears.

And she remembered Cousin Denarius putting his hand on her shoulder. When she looked up, the old man smiled wide and rattled his two false teeth—in out, in out, in out—with a clownish cross-eyed glee. Cadis giggled and sniffled and felt, somehow, that any horrible situation could be made absurd—and perhaps in most instances, should be. She had loved Cousin Denarius, who was as kind and doting and sloppy as a mountain dog. She'd eaten only with him, which meant she'd eaten only porridge with stewed apples, mashed corn, and oyster soup for his year with tooth rot.

Cadis had finished the speech and walked out with the Meridan guards. Before she stepped into the carriage, Denarius had squeezed her harder than she had ever felt and kissed her on the forehead.

"Be good, little bug," he had said. She had nodded. "And hearty, and joyous, and proud, and heroic, and magnanimous."

That got the smile he'd been wanting.

"Okay, okay," she'd said.

He'd hugged her again.

"You be heroic too," she said, with her cheek pressed against him.

When they'd finally parted, Cadis saw Denarius weeping for the first time in her life. Jesper chased their carriage all the way to the land gate and threw rocks at the Meridan soldiers. The soldiers, to their credit, let him have his ineffective rage. They were accustomed to the lamentations of orphaned children.

His curses on their heads were the last words she heard before the long, silent journey.

As Cadis entered the common hall, she did not anticipate such a flood of memory to wash over her—a cold and bracing reawakening of insecurities she had long outgrown. Immediately, she spotted the black fisherman's cap Cousin Denarius was so fond of wearing.

Cadis took off down the aisle to the front row.

"Cousin," she said, as she stepped into his view. "Cous—"

The wizened old man drooped in his seat as if the center mast had broken. His chin rested on his chest. He was fast asleep, or so she gathered by the spittle on his shirt. "Cousin Denarius, awake," said Cadis. "It's Caddy."

But even as she said it, she knew something crueler than years had assailed her cousin's body. The crook of the brow, the jagged lip, and limp cheek all spoke of the collapse. He was good only for feeding seagulls and filling theater seats now.

"Hmm," he said, tongue like a beached jellyfish.

"Cousin," said Cadis, kneeling before him. She hesitated to touch his arm—thin and brittle as it seemed.

The old man's eyes stayed closed. Perhaps the twitch of his mouth was a smile, but it could have been nothing.

"He's had the collapse," said Iren, when she reached the stage. Cadis's hand shook, hovering over Cousin Denarius's arm, still unable to touch.

The guildmasters filled the common hall, many taking their seats in the back to view the proceedings, while the larger guilds took rows in front. At the cardinal points of the stage sat the four equal—but perhaps a little more equal—parties: the archon, Terzi of the caravans, Kallis of the captains, Muto of the shipwrights—north, west, south, east.

It was time to begin.

In Findain they had no heraldic ceremony, no courtly oaths or magisterial show, nothing that lessened the dignity of any man or woman in favor of some continued notion of royalty.

Every man.

Every woman.

Made Findain together.

This was the reason that generations ago, the Emperor of Tasan had famously remarked, "A Fin at court has as much grace as a fish flopping on the deck of a boat." To that the Findish playwrights had replied:

> **A Fin can be as much a fish**
> **As any man or woman wish**
> **And flop upon a deck till dead**

Better that than be instead
The wooden boards nailed in the prow
A Dain would never deign to bow.

Though they had no courtly ritual, the Findish were never short of pageantry. To begin any session in the common hall, the Archon Basileus would stand upon the stage and recite a portion of *The Bones of Pelgard* and say at the end, "Findain together." The audience would reply with the same. And the floor opened to any who asked for it.

Cadis stood up and away from Cousin Denarius, expecting that he would rise and recite out of some miraculous duty to his position.

The old man hardly moved, even to breathe.

"You may begin," said Lieke Terzi, sitting in the front row.

Cadis was only half certain that the woman was speaking to her—and that only because she was staring directly at Cadis with the studious and dispassionate glare of a magister studying a frog's belly.

"Does the archon not speak?" asked Cadis.

"Not for two years hence," said Lieke.

Beside her sat Hypatia, her daughter and younger twin—annoyed already by the delay.

How could the office of the archon be empty for two years without me knowing it? Cadis wanted to ask, but noticed Iren standing erect before the masters of Findain and remembered a comment she had once made. "Never ask a question to which you don't know the answer."

Iren read constantly from the academy scrolls on elements of power. She believed it to be like a game of shatranj. Cadis rarely listened, believing in nobler truths—that she could win the respect of the masters if she proved herself wise and capable.

But there, standing before the common hall, she decided to heed Iren's advice. Cadis stepped onto the stage. She almost bowed, as she had done for ten years in the court of Meridan, but thanks be to Myrath, caught herself.

Her training—for stage and combat—took over. She whispered the words that calm and breathed the rhythm of a ship at sea, a metered verse, an even fight. In her chest was a full orchestra—tuned, tamped, ready.

"Masters," she said, "we've come bearing news of—"

She was interrupted by Hypatia. "Findain together."

"Ah, yes," said Cadis, cursing herself for falling into the double bind. Either she would have opened as the rightful Archon Basileus and disrespected Cousin Denarius, or this. She pushed forward, "Findain together," she replied.

Hypatia sat back in her seat, arms crossed, with a grin that pinched her face.

"Welcome home, Archana," said Arcadie Kallis, sitting in the front row, opposite of the Terzis. Cadis had to turn around to acknowledge it. Next to Arcadie was the stout Genio Kallis—famed captain with his famed black beard and markings on his arms, neck, and face that spoke of the many exploits that had enraptured the poets of Findain for so many years.

Arcadie sat shoulder to shoulder with her father as his second-in-command. Both nodded to Cadis.

"Tell us the news, sister, that we might fight with you," said Arcadie.

Cadis felt a rush of gratitude for the kindness even as she heard a click of the tongue coming from behind her, where the Terzis must have been sitting, disgusted.

"Meridan has been attacked," said Cadis. She made sure to turn as she spoke, to include all the masters.

"At the Revels, a ballista smashed through the wall of the ballroom."

A murmur from the crowd indicated the sheer improbability of such an attack.

"A boarding party entered through the breached wall and another flanking party through the east gate—"

"Would you like to sit?" said Hypatia Terzi, interrupting once again. She was speaking to Iren, who stood beside Cousin Denarius, at the foot of the stage.

But Iren seemed far less interested to win friends. "No," she said. "Let her speak."

Across the way, Pentri Muto leaned in to his aunt, Artesia of the shipwrights' guild, and whispered—no doubt a venomous recount of his and Iren's exchange in the marketplace.

Hypatia had no intention of letting Cadis speak, it seemed, and her mother had none to curb her daughter. "It's just that *we* are all equals here."

"Good for you," said Iren. "You don't have the floor."

"But by standing, you elevate yourself."

"I don't elevate myself above you," said Iren.

"*Above* me? Even seated I'm taller than you."

Cadis whirled around to take on Hypatia. She was standing in the crossfire and refused to let Iren fight alone. But Iren needed no help. "You misunderstand," said Iren. "I don't elevate myself, because every aspect of our existences does so for me. I'm the queen-apparent of Corent, first vice magister of the academy, and three of *you* would still fall to *me* in combat. So I will stand where I please, above you all, who may equally look up the mountain that elevates me."

Every mouth in the theater hung loose. Then Iren continued, this time sweetly. "But we are in the common hall of the great nation of Findain, and customs are courtesies. So you need not bow to me today, Hypatia Terzi, but you do need to quiet yourself so we can get something done."

Behind the scorching hate of Hypatia Terzi, Cadis spied Jesper, sitting as if on a hill of anticores.

Cadis waited a moment to relish, and another because the first felt nicer than she'd expected. If she was honest, she was also fearful of the next part. "The attack was assassination. The court of Meridan is dead, also the Findish envoy and the dons of Houses Sprolio and Sesquitaine. We don't know the fate of Declan, Rhea, or Suki of Tasan, but they were surely targeted."

Here came the crescendo.

"The assassins were Findish rebels," she said, as steady

as she could make it. An uproar from the back rows and throughout the hall.

Everyone spoke at once, interrogating their future arch-ana.

"How do you know?" demanded Hypatia, standing.

"I know."

"It could be anyone presenting our colors," said Pentri.

"They didn't wear our colors."

"Then you don't know," said Hypatia.

"Three of them were marked with the Munnur Myrath."

Another outcry.

To many, the Munnur Myrath was just a spook story of a secret society of revolutionaries fighting to dissolve the Treaty of Sister Queens and win independence for Findain. They took their name from the last work of PilanPilan—a minor tragedy. "The Mouth of Myrath" was the prominent feature of the goddess of change. The goddess's mouth was often described as two goldfish hooked to either end of fishing wire. When they darted up and down, and past one another, the line of her mouth twisted from grimace to grin, a horrified circle, a queasy wriggle—shifting every second.

Sailors at sea knew well the winds of constant change. "One may ask the goddess when she is happy; she may answer when she's not." And mothers would often call naughty children "As fickle as the fish mouth." To the Munnur Myrath, change meant freedom from Meridan rule by way of bloody chaos.

Amid the hubbub, Arcadie stood and spoke. "If Meridan claims our part in this, we've got war."

"We have to get word to the outward caravans," said Timor from the back, where the textilers sat. "They must return."

"And the merchant ships," said Pentri.

"Close the land gate!" shouted several voices.

"It doesn't need to come to that," said Cadis, trying to speak over the other voices.

"There is no way you could have known they were Munnur Myrath," said Hypatia, gnawing on the subject like a dog with a bone.

"We can avoid war if we—"

Cadis was interrupted once again.

"How did you know?" said Hypatia.

"She gutted twelve of the cowards," said Iren, who had stepped onto the stage the moment the audience began to lose its calm.

"What should that tell you?" said Hypatia.

"Nothing beside that they were trained poorly," said Iren.

Cadis added, "Several had the fish mouth tattooed on their necks."

"That means you killed your countrymen," said Hypatia.

The guildmasters erupted into argument.

"The rebels are outlaws!" shouted some.

"They fight for us!" shouted others.

"They fight and endanger us, you mean."

"How can Findain stand together at such cross-purposes with itself?" shouted a councilwoman from the back.

Cadis lifted both hands into the air—a conciliatory

gesture. "Good people. Good people! Now is the time to steady sails."

Cadis spoke with the same forceful calm of a captain in a storm.

"Soon all of Pelgard will hear of the attack and all the banner houses of Meridan will call for retribution. We are that target, whether justly or no. The killers were either Findish rebels or a party who wishes us ill. It does not matter. We will bear the weight of the blame regardless."

Another clamor of opinions.

"But—hold a moment more, good people, a moment more—but we can steer away from the shoals of war, where nobler thoughts run shallow."

"How?" shouted several in the back.

Cadis gathered herself for the blow. She was not so naive as to think everyone would like her plan. "We must hope that Declan survived. His loss would unmoor all of Pelgard."

"Good!" shouted a master of the lenders' guild.

"Good riddance to bad kings," said another.

Cadis pressed on. "If he lives, we condemn the actions of the Munnur Myrath, swear fealty, and send aid to Meridan for the inevitable infighting that will claim Houses Sprolio and Sesquitaine as they revise their orders of ascension."

By this time, Cadis was shouting into a raging squall of voices.

"Piss on that!"

"Help them? Are we nothing but lick-boots?"

"Sprolio was a profiteer!"

"Seize his house and lands!"

They were at full mutiny, thought Cadis, though they would run all of Findain to the ground. Anyone could see that their pride was ruling their better judgment. Did her countrymen hate Meridan so much? Declan was prideful and unyielding, but he had not been cruel to Cadis. He had never harmed her. They must have realized that chaos in Meridan court would harm Findain more than the stability that Declan promised. Or perhaps it was not Declan's rule that they hated so much, but hers.

Cadis looked at the Terzis. If they agreed, then others, like the textilers, would fall in line.

"Surely you see the reason in this," she said. "The land routes would be cut to ribbons in a war."

Hypatia Terzi stood and turned around, speaking to all behind her and throughout the theater. "That is exactly why the Terzis understand the stakes, whereas our good archana, long in the lap of Meridan, can never know."

Cadis would have thrown her glove if she had one, to challenge Hypatia to duel.

"If the Munnur Myrath have struck at the heart of Meridan, then I say they've done us good service."

A disconcerting chorus of cheers.

"We should not abandon our fellows so easily," added Hypatia.

Cadis knew the jibe was meant for her. She'd had no choice but to enter the Protectorate, but here she stood, accused by her own as a deserter.

Over her shoulder, Cadis heard the voice of Iren. "Don't acknowledge her," said Iren. It took Cadis a half moment longer to remember the lesson from Magister Hiram. *A queen cannot be rivaled by any foe unless she first makes the mistake of acknowledging the possibility.*

It went against every instinct she had, which begged her to challenge Hypatia, to win their hearts by winning their respect. But it was sound wisdom, and so Cadis waited for Hypatia to sit.

"And what say you, Guildmaster?" she asked of Lieke Terzi. But the mother was no better. She said simply, "The caravaneers will fight for the people of Findain." Behind them both sat Jesper, with a look on his face like a weeks-dead trout.

Cadis cursed the opportunism of the caravaneers and turned instead to Genio Kallis and Arcadie—of the captains' guild. "And you, Captains?"

She made a special pleading to Arcadie, who seemed like a sister-in-arms. "You, Arcadie? Can we not agree, even with our enemies, that this will lead only to chaos and the ruin of both kingdoms?"

Cadis had always been the best orator, speaking with a sincere passion that moved even Hiram and Marta. The common hall of the Odeon waited for Arcadie Kallis to respond. The heir to the captains' guild, at least, seemed to be considering the substance of Cadis's plea, as opposed to playing some political game.

Genio Kallis remained silent, as he had famously done

when Meridan border patrols cut the ring finger from both his hands. Arcadie—whose eyes were nearly as black as Endrit's—stared ahead and said finally, "No."

"We cannot agree that the slaughter of innocents at a festival is wrong?" said Cadis.

"No," said Arcadie. "We cannot agree that they were innocents."

The meeting was over—effectively scuttled by the rarest of ordnances, the agreement of House Terzi with House Kallis. The common hall was empty, save for Iren, who sat beside Cousin Denarius, both silent as the dead; Cadis, who stood stupefied upon the stage; and Jesper, who remained in his seat, even as all the guildmasters filed out of the theater.

For Cadis it had been a disaster. Her return was about as welcome to her country as a ballista in a ballroom. When the last of the masters left, Cadis finally turned on her so-called friend.

"You can speak now, little pup."

Jesper diverted the blow. "It didn't have to go like this."

"You didn't help."

"How could I? You were lashing in all directions."

"They wanted war."

"You wanted them to bow."

"I'm the archana," said Cadis.

"Not to you," said Jesper. "They might have bowed to you. To him."

"He's won!" shouted Cadis, her voice booming across the amphidrome. "By all the gods, are all you people blind? He won ten years ago, and we bow, whether we like it or not. We all bow."

Jesper rose from his seat. "Cadis, you don't know—"

"I know plenty. I know all of Findain wants another sea of blood to bathe in, even though the blood will be their own. And I know you are a wet loaf of bread before your aunt and cousin."

Jesper's skin was too dark to blush red. The heel of his jaw ground like a millstone. She could see him struggling to control his anger and realized he had become adept at bearing unjust words. A life with Lieke and Hypatia must have annealed his temper like Tasanese steel.

"You don't know the troubles here. You don't know the heart of the people." His hands gripped the back of the seat before him. His voice was a shuttle moving steadily through a loom.

"The market is suffering. Go out and see for yourself. Go. Where are the builders? They have dissolved their guild for want of employ. The potters, the glassers, both gone. We cannot trade directly with Corent or Tasan. Meridan twists us for our last penny. The country chokes, but you ask the drowned to sing."

Cadis wished she could interrupt him. Halfway through she knew she had been wrong to enter with demands instead of questions. It was obvious that over the last ten years what she had gained in craft of combat and courage of command she had lost in the confidence of her people and the knowledge of her country.

She had a lot of ground to gain before the Odeon would truly hear her. And here she had attacked the one person who had stayed with her for all those years.

"Don't go," she said, but Jesper was already walking up the aisle.

Cadis couldn't understand why she had felt so betrayed by Jesper's silence when it made perfect sense in the moment. Perhaps she simply wanted her friend to back her position. Or, if she was willing to admit, perhaps she wanted even more than that from Jesper.

"Have you got a house or something?" said Iren as she wiped Cousin Denarius's chin with his own sleeve.

"We're in it," said Cadis. "The rest of the castle is the Archon Basilica."

"Isn't he still the archon?" said Iren. She used his sleeve to wave hello to Cadis with his limp hand. Cadis laughed at the image of the man as marionette and felt worse for laughing.

"Why didn't he tell me?" said Cadis.

"He's collapsed," said Iren. For her the diagnosis was enough.

"No, I mean Jesper. Why wouldn't he tell me?"

"What could he say? You couldn't come back. You would eat yourself alive out of a sense of duty to your people."

"You make it sound like a bad thing."

Iren didn't say anything. Of course she thought devotion

to a sense of duty was nonsense. Cadis knew that already. "What would you do," asked Cadis, "if you were me?"

Iren sat back and thought about the question as she removed a ring from Cousin Denarius's finger and looked at it in the light. "I'd declare your cousin dead of mind and push the masters to instate you as the rightful archana immediately."

"Why?"

"For them to bow in ceremony before the people."

"How would that help?"

"It would enrage the Terzis. They would seek to consolidate power, and so they would need to reach out to their closest allies. A few days of watching would tell you everyone who is in their pocket."

Spying again. It seemed Iren had learned as much from Hiram the spymaster as from Hiram the magister. "If I continue to make enemies of the Terzis, won't they continue to oppose everything?"

"Certainly," said Iren. She put Cousin Denarius's ring in her pocket and looked for another. "Hypatia will hate you forever. But Jesper, you could have him if you wanted."

"Really?"

Cadis knew she had jumped too quickly. Iren grinned. "He has already bedded Arcadie Kallis. That much is clear. If you turn his head, he might turn hers, and you would have both guilds in line."

Cadis's vision swirled with Iren's too-cynical love triangle of eros and intrigue. She couldn't tell how much was even true and how much was the fancy of a bookish plotter. Had she really seen some feelings in the eyes of Jesper, or did she move him like a pawn? Was it all so easy and heartless as that?

"You're wondering why you would seduce Jesper if he's placed so low in the caravaneers."

That was not what Cadis was thinking, but she nodded anyway.

"Because the last thing I would do," said Iren, palming the last ring from the old man's hand, "is kill Hypatia Terzi."

CHAPTER ELEVEN
Suki

Suki woke up cold and dry-mouthed, with a stiff ache in her shoulder and the image of a crosshatched roof above her. She had never been here before (wherever *here* was) never slept under a hay (reed?) roof (not even at her father's hunting lodge—which had been built out of carved bituin trees—when she was a toddler). She had no idea how long she had slept under the thatched roof (when it rained, did the water just drip through?).

Everything felt oddly distant (the roof, the pain, the taste of water ever having touched her mouth). She had been shifted out of time and space (and she knew the return would be sudden (she could feel it like a wave looming over her (it was panic (it would hit her soon (as soon as she blinked (it would smash into her (panic that she was too stiff to move (and afraid (and maybe she didn't even want to (because an entire room of soldiers (or Declan could be hovering an inch away from her cheek like a spider with his mandibles extending out to feed on the flesh of her face)))))))))).

Suki darted up and back until she hit a wall and set fresh fiery pain through her shoulder (and screamed (but no one responded (so she must have been alone))). She sat for a while, panting. She was in a hovel of some kind (the bed was a cot (as hard as limestone)) and the floor was packed dirt. Helio's stable was bigger than the entire room (which had only a ragged old chair (wicker!), a clay basin (which she wouldn't use even if she popped), and a chest of drawers (ugly)).

It was all so impoverished and ordinary-looking that it reminded Suki of their tour of Declan's dungeons (which was supposed to prove he was a good king), which reminded her of Tola (which made her feel cold (and alone))—and that was when she realized she was naked (or nearly naked (in just her smallclothes (and her shoulder bandage))), and whoever had brought her there had probably seen her birthmark (shaped like dog splatter (that's how her mother had once described it (when she didn't think Suki was listening (on her inner thigh)))).

She couldn't see her clothes anywhere.

She had been wearing a dress at the ball (that was her last memory (Rhea acting surprised (though she was probably happy to see it (the sword, sticking out of Suki's shoulder (and then nothing))))).

It must have been somewhere around here (inside the ratty chest?). Outside her window was a bunch of bland countryside. Suki jumped out of the bed (steady movements, steady pain) and flipped open the chest (no dress). No one had the right to touch her dress. It should have been there, cleaned and waiting for her (instead, a stack of farm clothes). Suki grabbed a brown shift and shoes (equally brown).

The rough-spun material was as prickly as a cat's tongue (which was a horrible surprise to Suki (as she had always assumed the servants' clothes were worse than her silks because of all the hideous brown colors (because color dyes were expensive) and not because of texture (which was like wearing a briar patch))).

It was a farmhouse with more rooms and an open hearth (she saw after she dressed and left the room). Inside another room was another chest with a satchel (inside that was the precious jewelry Rhea was always boasting about (so she must have been nearby (even though her bed hadn't been used (the bedding was still folded up next to the satchel in the chest)))).

Suki rushed out of the house as soon as she saw the third bedroom (another chest, unused (Endrit's clothes scattered all over the floor (one large bed, tousled (two indentations in the cheap wool sacking)))) and kicked all the tomatoes off a tomato plant in the front yard.

She could have vomited (but had nothing in her belly).

She heaved a little anyway (but had the feeling of watching herself heave (calmer on the inside than the out)) and wondered if anyone else could see her.

Marta would be furious about the tomato plants (not really) and she'd disown Suki (she knew that wasn't true, but it felt befitting her disconsolate mood to think so (really, Marta would say, "Stay straight, Suki. Control your thinking." But no one can control their thinking. They *are* their thinking.)).

At the moment Suki was overcome by her own thoughts (with images of Endrit gently slipping the dress off of Rhea's shoulders (then the smallclothes (Suki could even see the gooseflesh on Rhea's arms as she stood before him in a moonlit farmhouse))) (but he doesn't yet snatch her into his arms, he takes her in with his eyes (his shirt is on—no, off—he is shirtless too (as he is always shirtless), and invites examination), he wants instead to reach into her hair and remove the bladed pins (one at a time) and then her necklace unclasps and lowers and there is nothing that either of them have not given to each other.), visions, and vituperations (voices that told her she was disgusting, that she was a fool to think she could have what Rhea had) until Suki had thrashed every plant in the front garden, ripped them out by the roots, and pushed over the white fence.

Suki found them in the hayloft (Rhea sifting and tying bundles, Endrit stacking (was she trying to impress, acting like stable help?)).

Suki snuck up the ladder and waited behind several bales (to hear how they spoke to each other (because if they had slept together, they would talk differently)).

"How did you let so much of this go to rot?" said Rhea (which was, again, either some kind of ploy to sound industrious, or a real question about an idiot subject).

She kept sifting through the hay, pulling out the dry, usable straw from the moldy piles. "Oh, I dunno. I guess I couldn't sneak out to keep a bunch of hay dry when I was busy playing manservant to four feckless queens," said Endrit (extremely playful and familiar (but that was Endrit all the time)).

"Manservant?" said Rhea.

"Mmm-hmm," said Endrit, grinning. "Of the very best quality."

Rhea laughed aloud and threw a handful of moldy straw at him (but Suki couldn't tell if it was a reference to his manhood (which Suki knew (or had heard) also meant something salacious (based on a jest she had heard between the guards))). It was impossible to decipher their flirtation as the flitting of horsefly (Rhea) to candle flame (Endrit) or the purring of alley cats after a tussle (meaning it could have been sweet talk in anticipation before, or boasting after, mutual pleasure).

"Fair enough, *boyservant*," said Rhea (smug and disgusting), "I suppose you're excused. We'll finish your chores."

"Very kind of you, my queen," said Endrit, bowing.

"Don't call me that."

(A long pause, while he shifted a large hay bale and cut the ties with a knife.)

"You okay?" he asked (real quiet (Suki had to lean out a little)) as if anyone would be okay in this situation (hiding out in a hovel after a vicious attack (and waking up with a gash in your shoulder)).

"Yeah," said Rhea (acting strong (but obviously also acting vulnerable (so that he would stay interested))). "Just don't call me that."

"What happened? A few days ago you were telling me the opposite."

Rhea smirked (and did that thing that makes people irresistible (looking up suddenly, as if through the veil of their own eyelashes (any courtesan from Walltown knew the trick (so obvious it was practically begging)))). And he fell for it! (Or if he didn't, he at least played along (smiled, squatted down beside her, and put his hand under her chin to lift it).)

She looked away. "Yes, I suppose." (Smile, smile, flutter, flutter.) "I just, I dunno. *You* don't have to call me that."

Suki wished she could call out Rhea's clumsy manipulations. She seduced like a mole rat scrubbing at an anthill.

"All right, then. I'll call you Captain Rheanon, the foolkiller." (Historic Meridan hero.)

"No! Not that either."

"Okay, okay. You're not very much alike anyway," said Endrit, sweeping the last of the moldy hay off the edge of the loft. They gathered the sifted bundles (Suki dove back down the ladder and hid behind a row of barrels).

"Rhys used to call me that," she said as they descended the ladder and carried the bundles to the horse stalls. A couple bent-backed mares slouched in the stables (the kind that Suki once saw when she was five and visiting the royal stable yard of Tasan (the horrible stupor in their aged eyes had made her weep for two days (but that was before she'd lost Tola (when pain had been so new)))).

"I'm sorry," said Endrit. (He spread some hay down on the stall floor. Rhea took the brush and dragged it across the horse with a limp wrist.)

"He would have made a great king," said Rhea.

Suki would have said, "Was he a maniac like his father?" but Endrit said, "I heard he was a good soldier."

"Not good enough," said Rhea, laughing, then wincing at her own carelessness. She was full tilt into her sob story now (and she had his attention).

"He was my father's obsession after I was born and he was widowed. Everything rested on Rhys, all of my father's ambitions. It wasn't as if he didn't love me. It wasn't that way. I was just so young—five years old when Rhys was twenty. Rhys doted on me like a pet. I bounced on his knee. I loved him with all my heart. Everyone did. He would say, 'Rheanon,' and I would shout, 'foolkiller!' and poke him in the chest like I had slain a fool. He would laugh, and I realize now the entire court must have been watching. He was all I ever noticed."

Rhea paused (to wipe her eye secretly (but not so secretly that Endrit wouldn't see it)).

"When the Fins murdered the king and queen, all the house was astir—mourning, of course—but my father's banner lords all agreed on the course of action. We would crush the Fins, Rhys would marry Emilia Sesquitaine, connecting the eastern- and westernmost houses of Meridan. They would rule, and all would be well again."

Suki scoffed to herself at the simplicity of it (that wasn't how it had gone).

"Well," said Rhea, "Corent failed to uphold the alliance and refused to enter battle. Tasan jumped on the opportunity to grab land in the Corentine foothills. And suddenly war was everywhere. Emilia Sesquitaine was a frail thing and died of glassers' lung. Rhys led the dragoons for two years, always as the future king. He wouldn't allow his men to pillage. Even in the Tasanese campaigns, the villages were spared. And suddenly, he was winning hearts in all the midland countryside. People started to wonder if he would marry Tola and unify both Meridan and Tasan—half of Pelgard."

Suki almost lunged from behind the barrels (to slap the name of her sister off of Rhea's lips). Rhea didn't have to finish the rest of the story (Endrit knew what happened. (Rhys took an arrow to the hand (tipped with chipatri mold (which spread rot through his whole body for five days and dried out his heart)) then Declan went mad, and pushed the dragoons deep into Tasan (then he caught Tola and killed Dato when he tried to rescue her, and then killed Tola too (Suki knew this was true (against every law of gods and honor and men, he'd slayed a royal prisoner (slaughtered the Tasanese army the next day at Crimson Fog (and took the daughters of the three kingdoms back to Meridan to "protect the peace" (hostages)))))))).

"By the time my father negotiated the Treaty of Sister Queens and created the Protectorate, Rhys was some months' dead. Father was a different person by then—closed, cold, rotted out—but nonetheless king of all Meridan. It wasn't as if he loved me less. It was simply that he, too, died in a way. I can't blame him, but there I was, his new heir. All that work that had made Rhys was undone in me. I suppose he was just tired."

Endrit had his back to Suki, but it was obvious that he was concerned (he'd finished spreading the hay and now stood beside Rhea with a hand on her shoulder (which she must have relished)).

"You can't blame him," said Rhea (when obviously, yes, you could blame a cruel, despotic man for having no love left for his daughter (who had become no more than a lapdog begging for his approval)).

Endrit took the brush out of Rhea's hand and turned her to face him. He looked in her eyes (which were wet (but prettily so)), she turned her face so her cheek would rest in his hand for a moment, and then he kissed her temple.

Suki made a silent cheer (if they had been lovers, he would never be so chaste (they must have only slept together as cousins do, for warmth or comfort) or she might have snuck to him at night and failed her seduction). But Suki's triumph was short. Rhea lifted her chin and rose onto the tips of her toes and kissed him (a long, urgent kiss (with her body pressing into his (her hands on his neck (his on her hips)) lasting forever (for the span of three full breaths (rise and fall (chest to chest), rise and fall (joined together), rise and fall (and twice as many heartbeats))))) until Suki turned and ran from the barn (stumbling) (blinded) weeping (unprettily so) back toward the farmhouse.

When they walked back up to the house (and saw the garden destroyed) (and saw Suki awake (and dressed) and eating the last of a rind of cheese from the pantry), Rhea and Endrit acted like *she* (Suki) was the one hiding things and not them.

"You're awake!" said Rhea (no opinion one way or the other).

"Mmm-hmm," said Suki.

"What happened to the fence?" said Endrit.

"I dunno," said Suki (shrug (who cares)). "A deer in heat maybe."

Endrit laughed at the idea of a deer razing a garden. Rhea made an incredulous look with her eyebrows. "Well, anyway, it's good you're up," said Rhea. She approached and hugged Suki around the shoulders. Rhea didn't touch Suki's wound, but Suki winced anyway (just so she could pull away). "Ow!"

"Sorry!"

"Be careful."

"Sorry, sorry. Does it hurt bad?"

(Yes, but not at the moment.) "Of course it hurts," said Suki. "How long have I been asleep?"

"Two days," said Rhea. "We gave you paste of the poppy."

(To get her out of the way, thought Suki, so they could tumble in bed together.) Suki tried not to stare at Endrit too much. She couldn't even look at Rhea (too disgusted). For the next few moments they loitered around one another in an awkward conglomerate, with Suki sitting on the porch, Endrit pushing the fence back up (tying up the broken slats), and Rhea standing around (uselessly).

Rhea fished for more information ("Can you rotate the shoulder?" "Would you like more poppy?").

Suki ate the cheese without offering any and refused to give her the satisfaction (or advantage) of knowing her weaknesses ("Rotates fine." "I've slept enough, you?").

Rhea acted like a babe in the woods, ("How did I sleep? Fine, I suppose. Been worried a lot.").

(Worried she'd scare the horses, perhaps. Suki didn't respond, so Rhea pushed further, ("We still haven't heard from Cadis or Iren."))

Cadis had told Suki during the melee at the ball that she was going to Findain. Iren was probably with her, since the fastest route home was a ship up the River Oxos, inland until the Corentine port city of Takht-e-Malin. (And because they were friends and looked out for each other (unlike Suki (who had no one)).)

Suki had no desire to share the information with Rhea.

("You've been busy.")

Rhea started to get annoyed, or at least, finally revealed it. ("What does that mean?")

It meant she was too busy diving at Endrit the moment she had him alone and hadn't even the decency to go ask a highwayman if perhaps all of Meridan had burned down.

"Do you have any idea what has been going on?" said Rhea.

"Don't be daft," said Suki. Obviously, she had been unconscious. And what had happened was that Suki had missed her chance to escape and go back to Tasan (to be empress (if she managed the long journey back home and (if they even recognized her after all these years when they had sent no one, not her siblings, not any letters, nothing to give Meridan the satisfaction of knowing it held a princess of the empire as prisoner (or maybe because they'd just given her up for dead and made little Kasem heir-apparent (maybe she was homeless))))).

Suki didn't say any of that (Rhea would have relished it). She struck a courtly pose of impatience.

"The Meridan dragoons either revolted in favor of some other house, or sided with the Findish rebels. They attacked us. We barely escaped. Marta has been arrested, for what, we have no idea. Cadis and Iren could be captured as well, for all we know. My father could be dead."

"Then what are you doing here?"

"Taking care of you!" said Rhea. The exchange had suddenly turned (Rhea was so good at doing that (twisting everything)) and Suki was made to look childish in front of Endrit.

"Will you talk to her?" said Rhea to Endrit (as if they were the parents of a petulant toddler).

Endrit gave up on the dangling pieces of the fence and wiped his hands on the back of his pants. He looked up at Suki without acknowledging Rhea's condescension. "We were thinking of going to Walltown for some news, and some fresher cheese."

He smiled. He was so much better than her.

She would challenge Kasem if she had to (and demand her throne (and demand to marry Endrit)).

"What do you say, Princess? If you say it's a good idea, we go right away."

It was obviously a good idea. Suki stood up so she towered over Rhea at the foot of the porch and said, "Cadis told me she's going to Findain. But we still need news and dinner, so we should go."

Rhea rolled her eyes (probably unable to accept the fact that Endrit wanted Suki's advice (and that Suki was queenly and decisive (instead of anxious and wormy) and would have never holed up in a house for two days wondering what to do (and even if she had managed to wrap her legs around Endrit, it hardly mattered (she was just another low-hung peach (like the Cheapside maids) which she would expect Endrit to sample and discard)))). Just as any queen would want the best of everything, the most learned magisters, the loveliest troubadours, Suki also wanted the most experienced concubine.

Suki hadn't walked on a dirt road in her entire life. She had ridden, of course (on Helio) and driven (been driven) in a carriage, but never walked along the center (between the two ditches made by the wagon wheels) where the nettles grew (and the horse patties lay).

She preferred to walk in the rut of a wagon wheel, where at least she could avoid being next to Rhea.

"Does it hurt?" said Endrit, as they neared the outlying buildings of Walltown (a mill yard, a ranch for goats).

"Hmm?" said Suki. (She had heard, but she wanted him to lean closer.)

"You're wincing," he said, leaning closer. Suki realized that her face was squeezed tight and she let out a subconscious hiss with each misaligned step on the edge of the ditch (which sent pain shooting through her shoulder).

"Sorry," said Suki.

Endrit laughed. "It's no bother. I mean, you should keep it down, because it's distracting."

(He was joking (because obviously being distracted was not as big of a deal as being injured (that was the joke)).) Suki smiled (but not too much (because it was too late by then)).

"I heard you fought like a wolverine," said Endrit.

"They were badly trained," said Suki. (That way she would sound nonchalant about how good she was.) The walls of Meridan Keep loomed in the distance. A motley village lay scattered at its feet. Rhea seemed to be pouting (since Endrit was giving Suki attention).

"And now we have matching injuries," said Endrit.

"Huh?" said Suki. (She was busy trying to walk in a steady line (and also peek at Rhea without turning her head).)

"We both have cuts on our shoulder," said Endrit. "And you wrapped mine, and I wrapped yours."

Suki felt herself blushing. "Really?" (Really, had he wrapped her shoulder (who else would have done it?).) Endrit winked when she looked up at him.

(Then the unwelcome voice of Rhea.) "While you were passed out at the ball."

(She had to remind Suki (she had to humiliate her (in front of Endrit)) about being unconscious (because obviously she was uncontrollably jealous that Endrit and Suki could walk together on a disgusting country road in peasant clothes and still feel as if the sun were shining just for them).)

"Your tongue was sticking out," said Endrit (but he was just teasing (he made a face like a dead sheep with a lolling tongue)). Suki slapped his shoulder.

"Ow."

(But now Suki wondered—) "What else happened while I was out?"

They paused. A wagon clopped up behind them. They stepped off the road and let it pass (cabbages). Rhea and Endrit burst into laughter. (Was it the cabbage cart? (or a joke they shared?).)

"What?" said Suki.

Endrit spoke. "It's just that—you know I love you Susu—I'd never do anything to—"

Rhea continued to sputter like a chimp (she loved having secrets).

"What? Tell me," said Suki.

"I threw you at a couple dragoons," said Endrit.

Rhea laughed and laughed, as if nothing could ever be so funny. "Don't be mad at him," she managed to say. "It was my order."

He was obviously covering for her (she wanted to prove that Endrit would do whatever she told him (even throw her away)). It was so obvious, what she was doing (but Suki would have no recourse, no real weapons to fight her (and take him), no power until she was empress).

"It was a tight corridor and I needed my hands," said Endrit. Rhea started pantomiming a troll chucking a boulder and hysterically laughing (maybe the troll part was just her face).

Endrit quickly added, "You were safe. I picked you back up as soon as we finished the guards."

"Wait," said Suki, finally piecing it together. "Were you carrying me?" (Suki could think of nothing more humiliating than Endrit carrying her the whole time (and nothing more tragic (that she wasn't awake to feel it)).)

"Of course," said Endrit.

Suki cursed in Tasanese. Thankfully, neither of them heard it (because another wagon approached, this one full of soldiers). Suki, Endrit, and Rhea jumped off the road again (and pulled up the cowls on their wraparound capes (to cover their faces)). They must have looked like three farmhands on the way to market (maybe farmhands would have goods to sell? (Suki didn't know (care).) Itinerant bricklayers, then).

They were close enough to the outer yard of a tavern (a few drunks leaned on the wall by the door, watching pass-ersby), so they kept their heads down and cowls up (so no one would recognize them).

Walltown was probably always a mud-soaked madhouse of peddlers, beggars, and villagers living together in the shadow of Meridan Keep, but somehow it seemed even more agitated (crowded (edgy)) than usual. (It had been only a couple of days since the Revels.)

A few open-air merchant stalls still had revelers' masques on sale, along with ribbons and kites. Builders and soldiers elbowed through the crowds (the builders' wheelbarrows were full of material (to rebuild the damage at the keep) and the soldiers to add security).

At the central market, everyone shouted their sales (while casting glances at the tripled number of guards). Suki couldn't tell if they were king's men (or rather, which king). When Suki turned back from staring at all the market stalls, Rhea was already paying an old man for a slab of butter, four eggs, and some cured pheasant. She placed a silver coin in his palm and closed his fingers around it. "Keep it," she said. "It's troubled times, Father."

"Aye," said the old man, pocketing the silver. "Aye, it's that."

"Were you here, then, when it happened?"

The man spat, "When the scum Fins tried to kill our king? Aye, I heard it too. It shook half my eggs clean off the table. Then madness. Total madness." The man whistled through a gap between his teeth.

Suki wanted to ask if the attackers were really Fins (how were they so certain?), but Rhea didn't press the line (because obviously, it was better for her if they were (instead of what Suki suspected (which was that she and her father planned the whole thing in order to kill off the Protectorate (which was a little confusing (because then why wouldn't Rhea kill Suki while she was unconscious? (maybe because of Endrit? (didn't matter (Suki was certain)))))))).

There was a hubbub at the central court (an aisle over, where the market stalls opened up into a small plaza with a well and a gallows (the people of Meridan had such a keen sense of justice and such a deep love of spectacle that a permanent stage for public execution was as important to their cities as the aqueducts)).

Suki looked around for Endrit. He was buying dried figs from one of the village beauties (he whispering and touching her hand) (she giggling and putting extra figs in his bag). It looked like dragoons were marching onto the gallows.

Rhea asked the old man, "And is everyone all right?"

"All right?" said the man. "Sesquitaine and Sprolio have fallen. Half the royal guards—children of Walltown some of them. Most of the court—rich bastards the lot of 'em, but deserved better."

"Yes, but the king—"

"Oh. He's just fine, thank the gods. No one's heard of the little queens, though. . . ."

"Have they—"

Suki expected the question, "Have they declared war?"

"—captured any rebels?"

(Of course she would care only about herself (if they had captured rebels, they could torture information out of them (specifically, names of any Meridan guards who might have colluded with them (that was all that really mattered to Rhea, cleaning out Meridan Keep with her paranoid visions of assassins around every corner (not the fact that another war would mean countless Findish, or even Tasanese, lives)))).)

"Capture them?" said the old man. "Aye, they caught every last one of them water rats."

Rhea and Suki both looked at the old man, confused (the dragoons couldn't have possibly caught the entire raiding party (the attack was too well planned (and last they saw of it, the attackers had breached the inner defenses (it was chaos (one or two could still be hiding in some unlit corner of a pantry somewhere, deep in the castle, waiting to spring out (a paranoid thought, but still possible (no one could have rounded them all up)))))))).

"They caught them *all*?" said Rhea.

"Aye. Meridan soldiers don't wilt. Got all the cowards, and the traitors too—"

Before Rhea could ask what he meant, the clamor at the

scaffold rose and was pierced by a herald's call. "Hark! Harken me, citizens! The king has come!"

A cold shudder ran through Suki (that Declan was nearby). Endrit had heard as well (he let go of the beauty's hand and ran over). Rhea was already pushing her way down the center aisle toward the plaza. A full regiment of dragoons had already taken positions at every alley and doorway surrounding the plaza. Their helmets shone from several rooftops and balconies.

Endrit ran up to Rhea and grabbed her arm (gently (so not to catch any attention (Suki followed))). "Keep your hood on," said Endrit.

"Why? It's my father."

A procession of guards had already approached the scaffold (Declan was dressed in military garb and climbed the stair with a slight limp (as if he was in great pain (but didn't want his people to worry (how brave)))) but where was Hiram? He would have been the one to dirty himself in a crowd.

"I know," said Endrit. "It'll all be over soon."

"It's over now," said Rhea. "He'll take us back. We'll be safe."

"Maybe you will," said Suki. (Endrit's look said she wasn't helping.)

"We all will," said Endrit, "but we don't know about Iren or Cadis."

"They're long gone," said Suki (not certain why she blurted it out; maybe just wanting to be helpful).

But Rhea whirled on her and made the peasants near them nervous. "What?"

"I told you, they went home," said Suki. "They're being smart."

(Was she only believing it now, because she didn't see them with her father? (That meant Rhea hadn't taken Suki's word for it back at the farmhouse (which was typical (and Suki didn't care))).)

"That's treason!" said Rhea. (Endrit had to step between them and quiet Rhea.)

"Let's hear what he says. We can go to him after. For now we have no idea who might be in the crowd." (Appealing to her distrust of her own people was a good idea.) Rhea quieted. They found a nondescript place to stand by a tin peddler's cart. On the scaffold, Declan let the crowd squirm a little before approaching—he was such a shameless showman that he might have been half Dain. "Good Meridan, I have been king only a short ten years."

Shouts all over the plaza. "A great king!"

"King forever!" (which must have been the castle servants planted in the crowd (or the people of Meridan just didn't care about the rest of Pelgard (it had been a prosperous decade for them, after all))). Declan accepted the praise with a modest smile, then raised a hand to speak again. "I come to you now, heavy-laden." ("Murderers!" "Traitors!")

Declan raised his hand higher. "So many compatriots, friends, good and honorable houses under our own banners were shamefully struck that a weak heart would wither and die under the sorrow."

(A pregnant pause.)

"But we are not weak hearts in Meridan," said Declan.

"Never!" shouted the people.

The guards on the scaffold pushed a row of prisoners forward (shackled together (blindfolded and gagged (tattooed (but newly tattooed (the skin still red) with the marks of the Munnur Myrath)))). The crowd threw apples (hard ones) at the rebels (who screamed into the rags stuffed down their throats). In Tasan, the king would never stand on the same platform as criminals.

The spectacle was unseemly. "We should go," said Endrit.

"No," said Rhea (she must have been enjoying it). As the Meridan soldiers executed the prisoners (all at once, blades gushing from their chests), the crowd gasped and then cheered (and Suki stared at the fishmouths (so new (and the soldiers so young (younger than those she'd fought (and none of them injured otherwise, as one would be if captured in battle))))).

"It's not them," whispered Suki.

"Don't be crazy," said Rhea. "They're the enemy."

Suki didn't respond (busy thinking about what Rhea had just said (*Whose enemy?* (Was Meridan hers? Or Declan Meridan's? Declan's was certainly hers, and Findain his (but who were these?))) *Think straight* (she said to herself in Marta's voice)). (*Don't get lost in there.*)

They killed the supposed rebels.

Declan wiped his shoe and spoke again. "Our own family has fallen. And the great experiment, the great hope that I myself thrust upon you—the Protectorate—has failed."

"What does that mean?" said Rhea.

Suki hoped Cadis and Iren had managed to escape (she searched the procession of guards and didn't see them (thank the gods)).

"I wished, naively, that war would never come to Pelgard again, and the sister queens would rule together in peace. Several villagers called out "Pax Regina" (the queen's peace), but most already sensed where this was going. Declan breathed again a visible sigh. "Iren of Corent and Cadis of Findain" (Hisses and boos at the mention of Findain.)—"have betrayed the Protectorate. They used the attack to escape to Findain under cover of night."

"They was in on it!" shouted some in the crowd. "They're with the rebels!"

Rhea leaned back to Endrit. "*How* could they have made the trip? Were they planning this?" Endrit had no idea.

Declan continued without correcting the accusations. "As I said, we don't know the reason of the attack." (But the crowd was convinced it had solved the mystery ("to help them run!")) "All we know is that they abandoned their sisters, and the truce, and are hereby declared fugitive."

The crowd erupted once again.

"Sink their ships!"

"Topple the spire!"

They were calling for war.

"They were daughters to me," said Declan (Suki nearly choked (a woman standing behind them mumbled, "Child brides, more like," (at which point Suki did choke))). "And they stabbed at the heart of everything I have worked for. For *you*, good Meridan. A weak heart would puncture and die."

(Another pause (He was good at this.).)

"But we are not weak hearts." His stride steadied as he paced the scaffold (as if the limp didn't matter). "They are criminals now, fomenting the downfall of your kingdom. And with sadness, I admit that my own blood, Rhea, may have been corrupted by their lies."

Endrit had to hold Rhea back from shouting out her presence.

"She, too, is gone," said Declan. "My own fault for thinking she could take the seat built for Rhys."

Endrit didn't have to hold Rhea back any longer. (She nearly buckled (Suki couldn't see her eyes, but a single sob racked through Rhea).)

"My hope misplaced," said Declan. "My daughter and Suki of Tasan are wanted for questioning."

"We'll find 'em!" shouted the crowd.

"Use of force," said Declan, "is advised, for they are well trained. Such is the state of our disrepair, good Meridan. We are injured. A weak heart would crumble and fall."

This time the crowd answered, "We are not weak hearts!"

"That is right," said Declan. "We are at war. And so I declare Meridan in martial state. I hereby seize the holdings of Houses Sprolio, Sesquitaine, Tulla, and Ferimore for the people of Meridan. The seventh and eighth division of the light cavalry has been recalled and will station in Walltown. Tomorrow they arrive."

For the first time, the crowd murmured (the news meant

a thousand soldiers would descend on the village, bringing money, but also new authority (new cruelty)).

"Stay strong, good Meridan. Tomorrow we begin the fight to avenge our fallen, to reclaim the peace that was stripped from us, the hope that was shattered, and reckon with our traitors."

The crowd bellowed their approval. Even the guards drummed their spears on the stone and shouted, "Here, here!"

"And tomorrow," said Declan, "we begin with the ringleader of the rebels, the worm in our midst who whispered treachery into the ears of my daughters and walked among you as citizen. Tomorrow I bring you the head of Marta from Walltown."

(Roars. Endrit turned and pulled Rhea with him (she had been crying ("We have to go," he said to Suki)), who had been thinking (fake rebels (Declan's a liar (Rhea sleeping with Endrit (manipulating) (sex) wasn't he kind to bandage her (embarrassed) Marta (Marta (Marta (think straight (they're killing Marta (framing her) and Endrit will need comfort (what a horrible thing to think (but none can save her now (maybe Rhea if she goes to him (if he cares (would he? (does he?)) she's "corrupted" too, he said (lied?) and would he really kill his heir? (if he did, and they escaped (the two of them (oh gods, Marta), I'm getting lost (and sorry) sad) sex) sisters) sabotage) Cadis) Iren) Tola) Tola) Tola and Marta taken apart, taken forever))))).)

They lowered their heads and left the plaza as the procession escorted Declan in the opposite direction.

CHAPTER TWELVE

Iren

Day two.
Findain. Archon Basilica. Midday.

In the giant-domed bathhouse, miniature aqua gardens gave privacy for a variety of activities.

Children played in the wading pools.

Old women played dice in the butterfly jungle.

Iren and Cadis sat by the steam fountain alone.

Servants brought in cold melon on the hour.

Cadis lounged, fully naked, unraveled her braids and removed the beads. Iren sat in a towel and scraped the dirt from her arms with a decorated seashell.

"You could always stab her in here," said Cadis. "It's so foggy, no one would see."

She meant Hypatia. She wanted to know everything Iren would do, if she were in Cadis's situation.

"Not enough exits," said Iren, only half present in the conversation.

"You could pay a servant to take you through the boiler rooms."

"They don't know me."

"That's why you'd pay them."

"Money is a cheap substitute for trust."

"So you'd need them to trust you?" said Cadis.

"No, I'd need them to fear me. But to do that, they must first trust that I can follow through with my threats."

Cadis let out a whistle. "Are you sure we grew up together?" she asked.

"I needed to do something while you braided your hair."

Cadis laughed and threw a bead at Iren. They ate some melon. Cadis seemed curious about everything—as if she no longer believed even the parts of Iren's childhood of which Cadis herself had been a part. She had concocted half a dozen assassinations for Hypatia, all amateurish and all in sisterly jest. She didn't truly acknowledge the option—and seemed to believe that neither did Iren.

Maybe she just wanted some distraction from the outer world, where she was quickly to become a queen or a pawn in a war too big for Findain to win.

"You could poison her cider," said Cadis.

"Where would I get the poison?"

"You put that poison in our travel packs."

"And you should hold on to it. It's for emergencies."

"And you don't carry non-emergency poison with you?" said Cadis.

"Only my venomous tongue."

"Well, then, you could blow up her house. I dunno."

"Too loud. Too much attention."

"And too many casualties," said Cadis, rethinking it. "This is difficult."

Iren smiled and shook her head. It was nice to have a kindhearted friend—to remember what kind hearts were like. She knew her assignment would be to return immediately to Corent. Her mother had given it first. Assignment #1. If ever anything went wrong—if Declan tried to imprison them, if he died suddenly—anything that shattered the fragile peace, then all other assignments were aborted. Her only task was to return.

For years Iren dreamed of it. She'd wondered if she might even help it along by stealing away at night. She hadn't imagined that the day would come and she would find herself reluctant.

"Okay, how about this?" said Cadis. "You take her hunting and push her off a cliff."

"She'd never go with me if I asked."

"Well, you'd leave out the part about the cliff," said Cadis, giggling.

"Oh," said Iren, smiling.

"Fine, then, clever sister. How would you do it?" Cadis ate a wedge of melon and poked at a palm frond with her toe. Iren thought on it for a moment.

"Her weakness is her company. Pentri is an arrogant mule. Arcadie hates her."

"How can you tell?"

"When someone speaks, don't look at the person talking. Look at how others react. It's amazing what you'll see on their faces."

"How does Arcadie react when Hypatia speaks?"

"Like she's watching a rat eat the carcass of a frog."

"Is that how you knew Jesper had bedded Arcadie, because they look at each other?"

"No. I guessed. Then I paid a servant for the information. They love pillow gossip."

Cadis laughed.

"Besides, have you seen him? He could bed the queen of the moon if he wanted."

They laughed together. An attendant brought in a pail of orange coals and threw them into the fountain. Steam rose up in giant plumes. Iren finished with her shell and washed her arms from a nearby basin.

"So you'd use Pentri's pride?" said Cadis, once the attendant cleared the area.

"I would spread rumor that Hypatia had insulted House Muto. Something vapid and irrelevant, but it would infuriate Pentri. He would demand to see her. She would acquiesce, because House Muto has votes in the council that she requires. Most important, he would demand they be alone. None of his entourage, none of her lieutenants. He would be too embarrassed, and he's the type who hasn't gained the fear of his servants. They must gossip about him incessantly."

"Okay, so they meet."

"Following Pentri is easy. He's a peacock."

"Then?"

"A magister's long surgery needle. Sneak up as Pentri does his shouting. Strike Hypatia first. Skewer through the neck. Then the ear. Catch Pentri as he runs away. Two pricks into a kidney."

By the look on Cadis's face, Iren realized she might have misjudged the request. Cadis wasn't truly envisioning an assassination. Not a real one. Not the kind that leaves any blood.

"You asked," said Iren.

"I was making idle conversation."

Iren sighed. "You're in the bathhouse of your own castle, playfully guessing at how to kill your greatest rival for a throne about to burn up in a war. Maybe now isn't the time for idle conversation."

"Okay," said Cadis. She finished unraveling her braids. Her hair lay about her like a sea maid. "I have to go to the wash tub."

Iren tried to revisit the entire conversation. Maybe Cadis had taken parts of it personally. Maybe the part about trust made her suspect that Iren never really trusted anyone.

She shouldn't have indulged in idle conversation.

Her secret life in Meridan, her assignments, was some kind of betrayal to Cadis. And for now her vision was clouded by it.

In time she would see clearly. That Iren's mother had done everything for them. Iren's assignments helped Corent, yes, but also hurt Meridan, which was a favor to Findain.

In time Cadis would recall the good memories.

In time they might see each other and embrace as sisters.

In time she hoped Cadis would love her again.

But until then it was best for Iren to return immediately. Her presence seemed to cause nothing but damage for Cadis.

Iren rose and left the bathhouse.

She took with her the beads that Cadis had thrown. In her hands, they made a dull clicking sound that reminded her of her friend.

She turned her attention fully to her assignment.

Assignment #1.

Find Mother.

Day Three.

Findain. Dockside. Sundown.

A tri-mast galleon sat in the bay.

At sunrise it would sail for Takht-e-Malin. The crew loaded it with cargo. They took leave to enjoy their last night. Iren approached the captain.

A short man, bald, unsmiling, marked for fifty or more expeditions without loss, wreck, or mutiny. A cautious man. The type to trust with business.

"Captain," said Iren.

She wore her travel clothes.

Nothing to stand out.

Old Dains were all broad and blond, like Cadis, but Findain was a market hub full of merchant ships, and the Findish caroused with everybody—the city had all types. Iren's short black hair wasn't the calling card here that it was in Meridan.

The man turned from inspecting the moorings. "Only on my ship."

He held a ship's log, on which he took notes. His fingers were steady. He was no poppy eater.

"We're close enough," said Iren. An attempt at familiarity.

"What can I do for you?" No smile. Iren would have normally liked the guy if she didn't need something from him.

"I hear you're the one to speak with about passage."

"On the *Queen's Constance*?"

"To Corent."

"We're a cargo ship."

"I can feed myself. I can crew if you let me."

"We're not a passenger ship."

He eyed her with suspicion. Iren had never been so reckless. She had little choice. She felt uncomfortable in Findain. Always watched.

Severed from her intelligence network.

She hadn't written or received a message from her mother since the attack.

She had assignments. In case of emergency, rendezvous at Takht-e-Malin. They had a safe house in the port city.

An old landlord kept it supplied with food for ten years, and tended the birds. Iren would release the birds up the mountain, to the academy spires.

Her mother would come.

But first she needed a single Fin willing to take her. "I have money," said Iren. A mistake.

The captain returned to his tablet.

"I don't take bribes, miss."

She had stumbled upon the most upright sailor in the entire captains' guild. Iren turned and walked back to the alleys.

For two days she had stalked the taverns on the dock. The eavesdropping, the sneaking, that was easy. But ships upriver were rarer these days. The tariffs imposed by Meridan were too high.

Captains were on edge. Merchant nobles called off the expeditions until the specter of war passed.

The hard part for Iren was all the talking. The chummy nature of the Fins, who seemed to think one had to be a friend in order to do some business.

Most of them knew she was Corentine just by the discomfort. She didn't understand why Fins needed so many friends. This wasn't the time to take foreign stowaways on board, they said.

The *Queen's Constance* was the last chance. Iren cursed under her breath.

She turned on her heel and walked back down the dock.

The captain must have been in his third pass of the ship's log. He didn't look up.

Iren searched for words. "You're diligent."

"Mmm," said the captain.

Iren croaked out another compliment. "You must be well regarded among your peers."

"I suppose." He still read.

Iren was finished with the niceties. "Look. I understand you won't take me."

"Good."

"Because we're not bosom friends."

"Because you have trouble written all over you."

"Nothing is written all over me."

"Very well."

"If you're an honest man, then I would send a letter."

"I'm no shinhound."

"Please," said Iren. She placed a small parcel including an encrypted letter and her signet ring onto the ledger the man read. Next to it she placed a bag of silver.

The man sighed.

"That's the most I've begged anyone," said Iren. "There's a woman, a landlord. She keeps a flat on the riverfront. Ask anyone for Dokhtar Zafira."

"Dokhtar Zafira," said the man.

"I wrote it on the parcel."

The captain nodded. Iren turned and walked away. The captain reminded her of her father, sentimentalist that he was. The king of Corent, off to be medic, on the front lines. Honor-bound. Dead.

The captain would deliver to Zafira.

Zafira would see the ring and send the parcel immediately to Queen Malin in the capital. Her mother would decrypt the message—a brief of all that had happened.

Iren walked up the alley toward the Odeon. The streets were alight with torches, and crowded. Taverns disgorged their diners toward the theaters. Jugglers and bards played at the entrances to welcome guests.

Iren moved through the crowds like a wind-swept leaf. The signet ring was the last piece of evidence that she was heir to the Corentine spires.

She was alone.

A pack of children surrounded her in a plaza. They offered trinkets and a shoeshine. Iren waded through them. A juggler in front of a theater shouted to her, "Careful, miss. They'll pick your pocket."

As Iren passed by, she dropped a handful of souvenirs and a few coppers into the juggler's upturned hat. "I picked theirs," she said.

She liked the sound he made.

"Whoa."

She liked being alone.

She was the shade scarab. A creature grown in the darkness. In Corent the magisters kept the vicious things in cages at the very tip of the spires—where they would get the least amount of shade. They stayed the size of a human hand. But deep in the mountains they grew into bulls. Their chitinous *click, click, click* haunted the caverns. Like the scarab, Iren was kept small by the constant glare of Hiram Kinmegistus, Declan, and the Protectorate court.

She hid her talents from the light.

Always withdrew.

Always pretended.

Dainty Iren.

Delicate.

Domestic.

But she was free now. In the shadow of the great wide open, where she was just another homeless child roaming the streets.

Iren smiled as she crossed the bridge to the island of the Odeon. The guards had no idea. The guildmasters. Even Cadis. That she had been loosed onto the world. Its shade would be her food, until she could reach her mother.

She ascended the stairs and entered the Odeon.

She nodded to the doorman.

She smiled.

She made a *click, click, click* sound.

The Odeon was built for gatherings. Outside the common hall was a garden palisade. None of the usual balconies designated for nobles. No inner sancta where royals distinguished themselves, even from their lesser cousins.

Just long garden paths.

Open porticoes where everyone strolled in leisure.

What social creatures these Findains must have been.

Iren crossed the garden without looking up.

Past two picnics.

Past a poet's recital.

Past three separate games of dice.

The castle of the Archon Basileus was the only other structure on the small island in the mouth of the harbor.

Cadis would be within.

Butting heads with Hypatia.

Sparring with Arcadie Kallis.

Flaunting herself for Jesper.

She was made for such constant melodrama.

She was a fish back into water.

So much social pressure.

So much business conducted over jokes and a handshake.

It was a wonder to Iren that Findain ever rose to power.

They ran a country as if it were a primary school, with cliques and guilds and secret societies. Whispers and singing and talent shows.

Everyone equal.

Another way of saying everyone vying for attention.

Unstructured rule by popularity.

Iren preferred a few magisters, a good debate, and efficient action. Iren entered the gathering hall in the basilica.

To her credit, Cadis was studying the ledgers of the central banks.

Hypatia Terzi lounged nearby, writing a letter.

Jesper stood over Cadis's shoulder, explaining some of

the names on the ledger. Unwritten explanations.

Jesper stopped when he saw Iren.

Cadis turned. It was concern on her face.

Something amiss.

Iren checked the exits: the entry and two doors, none guarded.

Three windows, all closed but breakable.

"Where were you?" said Jesper.

"Dancing," said Iren. It came with a sharpened stare.

They all knew she didn't dance.

Now they knew she didn't answer to Jesper Terzi either.

Cadis stood from her seat. "Iren, it's nothing."

"What's nothing?"

"Come away from the door."

"I'd rather not."

"Oh, stop coddling," said Hypatia. "We know where you've been."

Iren didn't respond. If she had to, she could run. All she really needed was the brace on her left arm. It held her knives and thief's kit. She could sleep in gullies with the homeless.

At night she could steal into the basilica for her travel pack. A land route to Corent would take two and a half months at this time of year. The plan formalized instantaneously.

"What were you doing at the docks?" said Jesper. He spoke like a boy trying to speak like a man.

Cadis touched his arm. She seemed concerned. She was wearing more powder than usual.

"Now, hold on," said Cadis. "I trust Iren."

Hypatia snorted from her seat. "Then you're a fool."

"She's my sister," said Cadis. Then to Iren, "We didn't mean to ambush."

Iren needed more information. What could they possibly know?

Iren felt blind. "I was at the docks."

They must have been following her.

"What were you doing?" said Jesper.

"Hopscotch," said Iren.

"Why don't you answer the question?"

"Because I don't answer to you."

"Iren," said Cadis. "We already know."

"We?" said Iren.

"Did you think a ship captain of Findain would keep your little secret?" said Hypatia.

So much for finding an honest man.

Cadis looked at her with genuine ache and confusion.

"Just tell us," said Cadis. "Please."

Iren knew she was cornered. Both were. Cadis could hardly stand beside her and keep hold of her tenuous position. She would have to take a tactical loss.

"Fine," said Iren. "I went to the docks and asked the captain to send a letter to my mother."

That was enough. Cadis seemed relieved. "See?" she said, as if proving an argument she had made earlier.

"But what did you write?" said Hypatia.

"Daughterly things."

"Spying, you mean."

"We don't know that," said Cadis.

"Why else would you write in code?" said Hypatia. She held the letter aloft. It was Iren's.

The captain must have run it over immediately. Hypatia's underground network was more impressive than Iren had figured.

"We have our language."

"A spy cipher."

"So we like puzzles," said Iren with a shrug.

"Not such a clever one," said Hypatia. The noose was tightening. Iren remembered Hypatia had been writing on the parchment when she'd entered. Hypatia read from the letter.

Two days of surveillance on all of Cadis's movements, ending with, "Cadis is desperate for their approval as one of their own. She will break soon. The revolutionaries will have her."

Hypatia lowered the letter. A triumphant sneer. "I guess I just solved your little code."

Iren would have put three blades into her, center mast. But Cadis's silence was far more alarming. She had flushed into a deep crimson rage. She could never hide an emotion.

Her hands clenched.

Jesper seemed afraid to touch her.

She couldn't look at Iren.

She shook.

Then she lunged for Iren's face.

CHAPTER THIRTEEN
Rhea

Cadis would know what to do, surely. Always the one with poise under pressure. Like Rhys.

Rhea, in turn, was utterly lost.

Did my father really make a criminal of me? Would he have thrown Rhys away so easily? Does he really believe that Marta was the leader of the rebels?

As they sat on the farmhouse porch, Rhea couldn't look at either of them. Suki had a frantic tremor ever since she awoke. Her eyes darted, glared at Rhea, lusted after Endrit. Her motions were jerky and her sentences scattered. Rhea wondered what the true toll of the attack had been on her little sister—certainly, it was deeper than the wound on her shoulder.

At least she wasn't sneaking around the barn anymore, listening to their conversations and pretending they couldn't see her.

Suki sat on the grass, on the other side of the broken-down fence, as far away from Rhea as she could be, eating more food. The little thing had eaten twice the portion of Endrit, who busied himself fixing the fence she had obviously broken.

He didn't seem to mind. He was never upset at Suki. He always doted.

Rhea tried to help by clearing the broken plants in the garden bed.

Why are we even doing this? she thought.

Have we finally broken under the strain?

Endrit didn't seem broken. But the energy had to go somewhere. He dug at the base of each fence post, straightened it out, then packed the dirt again. He was searching for an answer that none of them had.

"What do we do?" said Rhea.

"Kill them," said Suki.

"The guards?" said Rhea. The plaza had far too many.

Even the three of them approaching from the rooftops couldn't hope to beat them. "There are too many," said Rhea.

"I meant all of them," said Suki. She stared a thousand yards into the distance, in the direction of Walltown.

She lifted both hands in the air, in the shape of a ball, and then splayed her fingers outward. "Boom."

She's completely lost her grip on reality, thought Rhea. She turned to Endrit and spoke softer. Maybe Suki wouldn't hear, or wouldn't bother returning from whatever mad fantasy she was concocting. "Endrit, we have only a day."

"What can we do?" he said, pushing the shovel deep into the dirt with his heel. Only a few days ago, she would have relished watching him at his work.

"I don't know," she said.

"We need more information."

Then why is he fixing a stupid fence? Why aren't we stalking outside of Meridan Keep? Why aren't we trying to save Marta?

"Do you have a plan?" she ventured.

"Mmm-hmm," groaned Endrit as he lifted a shovelful of dirt.

Then why isn't he telling me? Does he think me still loyal to my father?

Rhea snapped a broken stalk from a tomato plant and tied the salvageable remains to the fence for support.

Am I still loyal? Or better put, is he?

Rhea couldn't help but go over the events of the night of the Revels. In the light of her newfound suspicions, her father's behavior seemed suddenly intricate and insidious. He had escorted her to her chamber that night and stationed a guard at the door.

Was he protecting me from the attack?

If so, why didn't he tell me?

Was he unsure?

She had felt such a zigzag of emotions in the market square, when she saw he had taken some sort of awful injury to the leg. *Why had he protected only her, if he knew? And what of Hiram? Where is he? Was he killed in the attack?*

Declan must have barely survived. Rhea felt overwhelmed and empty at the same time. She knew the man who had raised her was long gone. And perhaps he had only ever been there in her near-blind devotion.

As she considered the depth of her father's involvement in the deaths of hundreds in the Meridan court, Rhea rolled a leaf of March mint, a Corentine medicinal plant, in the palm of her hand. It was known to have a calming effect. Rhea closed her eyes and thought of Iren.

How did we come to this? How did we let the years come between us? Will we all stand against one another on the battlefield?

For a long time the three were silent—Rhea reliving her childhood, revising each and every interaction with her father; Suki eating all of their rations while running some sort of hedge maze in her mind; and Endrit frantically digging fence posts as if it would save his mother.

Tomorrow they would execute the only mother any of them had ever had. It was nearly sundown when Endrit finally smacked his shovel into the dirt and cursed. "It's not here!" he said.

Rhea looked at Suki.

Did she know what he was doing? By the look of her, she didn't.

"What isn't?" said Rhea.

Endrit sighed. "When we left. Escaped. She told me to look in the garden."

"For what?" said Rhea.

"I don't know."

So that's why he was digging.

"What did she say exactly?"

Rhea had never seen him so worried. He who laughed at all the cares of the world. He who had giggled two nights ago when she'd snuck into his bed, afraid of the visions she had seen in her dreams. She had curled in to him for warmth and comfort. He had been both. A lighthearted rake. Nightmare, frustrations, fears—they were all moods too rich for the likes of Endrit. Now he kneeled before a broken fence as if all those blithe and bonny years had turned—in the span of a few hours—into the weight of the Great Ocean.

"She said, 'Don't worry and look in the garden.' That's all."

It didn't sound like Marta to be so careless in her instruction.

"Did she say it exactly like that?" said Rhea. "Don't worry? Look in the garden?"

"I think. Don't worry. Be careful. Be calm. I don't remember."

"Wait. She said 'be calm'?"

"Maybe. Yes. Why?"

Rhea held up the leaf to the March mint. "Maybe it was a clue."

Endrit grabbed the shovel and rushed to her. Rhea stood aside to let him dig up the plant. On further reckoning, it was the only foreign plant in the entire garden. Suki ran around the fence gate and helped dig by scooping with her hands. She had never cleaned so much as a dish, and here she was dirtying herself. *Is it for Endrit? Has she fully snapped?*

All other thoughts were cast away when Endrit stepped onto the shovelhead a sixth or seventh time and they all heard a muted but unmistakably metallic *clang*.

Endrit stepped back and dug a wider perimeter. Rhea joined in.

It was a soldier's strongbox, about the size of a loaf of bread, made of ironwork, with inset hinges to be water-proof. On long campaigns, officers kept letters from their lovers, ducal fiats, maps, and personal items within. Often, it was the only part of them to return from war.

Endrit pulled out the box and didn't bother looking for a key. He set it on its side and set the tip of the shovel into the tiny lock. He stomped onto the shovelhead and cracked the box like an oyster.

The night had snuck upon them. It was too dark to read anything. Endrit carried the box inside the house with Rhea and Suki right behind him. Suki was clasped to his heel like a pup, leaving Rhea to strike the flint and light the oil lamps.

When she approached with two large lamps to light the table, Endrit had already emptied the box.

Parchments, mostly. They each grabbed a bundle and began to unravel them. "This is a bunch of commendations," said Suki. "Medals from King Kendrick."

"This is a personal letter from Queen Valda," said Endrit.

Rhea knew Marta was a decorated general in Meridan's army, but she'd had no idea of such a close relationship with the king and queen.

Rhea unrolled a large sheaf—schematics written by a magister of the build. "What is it?" said Suki, pulling the front down flat on the table.

"It's a technical map," said Rhea. She recognized the upper floors immediately. "It's Meridan Keep."

All the dungeons and catacombs below it were nearly double the size of the aboveground chambers. Some they had never seen before.

"Why would she have this?" said Endrit.

And without waiting for an answer, he rose from the table and marched to a chest in the corner.

"We can get her," he said, as he opened the chest and pulled out a hunter's bag and light leather armor. "We can get her tonight."

"Yes!" said Suki. She ran over to pick out a blade from the weapons rack above the hearth.

Are they both mad? A map wasn't enough to storm a castle. A map that could have been well out-of-date. And what of the guards? Would they subdue and kill more of her countrymen?

"Wait," said Rhea. "Can we finish looking, at least? Do we know that *this* is what Marta wanted us to find?"

Suki sighed aloud. "It has to be," said Endrit. "She knew she'd be arrested. If I'd gotten her clue, we would have had days to plan."

He had a manic energy that Suki seemed to feed from. They crisscrossed the house, preparing for a stealth invasion.

But if Marta wanted him to have the map, she would have

told him directly, "Dig under the March mint." *Why give a vague clue? Did she think she would survive to meet them?* Her words were only meaningful if they were last words. If she had arrived at the house, they would be nothing but basic advice to stay calm.

Rhea untied the last bundle. It was another letter from Queen Valda, wrapped around a metal plate or talisman, which Rhea could not yet see, because it was itself wrapped in polishing cloth. Rhea began with the letter:

Marta, I hope you will remember me as we once were, in my father's house—two maidens, hardly come of age, on such separate paths. Do you recall how many hours you would train with the master of swords in the same yard as I would paint a bowl of olives? Do you remember eating an olive and setting the pit back in the bowl—with such elaborate care, as if not to disturb my work? How we laughed at the time. How much more we laughed when I unveiled the painting at Father's court with that pit rendered for all to see.

Oh, Marta, I know we have let our sisterhood fade. I had Kendrick to worry over. You—you were leading his campaigns. But love me, if you would, and pity a sister who comes to you now begging.

Taylin is all I have, and you well know he was hard-won. He has Kendrick's puckish smile already, and he is not a week old. I have never seen Kendrick frightened as he is now, even with all the banner houses of Meridan swearing allegiance. He hears whisper of horrible plots. This magister from House Ferimore calls himself Hiram Kinmegistus. Do you know him? He has returned from the academy as so many second sons do, with eyes as hungry as the shinhounds always slobbering at his heels.

I have not left the birthing chamber, Marta. I pleaded that Kendrick stay too, but you know him. I fear there are knives waiting for us in every shadow of Meridan Keep. And worse still, Taylin is their target. Marta, I shudder and weep and beg you. Take my son and hide him. Protect him from all the hideous scheming and betrayal.

Oh, Marta, take him for at least a while, until we can be sure of his safety.

Name him after that master of sword you liked so much.

Tell him the truth only when he is ready. Tell him his mother did not stop kissing him until the moment a cruel world pulled him from her grasp. And please, Marta, tell him to be a good king.

Love, love, love,

Valda

Rhea's hands could hardly unwrap the polishing cloth, they shook so hard.

Is it possible?

"Endrit," she said. Her mouth was dry, and she was

unsure the sound had made it across the room. "Endrit," she said again.

He must have made some confirming noise. She wasn't sure.

"Endrit," she said.

"Yes. Yes, what is it?" said Endrit.

"What did your father do? What was his profession?"

"Why?" said Endrit, then responded anyway. "He was the master of sword before he died. He trained my mother."

Rhea unraveled the cloth. Inside was the sigil crest of Kendrick and Valda Ironclaw. It rolled out of her hand and clattered to the floor. The lost heir of House Ironclaw had been found.

Endrit was king of Meridan, son of Kendrick and Valda. Her father had killed them both.

Rhea felt a crushing weight. She was not grieved, however. She was furious.

How could he have been so stupid?

How could he leave them so exposed?

Rhys would have never been so sloppy as to leave the heir alive, under their noses, already beloved throughout the city.

Rhys would have never been so disappointing.

CHAPTER FOURTEEN
Cadis

Cadis lunged at Iren's face like a feral dog. The shock and viciousness of it made both forget their training for a moment, as Cadis smashed into Iren and they both hit the stone floor. The moment passed. Cadis pinned Iren on her back and struck twice with her elbow. Iren raised her forearms in front of her face and took the two blows.

Iren rocked her hips and turned her shoulders, escaping the hold.

Cadis bounced up and wheeled around with a kick at Iren's temple.

A thoughtless move, motivated by the desire to hurt her as much as possible.

Iren brought her left arm up to her ear and blocked the

kick. Her brace, lined with lockpicks and throwing blades, took the blow. Cadis groaned.

In return Iren had an open strike at Cadis's other leg. Iren hammered her shin into the soft hinge of Cadis's knee, just as it strained to hold all of her weight. Cadis roared in pain.

Cadis had never felt so outmatched. It was as if Iren had been hiding her true gifts all those years, behind glasswork and needlepoint. Yet another secret.

Cadis could barely move fast enough to check Iren's attacks, and quickly her blocks would begin to break even if she did.

Her knee throbbed. Iren seemed to target it twice more, shifting the fight so that Cadis would have to present the swollen knee.

Iren fought angrily. Her strikes hit home. Cadis was as much taken aback by the skill as by the emotion behind it.

Cadis took another battering strike to the knee and nearly crumpled. Iren took the opening and jarred her chin with a right hook. Cadis blacked out for an instant and woke up on the floor. Iren was atop her.

It would be over soon, she thought.

An arm appeared around Iren's waist just as she was about to pummel Cadis, and she was lifted backward.

Jesper.

They were Jesper's arms.

Iren kicked twice, both heels striking his knees, but he held. Cadis wanted to shout, "Be careful. Pin her arms," but her jaw was so numb she couldn't even feel it. Iren thrashed in Jesper's grip, but long enough only to drop down a little to free her left elbow. With a flick of her wrist, a throwing blade—no more than a flat shaft of weighted metal, fell into her palm. Iren stabbed it backward, into Jesper's left thigh.

His hold loosened.

She pulled the blade out, turned, and stabbed it again into his side, near his lowest rib. She moved too fast for him to react. By then he was overcome by the tidal wave of pain. Blood began to flow from the wounds along his left side.

Iren stepped away from him. "Don't touch me," she said. "Never touch me."

Jesper looked at her without understanding. He put his hands on the holes but hadn't the strength to apply any pressure.

Jesper wobbled, then crashed to the stone floor. Cadis found herself already on her feet. When Iren turned to face her, Cadis was too close. In all her life, Cadis had never put so much behind a punch. Iren turned just in time to meet it.

She flew, as if kicked by a stallion, and hit a potted planter. Cadis ran over to Jesper, who lay on his back, pale and motionless. No one else was around. Hypatia, Pentri, and the others must have slipped out earlier. No one else was around to help.

"Are you out of your mind?" screamed Cadis, but Iren was still clutching the side of her face and couldn't respond. Cadis set about stanching Jesper's wounds. She tore his loose muslin shirt as bandages. If the cut on the thigh was deep enough, it could hobble him. If he didn't lose too much blood, he would live. That was if Iren hadn't tipped her blades with any poison or rot mold.

Cadis worked on Jesper with her limited field-medic training. She couldn't even look at Iren, though she made sure to keep her in peripheral sight at all times. "Have you been spying on me this whole time?" asked Cadis.

"Only since we got here," said Iren.

"Not before?"

"Not on you."

"Then why wouldn't you tell me?" said Cadis.

"Because you believed, like a child, you believed the war was over and that we would be 'sister queens.' You believed in the lie. And maybe that was necessary, for all of us to survive, but not anymore."

"It wasn't a lie."

"It was a lie, Cadis. Declan killed Kendrick and Valda. I've been trying to find evidence. The war was his doing. When he failed to take Pelgard, he took us as hostages. No one would accuse him of usurping the throne with us as his shields. He killed Tola because she was too old—she saw the maneuvering. Suki was only a toddler. She broke, of course, but at least she was controllable."

Cadis knew that Iren was the more unwilling ward of the Protectorate, but she thought it was homesickness, or the persistent belief that she was above Declan's authority. But Cadis never knew the depth of Iren's antagonism. And if she were to judge, Cadis could find no blame in it.

If Declan had started the war, then he was the cause of Iren's father's death, and perhaps even worse, her separation from her mother, Queen Malin.

It was so much to fathom all at once. And yet Cadis couldn't help but feel that if Iren had only trusted her all those years ago, as they'd held each other in the dark of her chamber, then they both would have been better for it.

Perhaps they would have succeeded where Iren had obviously failed. And all these years later, Cadis wouldn't be saddled with the false memory of them together, forging what she thought was a lifelong friendship.

"If all that's true, why not join the rebels? Convince your mother and ally with Findain?"

Iren shook her head.

"Why not?" said Cadis, already sick of Iren's withholding attitude.

"They had nothing to do with the attack at the ball. They've barely got their secret handshakes together, much less a strategy."

How did she know all this? And why in the name of all the gods had she been so distrusting?

"So the attack at the Revels was Declan again?" said Cadis.

"Well," said a voice from the doorway, "I like to think I helped."

Both turned. Jesper lifted his head from the floor. It was Hiram, with a shinhound at his feet. He must have been the recipient of the carrier bird—the one sent by the spy on the road. He had a giant bandage wrapped around his face, big enough to cover a severed cheek.

"How did you get past the guards?" asked Cadis.

She was all too aware that she had no weapon and he had a beast that had been bred to crush the shins of soldiers in its jaws.

Hiram made an open, conciliatory gesture with his palms, since he could not smile. "I had an appointment," said Hiram.

"Ismata, heel," said Iren, but the shinhound had no reaction. Hiram made a garbled laugh through his soaked bandages. "A good try. But I'm afraid I had to kill that one. All the ones you met, actually. This one stayed in the kennels."

Iren squinted at the dog, as if trying to recognize it. Hiram's kennels were in a vast network of rooms, deep beneath the castle.

Hiram looked around the room. "Where is that Hypatia Terzi? So intrusive when she's not needed, and so absent when she is."

Cadis felt Jesper tense at the mention of his cousin's name. When she spared a glance at him, he winked, as if to say he was less incapacitated than he seemed and could help if she needed it. A gallant gesture, but Cadis knew a shinhound would get the better of him now that he had lost so much blood.

She turned instead to Hiram. She was still Archon Basileus of the castle, and she would not be menaced here. "Why would you meet with Hypatia?" she asked.

"Didn't you know that the little shrew is none other than first among the Munnur Myrath? Of course not. No one ever sang it to you on a stage. Why would Cadis—naive to the world—know anything about her people?"

Cadis couldn't tell if he was lying in part or in whole. It made no other sense, she supposed, for him to be there. But for Hypatia to lead the rebels when she could just as easily help Findain as master in the common hall—that made no sense at all.

As usual, Iren was a step ahead.

"Are you cutting a deal for yourself, or are you still lapdog to that usurper?"

"Lapdog, I'm afraid," said Hiram with a shrug. "We give Findain to Hypatia's rebels and support their claim to rule."

"You spark civil war here, to turn your attention on Tasan," said Iren.

"Close," said Hiram. "We'll climb the spire first. I'll say hello to your mother."

"I don't believe you," said Cadis. "Hypatia's second in her guild already. She doesn't need you to rule."

"She does if she wants your chair," said Hiram. "Leave it to the Dains to betray even themselves."

Cadis realized three things as plainly as if they were the choral soliloquys in a PilanPilan operetta. First, Iren was right about everything—Declan's plot, certainly, but also that Cadis had been woefully naive all these years and her people would pay for it.

Second, Hypatia Terzi would forever be her mortal

enemy. The old Cadis would have hoped a puppy-dog hope that they could make peace. But she knew that Hypatia had cleared the room of guards on purpose, to remove witnesses and to deny her involvement.

And the third thing that Cadis realized was that Hiram had come to do Hypatia a favor in return for the rebels inciting civil war in Findain—and that favor was to make sure neither Iren nor Cadis survived this conversation.

Cadis saw the metallic flicker behind Hiram, who had stood the entire time in such a way as to hide his right hand. It was a crossbow, sized for a one-handed shot. The bolt was for her, she knew, because Hypatia had made her the primary target.

The shinhound would be for Iren—a bit of poetic return for her meddling with his beasts, and also to give him the opportunity to reload. A shinhound was also the only creature in the room faster than Iren.

Cadis forced herself to think beyond the surface of the situation, where she would normally reside, trying to speak with Hiram and convince him not to shoot. Instead she thought of Marta and all her mornings in the castle yard shooting arrows at straw soldiers.

She had to ask herself what type of shot Hiram would take. One to the face? An emotional response, the most certain kill, but only if it pierced through the eye. Otherwise the bolt might hit her scalp, tear it like a rind of fruit, but leave her alive. Was he so confident for that, or would he aim for the heart—the most practical target? He could miss by a hand on every side and still be done with her.

Or would he shoot at her gut—the easiest target, and the one that guaranteed a protracted and excruciating death, as she bled out? A skilled magister could save her, but not before Hiram finished with Iren and came back for a second shot.

All Cadis had to do was decide: Was he arrogant, practical, or cruel? Unfortunately, she knew him to be all three.

"You were good pupils," he said, raising his crossbow, pointing at Cadis. "And you would have made good queens."

Cadis stood in a protective stance over Jesper. "Then why turn on us? Why destroy all the work of the Protectorate?" She was simply stalling for more time. Sure Iren had a plan. It couldn't be to wrestle the shinhound.

"Because good queens are not obedient queens," said Hiram. Then he commanded the shinhound, "Catch!"

The beast ran toward Iren, growling and watering already at the mouth. Cadis prayed that Iren was not so foolish as to think she could drop the hound with one of her throwing blades—or even three.

Iren stared it down. The hound readied to leap. Iren snapped her fingers twice.

The hound skidded to a stop and awaited instruction. Both Cadis and Hiram stared openmouthed at the sudden reversal. Iren spoke a few words to the dog in old Corentine and then answered the obvious question. "I spent some time in the kennels."

Then she spoke another bit of Corentine. The hound

turned and ran at Hiram. The magister took a step back, but even in a state of panic, he must have known he had no chance to get away. In the half second before the shinhound jumped toward his neck, Hiram remembered his mission, turned to Cadis, and fired.

Iren ran up to Hiram, whose screams had begun to gargle as the shinhound's teeth punctured his windpipe. She had a blade in her hand. The shinhound stepped aside at her command, champing its bloody jowls. For a long moment Iren stood over the magister and watched him grab his own neck, trying to keep the blood from spilling.

He struggled to speak, and when he did, it was airy, like wind through an open flute. Iren spoke over him anyway. "I should have killed you in Meridan," she said. She lowered to a knee and stabbed Hiram in the heart. Iren made sure the magister was dead with a technique that Hiram himself had taught her.

Cadis watched all this as if it happened on a stage.

Her vision, steadily darkening, would lower the curtain. Iren would smile and help their mentor to his feet. They would clap each other on the back for a brilliant show. But such a hope was an old comforting naiveté that she could no longer sustain, simply by virtue of knowing what it was. The real world was more complicated, more vivid with its pains and wonders. The real world was beyond the imaginings and theatrics that let her march blindly into the common hall, hoping the people would follow her command. And for that she had already paid in Jesper's blood.

Cadis looked down at the crossbow bolt that pierced the back of her right hand—all the way through, like a rotisserie rod skewered through a pheasant breast.

Cadis laughed. This was her second punishment, she thought, though the pain hadn't yet fully reached her. And this was her prize, she thought, for having finally seen it coming with clear eyes.

She had known Hiram would shoot for the belly, an irrational and hateful last swipe. Cadis had put her hand out at the last moment, as the bolt punched from the back, through the palm, and pinning it to her leather jerkin. Even through her hand, the bolt had cut through the hardened leather and stabbed a little into her stomach.

Cadis tried to pull it out. Her hand slid over the bolt—a pain as loud as a thunderclap, and a wave of vomit surged up to her throat. Her knees wavered, and she fell.

CHAPTER FIFTEEN

Suki

It was all over (they'd won (except there was no "they" (and "winning" was also vague (meaningless (so really, some people had done something that kind of resembled success, depending on what they'd expected to achieve in the first place (Declan was bleeding in a dungeon, so to bloody hell with definitions)))))).

But that was after.

And after that:

Black, black, black.

Nothing but. Cold. Hard.

(Hand on the wall.)

Hand cut at the wrist.

(For a second the meat looked like a salmon steak

(pink, raw flesh, round bone in the middle.)

A fountain of cherry sauce (his eyes horrified—who would dare unhand the king?)). (But he wasn't no king) (!).

Just another ambitious Meridan soldier (up-jumped) (class climber) with a house no older than a jar of Tasanese pickles.

Endrit (Taylin) was the real king.

Taylin, Taylin (even as she walked in the black, she said it (and it sounded strange (but no less welcome (on her tongue)))).

They'd hunched behind a wagon cart together in the keep yard (snuck past the walls through the smuggler's tunnel (walked past Endrit's home (door still busted (Rhea looked at it ashamed (that it was the rightful king they'd been abusing all those years))))).

If she had any decency at all, she'd beg Endrit for mercy (for killing his parents (or having a father who did it, anyway)).

Suki didn't feel the need to apologize, because she had been trying to tell him all this time that he was good enough for her (and the compliment turned out to be true (and Rhea was the one unfit for the king's bed (which she should have also apologized about))).

They snuck through Cheapside, so late that the taverns were closed and the bakeries were open.

No one stopped them.

(This time Suki had no problem walking between them and telling Rhea to move over (so she could be next to

Endrit (Rhea obeyed for once)).) She probably spent the whole time going back over every conversation they had ever had (their whole lives) trying to remember if she'd done anything worthy of execution by the new king.

She had dropped the letter from Valda (Endrit had read it next (took it like he took everything (in stride) as if being the lost heir was something every stable boy grew into)). He said, "Maybe this will save my mother" (meaning Marta (which was a good-person thing to say)). And that was all he cared to discuss at the moment (and so they left to go invade the keep (and Suki saw Rhea palm the crest (stuff it in her pocket (but Suki would kill her if she tried anything, so she didn't bother to make a fuss over it (and so she took it in stride (the confident thing to do)))))). The night wasn't even that dark.

Now it was all black, black, black.

Her hand on the wall.

Wet up to her waist in wastewater.

When they hid behind the wagon, Endrit offered Suki a drink of water from the wineskin. She took it and put it to her lips (but didn't drink) just to be close to him. They had a moment's rest. The moon was hanging low already. (Soldiers everywhere on the keep gates, balconies (and even patrolling the yard where the Revels tents had been just a few days prior (after her horse ride in the coliseum, Suki had presented a juggling routine (knives, torches, necklaces from the ladies in attendance))).)

She'd wanted a big tent with a trapeze, but Marta had said no (which meant Hiram had said no (which meant Declan didn't want any of them outshining his whelp)).

No more tents (only guards).

The wagon was as close to a basement door as anything (big enough to hide behind). The space between was twenty open meters.

Endrit drank the rest of the water and let the skin fall on the ground. Suki held a long straight dagger (the one she would break in a guard's mouth, when he reflexively clamped his jaw before he died (just the tip (on the bones in the back)) and later use to sever the hand).

All the guards would see them if they ran out. (So they waited.)

Suki thought about it for a long time, then put her hand on his knee. When he looked back, she said, "When this is over, we can go to Tasan (me, you, Marta) and I'll be empress. We can take the whole army and reclaim your throne together."

(He blinked a few times (he was probably overwhelmed (traumatized (his mind must have been a shambles (*think straight* (she could have said it, but it would have reminded him of Marta, and at the moment, she wanted him to think of his future with her)))))).) He smiled. "Thanks, Susu. But when this is over, I'll still be the stable hand." (Which meant he didn't think the Meridan nobles would bow to him, even though the keep was his by right (he was wrong about that (but he'd always been a stable hand and never seen the power that titles held over people)).) "But I'll still visit Tasan," he added, "just to see you be empress for a while." (Which pleased Suki (she thought the first thing she'd do was hold a meeting of nobles and kill anyone who opposed her (or acted like Rhea or Declan (overly friendly and manipulative)))).)

Endrit made an uncomfortable laugh (as if he'd heard her say some of it (and wasn't sure how to react)). Suki didn't know how much of it she'd said aloud.

In the black, black, black.

With wastewater up to her waist.

Her hand on the slime stonewall.

Hand at her hip, hand groping ahead.

Hand in her hand.

She moved her lips to words she wasn't thinking.

The words on her mind were "prison break."

(The word on her mouth was "Tola.")

The guards shouted "prison break" when they saw a shadow in the yard (because they were idiot recruits (just bodies on the wall (because it came from outside and walked *toward* them))).

It was Rhea (finally (she must have taken her time running to the other side)). She held her arms in the air. All the guards converged on her position, pointing crossbows (It was still too dark to see anything but her silhouette.).

"Come on." (Endrit.)

They (Endrit and Suki) ran out from behind the wagon cart (across the yard) (sprinting) (heads down) (shot full of bolts by idiot recruits while sneaking in the night would be an unworthy death).

At the time Suki suspected that Rhea *wanted* to get caught (distraction was her idea), that she had plotted with her precious father, but later she realized Rhea was just another pawn.

(When Declan turned on her too (she should have known (Rhea couldn't mastermind a tea party)).)

But that was after they got caught.

They ducked into the cellar door and used Marta's map to pass through the kennels (it was quiet (Hiram's shin-hounds must have all been out carrying messages)).

Endrit spied a guard at the entrance of the dungeons (but she was asleep (and Suki walked right up to her)). She could have slid the dagger down through the divot at the base of her neck (straight down like measuring the water's depth (but Endrit grabbed her wrist and whispered, "What're you doing?" (The guard startled (light sleeper) and Endrit had to knock her out with an ax handle))).

The dungeons had sconces with torches (but the flames were guttering and needed replacement (the morning guard would do it)).

They crept. Endrit was too agitated (to find his mother) to talk. They might have found her tortured (if they had found her at all (but instead, they were caught)). They had walked through the dungeons and found them empty (which meant only that Declan had a prison elsewhere). The hour was approaching sunrise.

Suki would have given up, but the evidence (no guards lurking, no one tending the sconces) meant they had it wrong.

Endrit opened the map (Suki was the one who'd discovered it (she'd idly mentioned that the entire keep was connected by the underground burrows (Declan could have spied on them, even in their privacy (and that led Endrit to the Protectorate wing, where each of the young queens had her own chamber (and below that, a training room (and below those . . . ? (the map showed only hidden stairs, leading farther down)))))))).

In the black, black, black.

Was it forever black?

With her hand on the slime stonewall.

Hand at her hip, hand groping in front.

With his hand. His fingers.

Waist-high in wastewater.

Tola.

She was always kept just a few hundred feet below in a dank, black hole.

So very close she could have shouted or howled and haunted the keep.

But never did.

For fear or for desolation.

Made silent.

Made animal.

When they descended to the lowest level on the map and came finally to a great circular room (under the Protectorate dining hall) that branched out in several directions (like a wagon wheel), Endrit stopped to check the map (and guards poured in from behind all the doors (even the one they had entered from (which meant they were followed (expected)))).

Suki thrashed like a cat in a burlap sack. Endrit lifted his ax (and a sword in the other hand) but took a hard armored fist to the back of the head. They surrounded him on the ground (kicked at his ribs and face).

Suki broke her dagger (she thrust it backward over her shoulder at the guard holding her (impaled his mouth (he clenched his jaw (she yanked it out (but left the tip snapped off in his bone))))).

He fell and let go.

Suki almost fainted (from the rush of pain (from the guard clamping on her wounded shoulder (and then releasing it as he fell))).

The moment's dizziness was enough (another guard swung her spear handle and smashed it into Suki's ear).

The floor was smooth bedrock.

(The guard said, "Yield or die" (as if she were playing in a yard game (she had her spear at the ready (so Suki yielded))).)

Declan was there later (walked in like it was another day at his own court (with Rhea flapping at his heels (and the king's dragoons (real soldiers (oath and honor-bound (trained not to eat daggers)))))).

A smug man (probably supposing that he'd won (again)).

(Torches at every door.)

(One hundred feet of rock above their heads.)

(Above that, another dungeon (where they'd all grown up).)

(The broken dagger at her feet.)

Endrit was held up by two guards (one stupid enough to keep her nose directly behind him (a snap back would drop her (later) (after Declan said what he said (and the killing started)))).

Declan approached Suki in the half-light (unbothered by the dead guard at her feet (squinting a bit)). "That's her," he confirmed (which meant he'd come to make sure the prisoner was the heir to Tasan (dressed in farm clothes)).

"Where's my mother?" said Endrit.

(He got punched in the kidney for the impertinence, but Declan smiled (still while looking at Suki).) "You'll all join her tomorrow."

Before (or after) he said it, Suki turned to Rhea and spat, "Traitor. Turncoat. Loser. Whore." (Anything she could think of.)

"I didn't say anything!" said Rhea. (Meaning she wasn't the turncoat whore who pretended to help the plan by being a distraction, only to tell the guards exactly where they were.)

Even Endrit's faith in her seemed shaken (he wouldn't look at her (which was something deep, because she had hooks the size of her legs around him)). "I didn't—" (Rhea exclaimed again, but a dragoon grabbed her by the arm to keep her in place) "—let go of me! Father!"

"Don't call me that," said Declan (stuttering with anger). "I had one child." (He whipped around (all smugness and calm suddenly gone and the frayed edges beginning to show).) "I had one perfect child, and all of this was for him."

(He'd intended Rhys to be king.)

"But look at us now." The soldiers all widened the circle (like spooked sheep). "We're stuck with you."

Rhea's face was twisted and breaking.

"So obviously less than. So weak that one sister leads you, one teaches and outsmarts you, and this one"—pointing to Suki—"even disdains you. You were the last of four. How could you ever rule Pelgard? I put my blood in the cup only to see it disappear. Only to watch you fret and stumble, even at the lowest bar I could set. You were going to help them? Were you ever my child?"

They watched as every nervous fear manifested before Rhea's eyes (every deep-held longing for her daddy's approval dashed and flung to the opposite corner (he hated her)). He hated her.

Declan gathered himself (he had been shouting (he breathed heavy and pinched his nose)). He was young still (he could have an heir come of age still (before he died)). He spoke (this time to the guards), "Lock them up individually. Set one guard at each door. Tomorrow bring them all. We hang this one for colluding with his mother"—(Endrit)—"this one for betraying her own family"—(Rhea)—"and this one"—(Suki)—"for—oh, does it matter? The people will love to hurt Tasan again."

Suki knew he meant Tola. He admitted it (he had killed her (he admitted it)). "They've only got two left in the passel," he added. (Suki's siblings, he meant (he'd taken Dato and Tola, and intended to take her (the third heir)).)

Suki flew, shrieking, at Declan.

Words she couldn't remember.

Scattered images.

A further tear in the gash in her shoulder.

A tussle.

A piercing jolt in her left calf (where the soldier behind her stabbed a spear (right into the meat of the calf)).

Suki fell onto her stomach at Declan's feet (the air rushed out of her lungs).

Endrit used the moment to snap his head backward (the guard's nose splattered blood (with a crunching sound)). Endrit turned on the second guard, a man twice his size (the one with armored gauntlets that had hit him the first time to the floor).

Endrit was already battered (his lip swollen, his shoulder from a hundred years ago (when Suki had helped him wrap it (his ribs))). They looked like a bear fighting a limping dog. The giant guard swung a heavy fist. Endrit didn't even see it coming (his eye was bruised on that side). Endrit fell again (blood pouring from his face. His sandy brown hair matted to his skull (wet and sticky from blood). The guard lifted his sword (a killing blow).

Rhea shouted, "No! He's the heir! He's Taylin."

The bear-man stopped at hearing the name of Kendrick and Valda's son.

Rhea pulled enough slack from the dragoon holding her

to reach into her pocket. She held the crest aloft (it shimmered in the torchlight).

"He's the true king of Meridan. You can't kill him."

Endrit sat up on the floor, bleeding.

The bear-man awaited orders.

Declan (with sword in hand) approached Endrit. "I most certainly can."

The usurper almost made the thrust (at Endrit's chest (but Suki was up (with the broken dagger from the floor (with enough blade yet to do good work (to sever Declan's hand fully at the wrist))))).

The sword (and hand) fell at Endrit's feet. Declan stared at where his hand used to be (for a moment it was just a raw salmon steak (with round white bone (and then it sprayed (a meager fountain (and he screamed))))).

Suki took the moment to push the dagger up and under the bear-man's rib cage (searching for the bear-size heart). He toppled like a tree.

Next would be Rhea (and then another for Declan). Suki bent to lift the bear's double-edged sword (she had the hilt (but Endrit grabbed her hand)). "Don't," he said. (But he'd never know what he was asking. "Don't, Susu.")

He didn't know (and she didn't want to be Susu anymore (not the way it was (sibling intimacy (instead of the other kind)))).

She helped Endrit to his feet (because he didn't let go of her hand). And when she looked up, all the dragoons (the king's men) were at salute toward Endrit.

They knew he was king.

(And they had Declan the usurper (a guard was already wrapping a belt around his wrist to stem the blood).) They'd have a trial. Endrit would marry Rhea, and kiss her.

It didn't matter. Suki wanted Declan dead (but Endrit didn't allow it (when she demanded her revenge (and the dragoons listened to him (and Rhea stood beside him (as if she weren't just as much a usurper (and Endrit even defended her (when Suki screamed exactly that (as if standing up for him absolved her (and so Suki ripped her arm out of the guard's grip and took the map from where Endrit had dropped it (and grabbed Declan's severed hand) and left (the guards had no right to stop her (and the last she heard was Endrit calling out, "Suki! Suki, just wait a minute and we'll straighten this—" (but Suki had opened and shut the door by then (the door that led farther down. Down to the lowest tunnel—where stairs led into water waist-high, that led into wretched depths so black, black, black that her eyes strained and nothing else (nothing guided her but her hand on slime and stone holding Declan's hand (when she reached it, she didn't even realize it was a door at first (Declan's hand jammed into the frame and she heard it rattle the hinge (and a whimper or howl from inside (and when she pushed it open, it wasn't even locked, it was just black, black, black (the deepest dungeon in all the keep (and Suki realized there was a creature inside, because it scuttled into a corner when the door opened (it said, "Don't, don't. I'll be quiet" (and somehow in her heart, Suki knew it was Tola (because maybe the voice? Or the fact that it was hidden so well? Or the sudden feeling that she wasn't even necessary for all this, Declan already had the heir to Tasan and Suki could have been home, she could have belonged at home and learned old Tasanese, the way all true heirs would and now she stood in the black, black, black, and she said, "Tola? Is that you?" (and she heard only raspy breathing ("Tola? It's me, Suki." (and the creature (she must have been broken (her mind must have been a horrible tangle of tortured half-part thoughts (like a beast, she must have been branded with the fear of her master (Declan) and Suki heard a "Su . . . Su . . . Su . . ." in stuttering breaths between sobs (and if they returned together, Tola would be the hero returned and Suki (the one who was barely even Tasanese (but the one who'd crippled Declan (would be shunted aside (and she would watch her crazed broken-minded sister veer the empire into ruin (and Suki could never return for Endrit (it was obvious from her sobbing, "Su . . . Su?" and the voice drew closer (it was dark, so they moved by sounds, and Suki heard the creature rise up and stumble toward her (arms open, probably (but she didn't move aside (Suki didn't move aside or warn her sister that she held a dagger (it was reasonable to draw it, when she entered (and she felt the weight, the horrifically light weight of a Tasanese queen running herself into the point of the knife, up to the hilt (they were face-to-face (Suki felt the gust of foul breath leave Tola (and she still held Declan's severed hand (which she used to keep Tola from falling forward (Declan's hand rested on her impaled sister's shoulder ("Suki?" was the last thing the creature said, and Suki replied, "Yes. I'm not Susu anymore" (and she ran out when she felt Tola fall backward, off of her knife, onto the dungeon floor (she ran out of the room, down the tunnel that Declan built (walked straight (and thought straight (only one thought (only *one* thought (that she would emerge from the dark hole as (Tola reborn (and return to Tasan (to go home (to take power (to come back to Meridan and burn everyone and everything to the ground)).

CHAPTER SIXTEEN

Iren

C adis fell.

But Iren caught her.

An awkward grab by the shoulders to avoid pushing the bolt farther.

It staked into her stomach, through her right hand.

Iren let Cadis down gently.

She grabbed the bloody hand.

Cadis screamed.

Every bone in it was shattered.

Steady. Steady.

Iren dislodged the wooden shaft from Cadis's stomach without shifting it in her hand.

The breaths came in spasms.

But at least they came.

Her stomach didn't bleed as much as her hand. Sacrificing it had saved her life.

Iren found herself admiring her old friend as she never had before.

She felt guilty that it had taken so long.

Iren helped Cadis over to the terra-cotta planter, where she could sit up. "I'll go get help," said Iren.

Cadis grabbed her arm. "You're not coming back, are you?"

"No, I'm not," said Iren.

She had time enough to take the land route through the badlands back to Corent before total war broke out.

Declan would hear of Hiram's death in a few days. He would march on Findain. Her mother surely had spies to keep her informed. But Iren could be of use, somehow. She would make sure of it. Cadis had not let go of her arm.

"Please," said Cadis. "You could join us. We could join with the rebels. We could stop Meridan. We know how he thinks."

"We don't," said Iren.

"You do."

"But I'm not coming back."

It was a naive plan.

The old Cadis.

But it was also shrewd for the archana to join the rebels.

Declan would never expect it.

Perhaps a new Cadis had arisen.

Iren should have gotten up then.

Something kept her.

"You'll do just fine," she said.

Cadis shook her head, no, as if telling herself not to cry. She looked away. She wanted something, some kind of momentous behavior.

So much of what Cadis wanted was born of understanding the world as a giant theater for the gods. She wanted Iren to exclaim her feelings, to be a fountain of emotion. To rend garments and shout, "Sister!" to a sky that Iren knew for certain did not give a damn.

She wanted to know Iren loved her.

"Just go," said Cadis. Iren made an awkward crab step over Cadis's legs and sat down next to her. Like before, when they'd first met. Iren hoped speeches wouldn't be necessary. She tucked her head into Cadis's shoulder and closed her eyes. She felt Cadis sobbing. She wiped her own eyes.

They weren't kidnapped little girls anymore. They didn't need to hold each other to survive a night.

They had killed and grown and escaped.

They were queens now.

And when they left the room, they would have new allegiances: Cadis to her rebel dream of rule by the people, Iren to the academy. It had always been to the academy and her mother.

Soon Rhea would take the throne of Meridan and fight them all. She was Declan's blood. Suki would ride to war just to win Endrit.

War was coming. Only sisters could stop it.

But they were not sisters.

Iren wished she could apologize for being the less loving one. For being so hard. "Thanks for being my friend," she said, remembering their first night and wondering if Cadis would remember it the same.

"Just go," said Cadis.

Iren got up. She snapped her fingers, and the shinhound ran to her side.

"Don't let Rhea take the midlands," she said. Hypatia and the rebels wanted bloodshed. Cadis should have been consolidating her power instead of giving it up to the vote of the uneducated, self-interested, and untrained.

Iren wanted to say all of this.

Somehow the words wouldn't form.

"Don't worry," said Cadis. "I won't look for assistance from the Corentine."

"That's not—"

It wasn't what Iren meant.

Cadis groaned as she got herself up to go tend to Jesper.

"You have safe passage through Findain," she said with her back turned.

Iren turned and left the room.

The shinhound followed.

She hoped her mother would be happy to see her.

CHAPTER SEVENTEEN

Rhea

For ten short years, Rhea had three sisters and she loved and hated them. She sat at the great round oaken table of their shared space as the sun rose and remembered it all.

Cadis, a gallant beauty, mounting the table and belting her orations, as if she stood in the Findish theater.

Iren, silent as the zephyr, cutting as the gale, sitting on three stacked books to see her glasswork on the table.

Suki, full of fuss and fear and fire, in turns vaulting across the chairs and pouting underneath the table.

It was all a ruin now.

Her father—king or usurper, guardian or prison guard, peacekeeper or villain—sat now in the dungeon awaiting trial. Would he get justice or vengeance from Endrit? The lost heir, returned from the grave—already beloved by the people, already plotted against by the nobles.

And what am I?

Just another for Endrit?

When they released Marta, she confirmed the history. The dragoons secured the castle immediately. Such transitions were bloody seasons. He would be inaccessible until magisters could verify the crest of Kendrick and Valda, until declarations could be made to all others.

Rhea sat at the table waiting to lose a throne she had never owned by rights in the first place.

Oddly, she did not mind.

Oddly, she found herself feeling certain of one thing: Endrit would need her. Whatever else he thought of her—as men think of women—she was still the only other to have lived as they had, in the gardened prison of the Protectorate. He would trust her for that reason. She was the only one sculpted to rule Meridan. And he knew it. He knew that she could be the mind of Meridan, even as he was the heart of it.

Hiram was her only rival in that knowledge—but Hiram was still missing. And if he returned, he was Declan's pet, not hers. And his whisperings could be silenced.

In many ways, Rhea realized, she would have a stronger grip on the crown of Meridan than she ever had before.

All she needed to do was keep the stable boy entertained—a dance to which she was learning the steps.

There would be plotting, of course. Always someone plotting. And there would be war. But her sisters had barely ascended in the eyes of their people, while Endrit was already a legend. There would be rumor and slander all through her father's trial. But Rhea smiled and watched the sun rise over the keep in newfound calm.

She was equal to it. She was stronger than Rhys, or if not stronger, at least better versed in the skills that mattered.

To meet rumor with quiet.

Treason with cunning.

And vicious with vicious.

> *Three little queens went riding into Meridan*
> *Three little queens who won't ride out*
> *The price of war makes a strange inheritance*
> *Dance little queens, but don't . . . fall . . . down.*

ACKNOWLEDGMENTS

I have looked forward to the opportunity to thank the many unsung and brilliant individuals who helped complete this book. They deserve far more than my thanks, but words are the writer's best currency, so I offer it freely.

Thank you first and foremost to Annie Nybo, who is the editor, babysitter, warden, tutor, and visionary of this endeavor. Editing is as difficult a craft as any true art form, and precious few practice it as gently and firmly, as insightfully and humbly, as precisely and clearly as Annie. For instance, if she had edited this paragraph, it would not have all the adverbs you just endured. Evidence, dear reader, that this entire book owes much to the craftsmanship of a good editor.

Wherever you find merit, please also credit the hard work of the Simon & Schuster team: editorial captain at McElderry Books, Karen Wojtyla. Citizens of Olympus Justin Chanda, Anne Zafian, and Jon Anderson. Managing editor Bridget Madsen. Our amazing designer, Sonia Chaghatzbanian, who created such a lovely package, and cover artist Charlie Bowater, whose magnificent hand gave our Rhea that delightfully inscrutable grin. And thank you also to Elizabeth Blake-Linn, a miracle worker in production, who gave us those special effects on the cover to highlight Charlie's work.

A special thanks to Zareen Jaffrey, Dani Young, Ruta Rimas, Emma Ledbetter, Amy Rosenbaum, Julia Maguire, Navah Wolfe, Kristin Ostby, and Ariel Coletti, who saw the book in its infancy—and Kirsten Dean, who kept with it throughout.

Thanks to Deane Norton, Christian Pecorale, Rio Cortez, Danielle Esposito, and Colin Shields for helping the book reach as many hands as possible, and thanks to Chrissy Noh, Michelle Leo, Candace Green, Anthony Parisi, Lucille Rettino, Katy Hershberger, Ellen Grafton, and Alex Del Negro for making sure people know of it.

Thank you all.

Much love,

KDC